No-one Loves a Policeman

Guillermo Orsi

NO-ONE LOVES A POLICEMAN

Translated from the Spanish by
Nick Caistor

MACLEHOSE PRESS
QUERCUS · LONDON

First published in Great Britain in 2010 by

MacLehose Press
an imprint of Quercus
21 Bloomsbury Square
London WC1A 2NS

First published in Spain by Editorial Almuzara.

This work is published within the framework of the SUR Translation Support Program of the Ministry of Foreign Affairs, International Trade and Worship of the Argentine Republic.

A CIP catalogue record for this book is available from the British Library

ISBN (HB) 978 1 906694 02 9
ISBN (TPB) 978 1 906694 03 6

2 4 6 8 10 9 7 5 3 1

Printed and bound in Great Britain by Clays Ltd, St Ives plc

PART ONE

Small Mercies

1

Five years ago, when I lost the last person I cared about, I vowed never again to answer the telephone after midnight. Since then, my resolve has seldom been put to the test. At my age it is rare for male friends to stay up late, and the women are not permanent fixtures once you are persuaded you are all alone in the world. All of them widowed or separated, and in the early hours they are snuggled up in bed, smearing themselves with creams, or warming their toes on memories of happier times and better lovers (if they have anyone to compare with). If they feel lonely, they call girlfriends. Or the Samaritans.

On the night of December 14, 2001, I went to bed early even for me. Not so much because I was tired, more that I was weary of playing along with such an uninspiring day. There was not a single bit of news I could cling to, none of those hilarious excuses Buenos Aires can be so generous with: an armed bank robbery just when you are trying to withdraw your meagre earnings, or paying the rent for the unheated apartment you have been living in for the past year. A demand from the tax people because you haven't paid the previous instalment. A friend in his fifties confessing he has at last come out, and could you please recommend an analyst, preferably a young, good-looking one. I had nothing to stay up for, not even bad news on the T.V., apart from the usual ridiculous celebrity marriages, resigning ministers, chaos in the markets making nonsense of the government's economic policies, and the inevitable run on banks. One of those days when midnight is a watery horizon and you suspect that your ship has sunk forever beneath the waves.

"Gotán, I need to see you as soon as possible."

"I'm in bed, with the duvet round my ears. The thought of getting up and dressed, taking the car out of the garage and driving half an hour to your place makes me feel quite unwell."

"Make that six hours. I'm not in Buenos Aires. And you have to leave right now, so that you reach here before dawn."

It took me a quarter of an hour to dress, pack stuff for two days into a bag, and leave a note to ensure that Zulema, the cleaner who comes on Mondays, put fresh water in the bowl and fed my cat Félix Jesús his balanced diet. He was out that night – with my permission – but he was bound to be back before I was, demanding food and a place to curl up in peace.

Half an hour after Edmundo Cárcano's call I was driving across the city as fast as a patrol car taking the special giant-size mozzarella from the pizzeria to the police station. There was hardly any traffic as I sped along the highway heading towards the southernmost stretch of the Atlantic coast. I was aiming for a tiny village of not more than a dozen houses, side by side on a bare, windswept beach, with nothing but sand dunes and sea to look at. Mediomundo was its name.

"It was called that by the estate agent who deals in these remote properties. He's a fisherman, but he uses nets rather than a rod. He catches all kinds of fish and makes stews for the few lost tourists who turn up here," Cárcano had explained. He reckoned the resort should be called Arsehole of the World. The estate agent owned a bar on the beach called All Kinds of Fish. He was the one who told me on this cold, windy morning that he could not believe it. "Why, just yesterday he was here eating sea bream and drinking sherry. How can he be dead? Poor Edmundo," he said, referring to my friend Cárcano, shot at point-blank and killed outright, which at the very least cast doubt on the suicide theory put forward by the policeman who had arrived that afternoon from Bahía Blanca.

Cárcano had built himself a simple, beautiful chalet with what he had saved from his oil-company salary. When I arrived, I could find no trace of the blonde, almost an adolescent and nearly as lovely as the house, who he had said he loved and with whom he planned to share this seaside eyrie. Not a lipstick or a sanitary towel, never mind underwear or a toothbrush. It looked as though no-one was visiting or living with Cárcano in his marine hideaway. That was the conclusion of the inspector, detective or traffic policeman from the provincial force who turned up in Mediomundo to investigate what he termed "this unfortunate event".

"If he called you at midnight it was probably because he didn't feel too good. Older people do get these bouts of depression at night," the inspector said. He was little more than thirty, and his nose for sleuthing had already been dulled by easy money from gambling and prostitution.

I asked him if he was going to check for fingerprints, but he said the forensic team would do that when they got here the next day or the day after. "We're up to our ears in work," he boasted, looking me straight in the eye. If the murdered Edmundo Cárcano was hoping for justice, he was not going to come by it by way of this bureaucrat, disturbed in his so-crowded routine eight long hours earlier by a friend of the victim. A friend who, rather than end up with the car wrapped round his head, had driven unhurriedly for six seemingly endless hours, and who as soon as he arrived felt sorry he had not once exceeded the speed limit, but had travelled singing a duet with Lucila Davidson on the radio, even allowing himself the luxury of closing his eyes for a few seconds so he could imagine her beside him, the two of them looking out over a sea of delirious fans. Closing his eyes up on stage with her, dreaming his erotic dream even if the car several times swerved onto the verge, blissfully unaware of what awaited him in this remote seaside village in the south-east of Buenos Aires province.

I knew I had arrived too late as soon as I opened the door of my friend's charming chalet. Day had dawned half an hour earlier, but even without touching the body, lying in a pool of blood, I could tell Cárcano had not lived to see its first pale light.

The house was clean and tidy; typical of my friend, for my taste a little too concerned with keeping things shipshape. No wardrobe door was open, and the only thing strewn on the floor was his body. The murderer appeared to have focused on what he had come for. He had not forced a door or window, so Cárcano must have known him and trusted him enough to let him in. Perhaps when he called me the man was already with him, pressing a gun to his head.

Edmundo was not the kind to get mixed up in anything dangerous. In recent years he had some wild scheme for making fuel from grain crops. He had found a backer, a banker willing to underwrite his research and then invest in the small business or co-operative Cárcano set up, of which he was chairman and general secretary. The other members were geeks, people obsessed with changing the molecules of whatever came within their grasp, building new worlds from the leftovers of the present one. In other words, people willing to give themselves a hard time to show uncaring humanity that if we have made planet Earth a dangerous place to live in, there is nevertheless still time to save it.

*

When I called Cárcano's daughter to tell her the news she sobbed at the end of the line, but said she had been afraid that something like this was going to happen. She is about the same age as her father's girlfriend.

"Since he left my mother for that tart he's been getting mixed up in funny business," Isabel said. She was as indignant as ever about her father's betrayal: to her way of thinking, his lustful adventure had exploded like a depth charge in their happy home. "He neglected his job. Thirty years with the same company! He was going to retire next year, and the firm was going to give him a gold medal. They had even promised to pay him extra to make up for the crappy state pension he had been contributing to all his life. He and Mummy had planned to travel to Italy, to visit our grandparents' house in Bologna."

Isabel cried for three pesos and forty-two cents' worth of my long-distance call. From the public telephone box I could see the sea and a cold, clear night falling over the deserted beach. I was thinking what a good idea it would be to have a little nest of my own in a place like this.

"What 'funny business' did your father get involved in?" I asked when it seemed the tears were drying up.

Isabel, in Buenos Aires, hesitated, sniffed, took a deep breath, sighed.

"We need to meet. I don't trust any phone in this country of informers, where half the population is listening in to what the other half is saying."

"O.K., but do tell your mother, and the burial is in Bahía Blanca."

When I mentioned the burial, a lump came to my throat. A steadfast friend who died in Mediomundo, a beach that does not appear on any tourist map, down round the arsehole of the world.

He and I met when there was still military service in Argentina. Serving the fatherland for eighteen months, preparing *mate* tea for the sergeants, cleaning the latrines in the officers' mess, going out in the early hours on sordid military operations to frighten the civilians. We were thirty-six when a drunken general gave the order to invade the Malvinas. Too old to fight a war that was lost before it began, and yet two decades later my friend abandoned his wife Mónica for a twenty-year-old blonde who was scarcely born when another general surrendered Port Stanley to save the lives of thousands of soldiers, not to mention his own.

Time can take on weird dimensions, like the elongated shadows in this sharp evening light. If, as the tango says, "twenty years are nothing", they are far too much when it comes to two lives as far apart as

Edmundo's and his near-adolescent and now-vanished blonde. All the past, all the memories you carry with you as a camel carries its hump simply do not exist for someone whose over-riding concern is the future. How could the two of them have set out on a journey together? Where could they go? Whichever direction they took, it would be tearing something apart.

The sun set over the beach. Rather than travel another fifty kilometres to Bahía Blanca, I decided to spend the night in my dead friend's house.

We take some decisions in only a few seconds, but soon find that the rest of our life is not time enough to regret them.

2

The house was better equipped for a good time than for a death. The fridge was full, there was a shed at the end of the garden piled high with firewood, whisky and cognac in the bar, two T.V.s with a satellite dish, bookshelves stocked with bestsellers enough for anyone not concerned to explore the mysteries of serious literature, a sound system with C.D.s of the Rolling Stones, Julio Sosa and the Leopoldo Federico Orchestra; Eduardo Falú singing Castilla and Leguizamon; Mozart, Charly García, Skinny Spinetta; Lita Vitale and Tita Merello. You could sit on the sofa in the small, warm living-room and wait peacefully enough for a giant wave to come and sweep everything away.

But tsunamis do not ring the doorbell. And it is only in the movies that beautiful women call to say hello after dark. That was why when somebody rang the bell I thought it must be Edmundo they were looking for and I would find myself confronted with a lovely face pouting with disappointment.

"Isn't it horrible?" the blonde said, as though we were old friends. She swept past me without explaining who she was, although it was not difficult to work out that she must be the Lolita who had brought a little joy to Edmundo's autumn years.

"Pablo Martelli," I said, holding out my hand, but she turned and clung to me as if I were a piece of driftwood on the high seas after her ship had gone down.

Her hair was damp from the evening mist. It gave off an enchanting fragrance of wild strawberries in a wood, if you could imagine that smell with your eyes closed when you're being clung to as though you were a drowning woman's only hope.

"I'm Lorena."

She said this with her head pressed against my shoulder, her face buried in my shirt – the only clean one I had brought, thinking I would be gone two nights at most.

"They murdered him. They shot him like a dog before he had the chance to explain he wasn't going to keep the money. Poor Poppa, dying like that just when we had all we needed to start a new life and be happy."

If what she said was true, I could well understand her dismay. Losing a still attractive, intelligent and healthy man in his sixties, especially someone as relatively well off as Edmundo, must be a real blow in times like these when there is so much unemployment and the young have to face so many existential uncertainties. As far as I could recall Cárcano saying, Lorena was not a career woman, although she had studied for a degree in something or other at a private university. She had been wasting her time in employment agencies or multinationals where they employ graduate students to run bank errands, when all of a sudden: bingo! she runs into Edmundo.

"Tell me what happened," I said, not at all impatient to come out of our embrace. "I didn't know Edmundo had enemies."

When I said this, she cast off her life raft. She headed for the bar to pour herself a whisky. It was only after she had gulped it down that she seemed to realise I was still there.

"You shouldn't stay here," she said. "It's not safe."

"You're right. Besides, as you've been living with Edmundo, this is your place, and I'm an intruder. But my only other choice was to go to Bahía Blanca. Isabel is arriving tomorrow."

My news disturbed her. She did not ask why Edmundo's daughter was coming because the answer was obvious. She went to the picture window as though she could see the ocean outside despite the dark night under a new moon.

"Poppa wanted to get away from his family," she said.

"But Isabel was his only daughter, and therefore his favourite."

She smiled a wan smile.

"We have to get out of here."

She walked back towards me. I wondered how long it had taken her to seduce her "Poppa". Two months, two weeks, two days, two hours, two minutes? She could have broken her record with me if the body had not been lying there still so fresh in its pool of blood, and Edmundo's eyes were not staring so intently at us, fixed at the moment of his death.

*

Half an hour later we were speeding down Route 3 on our way to nowhere. Lorena warned me not to call Isabel or anyone else from my mobile.

"They trace all the calls," she said. "They'll be onto us before you hang up."

"If I'm not at the funeral tomorrow, she's going to feel even worse than she does now."

As soon as the words left my mouth, I regretted them: the look the blonde gave me said it all – finding my dead body next to Poppa's would be no comfort to his daughter either. I did not do much better when I asked who it was who was tracing the calls.

"If I knew that, we wouldn't have been caught by surprise in such an isolated spot, playing the happy couple," she said. She lit a cigarette, drew on it as if it were a condemned prisoner's last, then passed it to me. The filter tip was sticky with fragrant lipstick.

"It's not so disastrous to die happy."

"Poppa didn't have many friends," she said. "People he could trust, I mean," she added, disturbed by what I had said.

"Who was with him when he called me last night? Who does the money that he wasn't going to keep belong to?"

A blonde silence, smoke drifting up between the windscreen and me, the straight line of the road disappearing ahead like the sides of a triangle whose apex we were travelling towards at 140 kilometres per hour. She did not know who he was with: she had gone on to Bahía Blanca on her own, and come back alone.

"My cousin is in hospital there. She's in intensive care. Her parents both died in a car accident; my cousin survived, but she's paralysed down one side of her body, and the rest of her doesn't know what's happened yet."

I gave an involuntary shudder. Lorena might be beautiful, but she could be a twenty-year-old Fate who spelled the end for any amorous, comfortably off old man who came within reach. She was making a big mistake with me, though. She obviously had no idea how uncomfortably off I was.

I did not believe a word of her story.

"We could turn off to Bahía," I said. "The city's only five kilometres from here."

At this, she dropped a delicate white hand on the steering wheel. I was forced to hold on as tightly as I could, then had to pull hard to straighten up to avoid the truck hurtling towards us, horn blaring, on his side of the road. I could imagine the curses he was screaming to himself in his lonely cabin.

"So where *are* we headed?" I said as we sped on past the turning to the city. "Why *can't* we go into Bahía Blanca, for Chrissake?"

She said nothing, and I relented. That was my second big mistake of the night.

*

Three more hours driving and we were leaving Viedma behind. At this time of the morning it was a ghost city, and the whole day through it would be the small, insignificant capital of Rio Negro province, a place to which an ex-president with grandiose ideas once announced that he was going to transfer the capital of Argentina. There must be so little oxygen in the stratospheres of power that the politicians' neurones stop working. They come up with ideas that even an astronaut lost in space would realise were the product of their delirium or the junk food they are given in their ration pills.

I asked once more who the money belonged to, and where we were going, but this time Lorena was fast asleep. When she was awake she scarcely looked the twenty-four she claimed to be, but lying there asleep she was Nabokov's heroine updated for the twenty-first century.

I stopped to fill the car with adulterated petrol – served by an attendant who looked as if he had come back from the grave. Sunken-cheeked and silent, all he managed to grunt was the price. When I handed him a hundred peso note, he gave it straight back.

"If you've no change, you'll have to stay here until someone who has turns up," he said with all the grim authority of a prison warder. He wiped his hands on a filthy rag and spat his phlegm onto the ground. "It's damn cold out in this desert. Come inside and have a *mate*."

I suspected that, apart from a thermos of hot water and the *mate*, and perhaps a packet of crackers, in his lair he was probably hiding a loaded shotgun, just itching to fire at the first client who used the excuse of having no change to drive off without paying. I bowed to the inevitable: the girl was sound asleep, and I had no urgent wish to carry on with a journey to the uttermost south.

"I'm going to the toilet," I said. "No sugar with my *mate*."

In the broken mirror, lit by an anaemic bulb, I hardly recognised the face staring back at me.

I thought of my cat Félix Jesús and the disappointment on his round, battered face when he got back and discovered I was not in the apartment. The only comfort he and I have is that we occasionally coincide, and can rub against each other like Aladdin's lamp and rouse early morning genies to make us feel less alone.

When finally I emerged from the toilet, my car and the girl had disappeared.

"Two men pulled up in a Ford Fiesta," the ghoulish attendant said. "One of them stayed in the driving seat; the other got into your car. He drove off with the girl, with the Fiesta as escort. Anything to do with you?"

"The car was mine. The girl was a friend's."

"Ah," said the attendant. He offered me a frothy, bitter *mate* with crackers.

3

Everything has its positive side. Pessimists say the world is going to end tomorrow or the day after; optimists insist it is born anew each day when we wake up alive. The sum of biological processes the earth is made up of are blithely uninterested in this sterile debate. The same nonsense gets created and recreated while poets wander about like scalded cats, skulking from their former loves so they can write about them.

The positive side to the fact that Lorena had been abducted in my car was that two hours later I was on board a Skania travelling up from Patagonia with a load of sheep, was able to jump down at the outskirts of Bahía Blanca at 9.00 in the morning, and arrived on time for my friend's funeral. I did not tell either Mónica, his distraught wife, or Isabel about my night-time excursion with Lorena. That would only have fuelled their hatred, and this, as everyone knows, is the enemy of consolation and not to be recommended in the peace of a cemetery.

The topic came up anyway, because Mónica could not get it out of her mind that if "that little tart" had not appeared in Edmundo's life the two of them would by now be on that trip of a lifetime in Europe.

"He was never a philanderer. I don't understand it," she sobbed. A couple of paces behind her, Isabel was waiting for the chance to tell me what she had found out about the funny business her father had been involved in. "He was never unfaithful," Mónica cried. "Never a hair on his clothes that wasn't his; never any lipstick or perfume that wasn't mine."

I envied my friend his widow's poor memory. As I put my arms round her so that she could let it all out, I recalled the nights Edmundo had turned up at my apartment because Mónica had thrown him out after discovering passionate love letters to him, or telephone numbers scribbled on paper napkins which were answered, when she rang them, by sleepy, sensual voices.

"The old goat," was Isabel's version when the two of us were alone together. "He used to drive her mad, but he had that knack of making us feel sorry for him which meant we all loved him despite his weaknesses. I thought that with his prostate problems he had changed his ways, that he would actually keep his word and give Mummy a peaceful old age, take her to see some of the world he had become so disenchanted with. How wrong can one be?"

"I suppose he wanted to play his last card, but by then he was already a loser. Why was he killed?"

We had arranged to meet at midday at a restaurant in the centre of Bahía Blanca. Exhausted by the journey and her distress, Mónica had stayed in their hotel. This might be the only chance Isabel had to share her discoveries and her theories with me.

"He made a very big mistake when he fell in love this time."

"We always make mistakes. Otherwise it wouldn't be love, it would be convenience."

"I found these papers in his desk."

Isabel took a folded brown envelope from her bag and put it on the table next to the bottle of mineral water. I opened it uneasily: after the night I had spent, I wasn't sure I wanted to know about any of my friend's little schemes. I would much rather have taken a bus back to Buenos Aires that same day, got home, shut myself in with Félix Jesús and taken a delicious, replenishing siesta.

If only I had.

"They're about the research my father and his group of assistants were doing," Isabel said when she saw me staring at a swirl of numbers and equations all over a hand-written report I could make nothing of, partly on account of the handwriting and partly because the technical stuff was beyond me.

"I know they were working on methods to change sunflowers into petrol or something like that," I said.

"It was maize," Isabel corrected me with a smile. "But a lot of people are doing similar research. In fact, they've already been successful in several countries. They call it bio-fuel. It's an interesting development, but it's not going to make the sheikhs paupers. Not in the near future, anyway."

Having discarded Al-Qaeda and the possibility that Edmundo and his friends' research might damage O.P.E.C.'s interests as the reasons for his demise, Isabel focused her anger on Lorena and her not inconsiderable charms.

"She used to call him at all hours of the day and night. I don't think Daddy ever seriously considered leaving Mummy, but it got so that it was impossible for them to be together. He would answer the phone in bed and beg the little tart to hang up, while beside him Mummy was crying her eyes out and could not understand why, yet again, when they were of an age to be looking after grandchildren, her husband's wanderlust was pushing her to do something she hated doing."

"Throwing him out."

That was what she did, and this time it was for ever, or so she said. And that was how it turned out, because a bullet fired at point-blank prevented Edmundo from coming back from wherever his lust had taken him.

"But it was three months from his leaving home to when he was shot," Isabel said. "If you had your glasses on, you'd see there's a telephone number in among all those figures and equations."

My prosthesis for myopia had been in the glove compartment of the car stolen by whoever had abducted the blonde. I told Isabel it had been taken the night before, but did not go into detail. I had more than enough to worry about with my own confusion and the sneaking feeling that if we stuck our noses into the reasons behind the murder we would be venturing into very dangerous territory.

"I called the number," Isabel said. "Daddy wasn't coming back, Mummy was worried what might have happened to him. Think about it, after all those years together, hate soon goes out of the window. All that remains are the shared memories, the need to have him near if only to curse him. It was the tart who answered. I recognised her voice: it was the same I had heard so many times, the same brazen insolence: 'Let him be,' she said. 'Your Dad has the right to be happy.' What d'you think of that, Gotán?"

Edmundo's family knew me by the nickname I had acquired forty years earlier at secondary school. I was into rock music, played an electric guitar and sang like Tanguito, but the words to the dreadful songs I wrote were pure Buenos Aires slang, so I got to be called Gotán, back slang for "tango".

"Gotán thinks lots of things," I said, using Maradona's absurd third person. "He believes some of them, understands a few more, and feels sorry about a lot he doesn't grasp at all. We all have the right to be happy: the tart was right there. Perhaps poor Edmundo really did fall in love."

Isabel leaned back in her chair, asked me to fill her glass with mineral water, then raised it in a toast, possibly to lost happiness. She admitted her father might have left home convinced he had finally found what he had been looking for all his life. But that was not the point, she said.

"Less than half an hour later, I reckon, my phone rang. A man's voice told me Daddy was going to die."

I could not suppress a shudder. Even though the threat had already been carried out, I could not help seeing Edmundo on his back in a pool of his own blood.

"What makes you think the tart was linked to the murderer?"

"I can trace calls," Isabel said. "The number the man rang from to tell me my father was a marked man was the same one I dialled to hear her voice and her words of advice. The same one that's written on one of those sheets of paper you can't see because you're so short-sighted."

"Talking of coincidences, chance, or destiny written on a wall somewhere, prepare to be amazed," I told her, looking over her shoulder towards the door of the packed restaurant.

The woman standing in the doorway was one of those who affect observers like an Arab walking into the Pentagon with a brown-paper package under his arm. Although Isabel had never met her, the little tart was reflected in my pale, unhinged face as clearly as in a mirror.

4

It was very plain Lorena had not expected to see me there. Only a few hours earlier she had left me in a petrol station toilet three hundred kilometres away in the middle of the Patagonian desert, so how could she expect that the handsome fellow sitting at a restaurant table in Bahía Blanca would be Cárcano's closest friend? It took a few seconds for the shock to sink in, and her companion was busy searching the restaurant for a free table, so that when she took him by the arm and whispered the news in his ear, he stared straight through me, then started pulling her towards the street door.

"Is that her?"

Isabel's question went unanswered, because by then I was getting to my feet, furious, and bellowing through my nose like someone with chronic sinusitis. A waiter carrying aloft a tray laden with dishes got in my way, and by the time I was outside all I saw was a car with an official number plate and tinted windows speeding off the wrong way down the street, then turning the corner, also against the traffic. I stood there expecting to hear the crash as it rammed a vehicle coming the other way, but there was only a babble of klaxons. After that the tree-lined streets were as quiet as usual. Isabel came out of the restaurant and grabbed me by the arm. Again she wanted to know if it was Lorena, and why had she run off like that if she did not even know who we were. As we walked back to the table I had abandoned so abruptly, I had to explain what had happened the previous night.

"Then the man with her must have been the one who warned me

Daddy was going to die," she said, stretching out her hand as if asking me to pass the salt. I did so, not looking for any ulterior motive. "Put it down: it's bad luck to hand it straight to someone."

*

We have no way of anticipating when our everyday reality is about to disintegrate. There are always signs, of course, but how are we to spot them? A telephone call at midnight, an unexplained journey with a dead body at the end of it: this should be enough to alert even someone who is fast asleep, but we refuse to make connections.

My friendship with Edmundo Cárcano in no way required that I give my life for someone who had already lost theirs. Nor did it demand that I swear over his dead body that I would not rest until I had avenged him. He had not been killed in his Buenos Aires home in Villa Crespo while drinking *mate* tea with his petite bourgeoise wife of thirty years, but in his isolated beach chalet, possibly (to my great envy) as he was making love to a twenty-year-old whose loveliness would guarantee anyone she was with almost anything but a quiet old age.

"I can see he wasn't in a position where anyone would feel sorry for him," said his widow of a few hours when we met that afternoon in her hotel lobby. By now she was much calmer and more resigned. "But nobody deserves to be shot simply for giving in to temptation."

She was looking down as she said this, putting me in the position of a priest hearing her confession rather than a friend.

"There isn't going to be an investigation or anything."

"I couldn't care less now," Mónica said.

"But his body should be in the morgue, not buried in the ground. He was your lifelong companion and my friend —"

"He betrayed me. He was unfaithful. And the sinner has to pay – although, as I said, I think he paid too high a price."

I learned later from Isabel that for years her mother had belonged to an evangelical sect. One of those electronic churches where God appears on demand and collects his ten per cent.

"Daddy's adventures started in earnest when she had her menopause," Isabel told me. "He went from being a typical office lover, a sad sack who falls for the woman at the desk opposite, to a roving Don Juan who came home late making the most ridiculous excuses. Since the Holy Catholic Church only offers punishment and penitence and no prospect of happiness, Mummy threw herself into the arms of those soul-stealers in search of a bit of relief."

"I never saw Edmundo that way. He never boasted of his conquests. He was a reserved, rather gloomy man. Lorena must have performed a miracle if she rescued him from that."

For a while at least he had looked jovial, with the exhausted but contented appearance of someone who spent his nights on the tiles. He was like one of those boxers who make a comeback in the ring: weary and flabby, but still with the courage of a true fighter. The crowds applaud them even if they get knocked out in the first round.

After all – and this is nothing new – love and death are the only stable couple I know.

5

I decided to spend the night in Bahía Blanca, in the same hotel as my murdered friend's widow and daughter. We shared a frugal supper and said goodnight until the next morning, when we planned to return to Buenos Aires in Isabel's car.

I felt depressed. I had lost my car because I had left a blonde inside it while I went blithely off to have a pee. The local police had questioned me as if I had been a crime suspect rather than the owner of a car reporting its theft. To add insult to injury, they growled at me that the robbery had occurred outside their jurisdiction, in Carmen de Patagones, so all they could supply me with was an untidy report that a bulimic inspector took half an hour to type on a rusty Remington. He was more interested in his *mate* and telephone calls that had nothing to do with his police work. In fact, it seemed as though he used his hours on duty to run a numbers game: he took bets quite openly, and even discussed the merits of such lucky numbers as twenty-two or forty-eight with his clients.

When I called the insurance company, they told me the crime report was a start, but that at some point I would need to go down to Carmen de Patagones so that the "relevant authorities could give me an official confirmation of the theft". I spent a good few moments cursing a system that washes its hands of anything that disappears, be it a car or a close friend. Typical, I thought, of a country that sends hundreds of cargo boats abroad piled high with food, yet allows more than half of its citizens to live off charity or scraps, with the age-old excuse that Argentina is a country that does not deserve what is happening to it, because we are a nation inevitably destined for greatness.

I went for a walk around the frozen streets of Bahía Blanca, half-hoping I might find my car parked on some corner or other. Luckily, just as I was about to freeze solid, I saw the universal neon sign with red lettering and a champagne glass flickering upwards. Pro Nobis the place was called, and if you looked as carefully at the sign as you might at a Goya painting in the Prado, you could see that alternating with the glass were a pair of female thighs.

I went in, hoping to find a drink and a woman who would not overwhelm me with demands or confessions. As a young man I had always avoided dives like this, frequented by desperadoes and sailors stranded on dry land, who dug into the dark corners in search of the fools' gold of their memories. Every lone wolf knows of long-haired women with perfect bodies who have betrayed them: the loss has remained with us for the rest of our lives, even though we are aware that if we met them again we would soon run into the same misunderstandings and contradictions, would yet love them as though they were the only ones for us, expose ourselves to ridicule, and believe for a while at least that what we cannot see or touch does not matter in the slightest.

"Get me a whisky, would you?" asked a redhead who came and sat beside me at the bar. The room's red light made her look transparent, the closest thing to an angel you could find etched in the filigree of smoke swirling round the dark surroundings. The barman was a blond bear with the face of a Swedish actor signed up by Bergman who spent his free time making porno films so he could have sex without having to spout nonsense about God and the human condition between fucks. He looked at me as I might have looked at him if he had spoken Swedish when I told him to serve the girl a real whisky, that if she was thirsty she could have a glass of water, because I had no intention of paying for a glass of coloured water when all I wanted to do was forget everything about the day I had just had.

"We can guarantee you'll forget everything in here," said the redhead. "And if after three glasses you start to cry, the fourth is on the house."

"And just when I was thinking there was nothing new in advertising."

"Do your zip up, darling. If anyone sees you like that they'll think I did it, and there are house rules."

Hearing her speak in that way confused me. She sounded more like a schoolmistress than just another woman I could spend some time with and never see again.

"You went red. Of course in this light it doesn't show, but you went bright red." She winked ostentatiously at the barman, and the two of them laughed. They must have been lovers, indulging in this kind of game to keep the nightly boredom at bay. She slid her hand onto my crotch and started fiddling with the zip and the little animal curled up inside. Poor thing, he did not even seem to realise the warm fingers caressing him were of the opposite sex.

Instinctively, I looked round the room. It was empty. Techno music was blaring out, strobe lights alternately blinded and dazzled, but there was nobody to enjoy them. I was the only customer in Pro Nobis, which must have been the only bar open at 2.00 in the morning in this southern port city. It was from here that the Argentine fleet threatened to leave to vanquish the British in the 1982 South Atlantic War, except that none of them ever weighed anchor.

With great relief, doubtless, the redhead realised I had not come into Pro Nobis for sex but to feel less alone, to share small talk or simply healing silence, despite the music and the lights that were an unavoidable part of the atmosphere for anyone who came here to escape the harsh emptiness of the early hours outside.

On the wall, a framed photo of the cruiser *General Belgrano* adorned with an anchor and a lifebuoy got us talking about the disaster when it was sunk by British pirates. The redhead told me she had a brother lying at the bottom of the south Atlantic. He was not yet twenty when the submarine *Conqueror* torpedoed them, on the direct orders of the British prime minister whose scorched-earth policies went on to inspire the 'new' Peronism of '90s Argentina. Today her brother would have been more than forty, and could well have been sitting at this same bar, making sure that his little sister (she was five years younger than him, she told me coquettishly) did not prostitute herself with the dirty old men who brought their moss-lined hulls into this particular berth.

"He could have been, he might have been, but he isn't. Sometimes I see him coming in through that door over there," she said. I gazed in the direction she was pointing, but all I could see were other girls, the barman and the dish-washer coming in and out.

"He comes in, sits down right where you are now, and bums a

cigarette off me. He never bought his own, but smoked all kinds, and marihuana too – it was all the same to him. 'Take care,' he says when he comes to see me, 'and try to find another job, because I don't want a sister who's a whore.'"

I had no doubt the redhead's story was true, that her brother came in just as she said, spoke to her, then stayed for a while, smoking his borrowed cigarette without saying a word. And that she waited until he had left to avoid upsetting him by seeing her sell her body, a body firm now only in this half-light, her flesh gouged by the toothless night-sharks.

I sat watching her silently, just like her brother who never reached the Malvinas. I only left when the Swede said he was no longer serving, that the evening was over. It was not yet 3.00. The Pro Nobis sign clicked off above my head, the woman's thighs frozen in the night.

I should never have left the hotel, I told myself. My words of wisdom proved prescient when two giants straight out of a body-building ad sprang from a car parked a few feet away and proceeded to wipe me from the map with a few well-aimed punches.

6

No way of knowing how long I was unconscious. It cannot have been for very long, because when I came round day had not dawned. I felt groggy and with a stomach pain that this once I could not blame on my chronic ulcer. I heard people speaking, but was afraid I might get another beating if I opened my eyes, so I clung stupidly to the hope that all this was a bad dream. When I began to tremble with cold I realised that it was not.

"Wrap this round you," said a hoarse smoker's voice. A leather jacket hit me on the head. More curious than fearful, I opened my eyes.

"Don't worry, you're with friends," the same voice told me.

Before I could properly make out his features, I saw the glow of a cigarette in the corner of his mouth. I pulled the jacket round my shoulders.

"The men who attacked you took your coat. They thought the beating was enough, but hoped you might freeze to death as well."

"I don't think they were muggers," said another, reedy voice.

The first man was sitting opposite me. They had laid me on a bare bunk with only a blanket on top of its springs. The one with the reedy voice was speaking from the corridor on the far side of the bars, as though he was a visitor. When I tried to sit up, the pain in my stomach paralysed me. My neighbour helped me with the jacket.

"Stay where you are for a while," he told me. "The doctor is on his way. We had to wake him, he was out flat. We don't get many emergencies around here," he went on, as though to justify the doctor being asleep. "This is only a small town, there's no dangerous violence like there is in Buenos Aires."

I understood that what had happened to me was not dangerous, simply a demonstration of small-town high spirits.

They had not taken me to the infirmary, but had dumped my unconscious body in a cell. It was lit only by a fluorescent tube in the corridor. The man opposite me was big enough to have been one of my attackers, and the man outside could have been his companion, but it made no sense for them to have beaten me up before they brought me in. They could simply have arrested me: I usually do not resist polite requests to accompany people to a police station.

"I wonder what led a middle-class guy from Buenos Aires to leave his warm hotel room in the middle of the night and end up in a dump like Pro Nobis? What was he looking for?" my hoarse-voiced friend asked.

"Who are you?" I managed to stammer, as if he could ever have been anything else but a policeman.

"Inspector Ayala," he replied, in a formal manner that took me by surprise. "And that's Officer Rodríguez," he said, pointing towards the man in the corridor.

I tried to draw breath, but the effort was a punishment.

"Don't worry, the doctor will soon be here."

"He must be cleaning his teeth," came the voice from the corridor. "He's obsessed. First of all he brushes them, flosses them one by one, and then gargles with mouthwash. It takes him at least half an hour."

"If I were a woman, I'd have him lick my cunt," said the man beside me. The two of them laughed so loudly at this that it sounded like a duet for two drunks, with a low and a high voice singing from very different scores.

"I spent all the money I had in Pro Nobis," I said, feeling my empty pockets. "So why did they mug me?"

Inspector Ayala wiped away his dirty cackle like crumbs with a napkin.

"You should know," he said drily.

"I've never been beaten up to thank me for something," Rodríguez said.

I realised then that I was not in a cell because there was nowhere more comfortable to accommodate me.

"As far as I'm aware, I haven't done anything wrong. I'm a single father. My daughter lives in Australia. Her mother abandoned her when she left me, so nobody is asking for any alimony."

"Why did you come to Bahía Blanca?" Ayala wanted to know.

From out in the corridor, Rodríguez offered him a cigarette. Ayala asked if he had forgotten he had given up two months ago. He was finding it hard going, so why didn't Rodríguez stop messing him around and just get on with poisoning his own lungs. Rodríguez shrugged and lit his cigarette, glancing at me out of the corner of his eye either for support or to keep tabs on me.

Ayala was still waiting for my reply.

"Am I being charged?"

He stood up and turned as if to leave the cell, asking Rodríguez if that wasn't the doctor he could hear, parking his sky-blue Volkswagen outside the station. As Rodríguez was saying he did not think so, the inspector wheeled round, leaned down, and slapped me as hard as he could across my left cheek.

"That pain in your stomach is going to seem like an itch compared to this," he said, knocking my head in the opposite direction with another blow.

I have only a few teeth left, and most of them are rotten, but luckily I have never gone in for false ones. If I had, I would have lost them all with that second backhander. I cursed him as loudly as I could as my mouth filled with blood.

"Blue Volkswagen pulling up outside, Inspector," said Rodríguez.

"If the doctor asks, tell him you fell over," Ayala explained patiently. "You were beaten up in the street, and when you tried to stand, you fell against the kerb."

"Son of a bitch."

"If you ever say that to me again, you're a dead man. Our good doctor doesn't have any scruples when it comes to signing death warrants. He wouldn't be a forensic expert if he cared a great deal about living specimens."

I believed him. I had no idea why I was so reluctant to answer their questions. There was nothing suspicious about why I had come all this way to Mediomundo, even if I had arrived to find a friend who had been shot and a young blonde who had jumped into my car and then vanished along with it.

The doctor came in staring at the floor and did not say hello to anyone. He was a short, bald, plump man in his fifties. He was sweating, although inside the cell it was as cold as an ice box. His breath anaesthetised me while he poked around my stomach with his stethoscope. When he pressed on my ribs, though, I howled with pain. He gave me a strip of gauze to wipe the blood from my mouth, and asked if I had lost any teeth. I said I had not, that I had a dentist who was perfectly capable of doing that for me.

"Did you see who it was?" he asked, keen to play the detective.

"I didn't have time to open my eyes," I said.

"This is a peaceful city. Violence comes from outside," he said, handing me a prescription. "Take this for the pain. And make sure you rest. There could be internal injuries."

He scribbled something else on his pad, then, as though prompted by Inspector Ayala, asked:

"What brought you to Bahía Blanca?"

"Nothing special. A dead friend."

Ayala, who had stepped back to give the doctor room, nodded his approval. I briefly wondered whether the doctor might be Ayala's ventriloquist's dummy.

"What did he die of?"

"The usual. Shot at point-blank range."

The doctor looked inquiringly at Ayala's impassive face. The inspector did not disappoint him.

"His name was Cárcano. One of the bosses out at the C.P.F. oil company. Five thousand dollars a month in his pocket, plus bonuses."

"His widow was right, the dirty old man spent it all on his fancy woman," I said.

"Five thousand dollars a month! Not even the King of France earns that!" said Officer Rodríguez, consumed with envy in the corridor. "I earn eight hundred and risk my life dealing with all the garbage out on the streets. And when I retire I'll get half that, dammit."

"Yes, dammit for two reasons. Dammit for the pittance you get, and dammit because the King of Spain might earn that, but not the King of

France, they got rid of him a long time ago," the doctor said. Then he turned to me. "Go back to your hotel or wherever it is you're staying and take a couple of days' complete rest."

Ayala seemed to agree with his advice. My face was still aching from the slaps he had given me, but I was warming to him. When he spoke, I changed my mind.

"I think twelve hours will be enough 'rest'. You could be on your way back to Buenos Aires tonight. I don't think Bahía Blanca needs you any more."

"I was intending to set off in a couple of hours, with Cárcano's widow and daughter."

The doctor put away his pad and stethoscope and said with a snort that he would not be held responsible if I died en route.

"When you woke me up I thought it was for something important."

I left the police station with him. Nobody asked any more questions, or apologised for the beating, or for slapping me around in the cell. The roly-poly doctor was kind enough to drive me back to the hotel. I would never have found it, although it was no more than six blocks away. As I was getting out of his car he told me I really should get some rest, but if the inspector was telling me to leave, then it would be wise to do so. I thanked him for his advice. I could understand his position: it must be unpleasant having to cut open the body of someone you were talking to only a couple of hours earlier.

I got out and went into the hotel.

"Room number 347," the receptionist reminded me. Day was almost dawning, and I had agreed to have breakfast at 8.00 with Mónica and Isabel before we set off for home. Exhausted, aching all over and still completely at a loss, I threw myself down on the bed without switching on the light. If I sleep on my back my own snores wake me up, so I turned on my left-hand side.

It is every man's dream to find a beautiful, naked woman aged no more than twenty-five in bed beside him. What happens next depends on one's condition and the circumstances. That morning (and from that moment on) my condition was not what it might have been, but there was still a little something there if sufficiently tempted. The circumstances however could not have been worse.

The naked woman was Lorena. She was dead.

7

One thing was clear. I was not going to be able to sit and have breakfast with Edmundo's widow and daughter at 8.00 that morning. It was also clear that if I ran out of my room shouting there was a dead body in there I would be thrown head-first back in jail, and I would be questioned even less politely. And this time they would not bother to rouse the police doctor from his nice, warm bed.

I am always upset when young people die. It makes me wonder what I am doing still hanging around, pushing sixty and with a body and ideas that stink to high heaven, unable to instil hope in anyone. I am not even one of those metaphysical gurus that are everywhere these days, the sort who line their pockets writing books and giving talks where they tell you without a qualm that God is in all of us, when it is obvious even to the numbest of skulls that God is not even where he is meant to be, that no-one can find him: he has not even left a note with a clue as to why he has abandoned us like this.

*

Lorena had not had the time to become disillusioned with mankind, still less to repent of her sins. A stiletto blade had pierced her body just below her left breast. Somebody had made love to her and then stuck the blade in her like a pin in a voodoo doll. The only sign of violence was the small circle of blood no bigger than the aureola of her nipple.

She was flat on her back. No more than thirty seconds could have passed between pleasure, pain, and nothingness. Her legs were splayed open, but I felt a mean-spirited sense of relief when I realised there was no smell of semen. There is nothing more unpleasant than the scent of another man's spunk. I suppose it has to do with the sense of having one's territory invaded; the same feeling a woman has when she sniffs someone else's perfume on her man.

Poor little thing, I said to myself as I examined her body for any other wound or mark. Poor little thing.

I had hardly spoken to her, and she was somehow involved with the people who had stolen my car, but seeing her like that I could not feel angry. She could not run away from me any more as she had done in the restaurant. I was the one who had to get away now. I could not imagine Inspector Ayala looking kindly on my explanation of events, although if he thought about it at all, he would have realised I did not have the time to seduce someone and kill her in the quarter of an hour between me leaving the police station and the discovery of her body. But until the forensic report confirmed this, he would adopt the standard police methods of trying to beat the truth out of me.

The forensic report, I told myself. Perhaps the doctor could help me. I did not even know his name.

"You mean Doctor Burgos," the man on the front desk told me when I asked him if he knew the person who had dropped me off at the hotel. "Who else in Bahía Blanca or anywhere else in all Patagonia would paint a V.W. Polo sky blue?"

He looked in his address book and wrote a phone number on a piece of paper. He even had time to recommend him.

"He attended my wife each time she gave birth. Four fillies, one a year." He added, confidentially: "And he got us out of a real spot of bother last year. There were twin girls on the way . . ."

A forensic doctor and an abortionist.

I did not see any contradiction there. It seemed to me legitimate to prevent the birth of beings who – as everyone knows – only mess up the environment and not only threaten the future of all the other species but of the planet itself. Seen in this way, an abortionist is only carrying out preventative medicine, and that is highly recommended nowadays as a means of avoiding the astronomical cost of keeping people alive in old age.

A forensic doctor, on the other hand, is a failed writer. Since he has no imagination, he rummages in people's stomachs to try to uncover the mysteries of death. It is not for him to discover them – that is the job of theologians and alchemists – but the forensic doctor is clearly (or obscurely) a stubborn dung beetle digging his own grave in the belief that he is burying others, and with them the answers to all the enigmas they could not discover while they were alive.

*

"Where's the body?" the roly-poly doctor said. He did not sound in the least bit surprised.

"In my room at the Imperio Hotel."

"You ought to be a thousand kilometres from Bahía by now. Abroad, if possible."

"I didn't kill her."

"Do you think anybody is going to believe you? Here people are pardoned *after* they're burnt at the stake. I can't remember your name . . ."

"It's Pedro Martelli. People call me Gotán."

"Don't go back to the hotel, Don Gotán. Whoever left the body there is trying to frame you. Do you have a car?"

"The dead woman stole it."

"Not good. Well then, take a taxi to the railway station and wait for me there. There are no police guards because hardly any trains reach Bahía Blanca these days, and there's nothing left to steal because the place was stripped when they shut the railways down."

*

I stopped a taxi in the street and told the driver to pull up outside the hotel for a moment. The porter was surprised to see me back only five minutes after I had left.

"Has anyone been here asking for me?"

When the porter shook his head I plucked up the courage to go over to the receptionist and slide a hundred-peso note under the register.

"That's for you to forget I asked about the doctor in the blue car."

His sphinx-like expression told me I could put about as much trust in him as an infant deer could in a lion reading her *The Jungle Book*. There was just the slimmest of chances he would not give me away.

*

Bahía Blanca has a Victorian railway station, built by the British. Once upon a time express trains came and went from Neuquén, Bariloche and Zapala, dust-covered carriages filled with passengers from Patagonia, still wide-eyed from the vast desert lands. These were once the domain of Mapuches, Araucanians and Tehuelches, until in the nineteenth century they were all wiped out by the campaigns of a general called Roca, that same general who the Peronist government decided to honour by baptising this railway line in his name.

Nowadays the station was nothing more than a stopping-off place sunk in desolation and melancholy. As if by miracle, there was still one train a day to and from Buenos Aires, although most people preferred to take the bus because they could not trust the railway timetable. The train left at night, so my taxi driver was curious to know what I was doing at the station at 7.00 in the morning.

"If you want to buy a ticket, the office only opens at midday," he said nosily.

"I'm a photographer. I'm working on a series about Argentine railways."

His eyes narrowed suspiciously as he peered at me through the rear-view mirror, looking for my camera. To avoid further scrutiny I got out of the taxi without waiting for my change.

"Be careful, there are lots of delinquents around here," he warned me as he pulled slowly away, still staring at me through his side window.

Day had barely dawned. The ramshackle station did not seem like the ideal meeting place, but if the doctor had laid a trap for me, it was too late to back out now. I did not want to leave the city with the police on my heels and no idea of what was going on. The doctor was the only person I could think of who might help.

Less than five minutes later I saw the sky-blue V.W. splashing its way through the mud along a side street, then turning into the station yard, where it came to a stop next to a goods van.

"The police never come here. They're afraid of getting mugged," he said. He did not get out of his car, but jerked his head to invite me to climb aboard.

"What a night it's been," I said.

"You can say that again. But now you're headed somewhere safe."

He sped off in reverse towards the beaten-earth street that was a sea of mud. The car spun round like a top then leaped forward. I did up my seat belt.

"If we overturn and the car catches fire, you'll be burned to a cinder with that belt on," he said. "I trust to fate."

I did not say it, but thought that what in fact he put his trust in were the layers of fat that would act as an air-bag if we hit anything. He groped for a cigarette from the packet on the dashboard. It was only when he had lit it and stuck it between his lips that he thought to offer me one.

"Homeopathy. Two or three fags a day are the best way of preventing lung cancer."

I accepted his advice and was soon breathing in the therapeutic smoke.

"Why do you trust me?" I asked him.

"What about you? It can't be because of my looks."

He had two days' stubble, and his eyes were bloodshot either from lack of sleep or because he was some kind of addict. No, it was definitely not because of the way he looked.

Nor did the aggressive way in which he drove inspire confidence. Or his agitated breathing, which suggested he had just killed someone and he was the one on the run.

"This is the third murder in similar circumstances" he said. "I doubt whether you could have committed all three."

He said it so matter-of-factly I was not sure if he was arguing his belief in my innocence or if he did not think me capable of anything quite so sophisticated. He sped off down a long, deserted avenue arched over with chinaberry trees. Eventually the road turned into an asphalted track, potholed by heavy farm vehicles.

"Rustlers," the doctor explained. "It's their trucks that make all these holes. They come out here and steal cattle. They butcher them at night, in conditions even Dr Mengele would have balked at, then sell the meat directly to the shops at half price. That way everyone wins: the rustlers, the butchers, and the customers – they get the best steak for the price of scrag-ends."

"What about hygiene?"

"I don't know what you're talking about," he muttered. "Look at those mad cows in England. It's all very hygienic, but they feed them artificial muck. We all have to die sometime, and I'd rather it were from eating a nice, tender, juicy steak."

We turned off down another track that was nothing but mud. The V.W. might no longer be sky-blue, but behind the wheel the doctor was shouting as enthusiastically as if he were piloting a speedboat.

"My little cottage in the country," he said when we finally arrived, switching off the car's straining engine.

From the outside it was nothing more than an adobe shack with a thatched roof. But once inside, I found myself in a large room that was anything but ascetic.

"I like luxury as much as the next man," he said. "But that doesn't mean I have to show it."

I could scarcely believe the contrast. More than a cottage, it was like an outlaw's hideaway. It had everything to withstand a siege or a period of exile: freezer, microwave, T.V., mobile phone, shelves full of books, a video player, racks of wine, and a barrel-shaped bar stacked with bottles of spirits. There were two reclining chairs and a bed, with a small kitchen at the far end.

"This is my refuge. Nobody knows where it is. They know I have a lair, but you're the first person who has been here: you're not from around here, and this is an emergency."

"It can't be easy being a police doctor," I said.

"It's far worse being a policeman, believe me. This society of arse-lickers is always sacrificing them on the altar of their hypocritical so-called morality. But for now, just try to relax – you're going to have more than enough opportunity to be stressed out."

I did as he suggested. We had taken off our muddy shoes when we came in, so I walked over and sat in one of the chairs while Burgos served us both whisky on the rocks.

"At this time of day we should be having coffee and croissants," he apologised, "but I don't have any."

He sat in the other chair, folds of flesh spilling over the green chintz.

Taking a sip of his breakfast, he began to tell me the story. As he outlined the details, I realised the maze I had got myself into, and how hard it was going to be to stay alive until I could find a way out.

8

Isabel's voice sounded agitated, as if she were speaking from a moving vehicle. Yet she was still at the hotel, waiting for me to come down and have breakfast with her. Burgos had advised me not to call her. Someone could trace the call, he said, and besides, it was his mobile I was using: "All I need is for them to think I'm your accomplice. I've only got a few more months before I retire." In the end he relented: "It's not 8.00 yet, which means the province's entire security apparatus will be busy drinking *mate*."

The Imperio Hotel was carrying on as usual. Lorena's dead body was probably still on the bed in my room, lying in the freezing shadows of death until a maid found it and ran screaming into the corridor. I warned Isabel that this would very soon happen: I did not want the news to take her by surprise, or for her to have the least suspicion I might be responsible for the murder.

When I told her she went so quiet I begged her at least to breathe out so I would know she was still alive.

"Where are you now?" she whispered.

"I'm safe, for the next thirty or forty minutes at least. You and your mother need to check out of the hotel. Pay the bill and take a taxi to Tres Arroyos."

"But my car is in the hotel garage."

"Leave the key with the receptionist. I can't explain now. I'll sort it out later."

"Mummy isn't well, Gotán. She's so sad. She's in no state to play cops and robbers."

"These people aren't robbers, Isabel. They're murderers. It wasn't a heart attack that killed your father."

It was only to be expected that this would make her burst into tears. I prayed there was no-one else in the hotel breakfast room, or that if there was they were paying her no attention. Even though boyfriends rarely break off a relationship in the early morning, it's the first thing curious onlookers think when they see a woman crying into the telephone.

I heard another voice – Mónica's – asking what was going on. "I'll explain in a minute," Isabel said, then, choking back her tears, asked what they were to do in Tres Arroyos.

"Take a room at the Cabildo Hotel," I said, following Burgos' advice. "Wait for me there."

"What will happen if they arrest you?"

"Something terrible, I imagine," I said, suddenly catching my breath. "If I'm not there by nightfall, take a La Estrella express bus to Buenos Aires. It leaves at 11.00."

"Reclining seats with a stewardess," the doctor said at my elbow.

"Who's that with you?" Isabel asked in alarm.

"My guardian angel."

*

A breakfast of whisky on the rocks seemed to have loosened the roly-poly doctor's tongue. Serial killers apparently prefer cold climates, he said: southern towns and cities in a country like Argentina, northern ones in Europe or the United States. For some reason, these attacks are more prevalent in Scandinavia than in the Caribbean banana republics, he went on, as if setting out the introduction to a student lecture.

"So, that blonde in your hotel room is the third in three weeks, Don Gotán. All following the same pattern: first the love-making, then after or during the orgasm a stiletto under the left breast, straight to the heart. None of the three was a prostitute. I'm not saying they were nuns, but they were well-educated girls. At least the first two were, and I'm sure this one was too if she was your dead friend's partner."

I told him about our one and only meeting, how we had been forced to flee, her obstinate refusal to speak during our night drive to nowhere, racing at 140 kilometres an hour along Route 3 until I almost ran out of petrol.

I do not know whether he believed me when I said we had not stopped for a quick fuck. He would have done, he said in the same tone as one would warn a companion on a long journey that you needed to stop for a pee. Evidently he did not consider the possibility that a beautiful young woman like Lorena would be revolted by the idea that a toad with a stethoscope round his neck might jump on her.

"You're not gay?"

It was a question, but it sounded like a statement as he sat there holding his whisky glass up high like the Statue of Liberty's torch.

"Me?"

"Yes, you, Don Gotán. I'm just curious."

I felt as though I had been slapped as hard as in the police station, but this time it gave me a surge of adrenalin.

"Don't worry," he said. "Nor am I."

I breathed a sigh of relief.

"I lost my wife ten years ago. A galloping cancer that finished her off in a matter of days. It tore into her like vultures eating carrion, but she was lively and lucid to the last. Since then, I take on any job at all hours of the day or night."

"Such as being the police doctor."

He moistened his lips with a fresh glass of whisky.

"And you?"

"I'm not a police doctor."

"So what are you?"

"I'm a policeman."

*

My tango woman Mireya could not believe I was a policeman either. Her real name was Debora, and she hated being called Mireya almost as much as she hated my profession. But who on earth in this day and age is called Debora?

Burgos said this was no time to tell each other our life stories. Plenty of time for that if I was arrested, long years inside waiting for hearings that would be time and again postponed, judges and sentences coming and going, legal chicanery until my dying day. A policeman where, he wanted to know.

"In the capital."

"Ah yes, the National Shame," he said.

"Don't worry about my job, they threw me out."

He did not ask me why. Perhaps he was saving the question for my years of retirement in jail, but then again if you're about to go into battle it is best not to fill your rucksack with books and Bariloche chocolate. Too much information can slow you down. What is the point of discovering that the person meant to be on your side is in fact a psychopath who could dispose of you as easily as a computer virus?

If we have to put our trust in someone, it is as well not to know too much about them.

9

In spite of my being from the National Shame, Burgos seemed relieved I was a policeman. At first, his idea that we meet Inspector Ayala and Rodríguez in what he called "neutral territory" seemed crazy. It was like proposing that the Palefaces had something to offer besides pillaging and massacring the wretched natives. I was the Red Indian here, and normally I do not share a single puff of the pipes of peace I smoke locked in my bathroom.

"I'm innocent. I hope that you at least are convinced of that. Otherwise you'll think I'm double-crossing you."

"That's part of any game between card-sharps," he said. "I'd do it without a thought. Cheating on a Buenos Aires policeman wouldn't ruffle my conscience for a second, but it wouldn't help me achieve the one thing that made me agree to come here: to find the son of a bitch who's getting a kick out of butchering the sweetest, most interesting young women on the coast."

Burgos was driving back along the rustlers' road, avoiding all the potholes by wrenching the steering wheel from side to side so violently that I was afraid we would find ourselves upside down in the ditch. He laughed at my terrified face. "You must have been a desk man, a bureaucrat who never ventured out onto the streets," he decided, unable to otherwise explain why I was so alarmed by his driving. He was wrong, but I had no wish to correct his impression. Better that he feel in control, carry out his own investigation in the same carefree way as he drove.

"Ayala is an intelligent sort, though he does his best to hide it. He's a Dr Jekyll who in his more lucid moments is able to see why he turns into Mr Hyde when faced with a suspect."

"It goes with the job," I said. The last thing I wanted to do was analyse the personality of some dumb provincial policeman, but Burgos wanted to go on talking about him.

"He wants to retire. He has a family, God help us. A fine wife, and two kids. 'I'm not going to let the criminal scum ruin my life,' he tells anyone willing to listen. 'Every thug I kill without the press kicking up a fuss is one more step towards my leaving the force with honour.'"

"He wants a medal," I said, as innocent as a schoolboy.

"No, he wants money," the chubby doctor corrected me, steering his way round a series of gaping holes in the broken asphalt. "What 'leaving the force with honour' means down here is to retire but keep the money coming in."

By which he meant the shares in prostitution, illegal gambling, moonlight rustling, kidnaps for ransom, and all the other little sidelines that never show up in the abundant official statistics on economic activity and employment, but which are such an important part of the overall police product.

The doctor went on and on about Ayala's virtues, while I felt increasingly stupid, thrown out of my job and now a fugitive, a Richard Kimble with no degree and none of the women the Yankee doctor managed to pick up in that old black-and-white T.V. series while he searched for the one-armed man who had killed his wife.

When I mentioned this existential anguish, my companion said I had picked up a real beauty myself when I answered my friend's call.

"But you have to look after these sweeties," he lectured me. "Soften them up a bit, then go for it. Did you really not fuck her?"

I had no wish to answer him, and no time either. We were approaching Bahía Blanca's station again.

Ayala and Rodríguez's silhouettes stood out against the bare brick arch of the station like characters from Cervantes. The inspector was tall and lanky like Don Quixote, and his sidekick was almost as round as Sancho Panza (though not as plump as the doctor). They went on smoking, oblivious to our presence while Burgos parked his exotic blue V.W. alongside the black Ford Falcon without number plates that the policemen had come in. Rodríguez was giving his version of the game between Rosario Central and Chacarita he had seen the previous evening before he went on duty. Ayala seemed far more interested in the details of the game than in our being there. Apparently the game had ended nil-nil as fixed beforehand by their managers, anxious to add another couple of games to a tournament designed to fleece summer holidaymakers.

"Look, the tin-opener's arrived," was Ayala's greeting for the doctor, spat from the left-hand side of his mouth directly at Rodríguez, who finished the sentence for him:

"And he brought the sardine."

I stayed in the car while Burgos got out and whispered in Ayala's ear what he had learned about me being from the Federal police force. I heard Ayala growl "So why the fuck did they throw him out," at which Burgos shrugged and looked back in my direction, winking at me as if we were on the same side, although I had no idea if he meant I should join in or carry on sitting there quietly without a word, like a penitent who has just left the confessional.

Ayala pushed him aside and came over to the car. I have not carried a gun for years, but no sooner had I instinctively felt under my arm for my revolver than I was squinting down the barrel of the .38 that this provincial Quixote had stuck right between my eyes.

"I've had it up to here with you, Martelli. What the fuck are you doing so far from home? At your age you should be wrapping up warm and going to bed early."

"I've already told you why I came here."

"I don't like men who stick their noses into other people's business, especially when it's someone who's been kicked out of the force, pushing his snout in where nobody's asked him to."

"The person who asked me was a friend. When I arrived, he had been murdered – something that doesn't seem to bother you, but which explains why I'm pushing my snout in here."

"Get out of the car," he ordered, taking a couple of steps back but still aiming the revolver at me.

I did as I was told. I get hot under the collar when I have to deal with bureaucracy, and sometimes women drive me crazy, but I am never bothered by the sight of a gun. I have spent too long handling them, shooting and being shot at. Even though I no longer carry one, I accept my destiny. To be surprised that one day I might end up riddled with bullets would be as hypocritical as a habitual smoker who refuses to accept he has cancer because he gave up smoking at sixty.

"I could arrest you right now, and you'd spend the rest of your life on remand, waiting to be tried for the murder of three women."

"But he didn't do it!" shouted Burgos. Rodríguez was filling him in on the rest of the game now that Ayala was busy threatening me.

"You could," I said to Ayala, "but there are a few things I need to know so that my friend's widow can hate him in peace without feeling any remorse."

"That's not going to be easy," Ayala said, slowly lowering his gun. "Cárcano was a womaniser, but he wasn't mixed up in any shady business."

"So why did they kill him?"

"We had better talk in the waiting room of this magnificent Victorian-style railway station. It's a pity it's crawling with tramps and drunks, but I'll get Rodríguez to clear it out for us."

He did not have to insist. Rodríguez had already broken off his match report and disappeared inside the station. We heard him call out a couple of times and then, perhaps because one of the occupants was taking his time getting up, a bullet whistled through the glassless window. There followed shouts and the sound of running feet, and then I saw a pair of hobos leaping across the tracks in their socks and shredded underwear. One of them was whirling a pair of trousers round his head like a gaucho waving his poncho.

"They'll be back," Ayala said, with paternal concern. "Even if we get thrown out, we always return home."

10

We made an odd foursome following our meeting in the Bahía Blanca station waiting room. Three musketeers and a D'Artagnan who doubled as Don Quixote.

Burgos had hardly anything to say, even though, as he admitted, the idea for our little "off-the-record" chat had been his. "I'm a doctor, not a policeman," was his only contribution. "My profession is a priesthood. I cannot kill without betraying Hippocrates."

"Go and take a shit, then," Ayala said, no doubt aware that the toilet in this splendid station would be a den of rats and cockroaches.

All three of them wanted desperately to find the man who seduced beautiful young women and then sliced them like watermelons. They could not give a damn about Edmundo's death in Mediomundo. Ayala had dug up nothing in Cárcano's life that was of interest to him: he ran no rackets or brothels, and did not seem to be a drug trafficker. Solving his murder would not get Ayala on the front page of any papers or on the T.V. news, and might instead open a Pandora's box that, as a humble provincial policeman, he would find impossible to close.

The only virgin whose death I was interested in was the third one.

My name would soon be tossed into the nearest prosecutor's office like a stone in a pond, and within a few hours I would be on the wanted list in all the police stations in Patagonia. I could hardly rely on Don Quixote and Sancho Panza for protection. That was limited strictly to their own small area of jurisdiction and to their even more reduced authority. As for the doctor, his network was altogether virtual, and seemed to consist of a handful of characters who could only be seen as important from the point of view of a forensic expert used to peering at bloated wounds or the entry hole made by a bullet in a corpse's skin. Some local magistrates and a few cheap criminal lawyers as putrid as the bodies he examined.

In spite of this depressing scenario, I was happy enough to talk things over.

"That Cárcano wasn't mixed up in anything shady," Ayala said, "doesn't mean he was never tempted, the little mouse. Perhaps he saw the cheese and went for it."

"The cheese in this case being the girl," Rodríguez concluded, briefly raising his head from the sports newspaper he was studying. "Catalina Eloísa Bañados by name, although she used Lorena for her modelling work in agencies that are little more than a front for the white slave trade."

"What agencies?" Ayala said.

"You know the ones, Inspector. They use cheap motels here on the coast, less than three stars. Five-star places have a different class of clientele."

"Lorena didn't look like someone who was three stars or less," I said, annoyed by Rodríguez's scorn.

"You should have fucked her, Don Gotán. In bed after a good workout, women make the best informers. They fall for you, if only for a few moments, and blab about anything and everything."

I wondered just how often the doctor found voluptuous young women falling for him, or what arts not learned in the morgue he used to seduce them.

"Well, I didn't," I said, indignant. "I didn't have the opportunity or the inclination. She was with a friend of mine who had just been murdered. Whenever I looked at her I saw him lying there in a pool of his own blood with his eyes wide open, obviously killed by a professional."

What I did not tell my fat friend and the Cervantes duo was that I was in no mood to fall for anyone. After all, this was not a cosy tea-time chat among girlfriends.

It was time for us to leave. The toilet next to the waiting room stank to high heaven, and as the morning drew on our cars parked outside might arouse suspicion. Ayala and Rodríguez were off duty, and should have been either asleep at home or putting in a few extra hours as security guards at a factory or for one of those gated communities being built like medieval fortresses outside our cities to protect the haves from the have-nots.

What we agreed in the end was that I would leave that night for Buenos Aires with brand-new papers that a friendly counterfeiter in Bahía Blanca was already preparing for me. I could use Isabel's car to pick them up in Tres Arroyos. If I was stopped at a road block, I could use the documents and a ten-dollar bill to see me through. No local policeman wants to try arresting fugitives, because they are generally armed. The police are in more danger than the people on the run, because when they go up to a car they are on their own, even if they have an army battalion backing them up at the roadside. Besides, if saving their own skins were not motive enough, in summer they are too busy shaking down the dimwits who go on holiday without warning lights, or with out-of-date insurance or a broken left-rear light. The police know they are on to a good thing: they only have to threaten to write a ticket or impound the vehicle and the harassed family man or lover reaches into their wallet for twenty or thirty dollars "for the police widows' and orphans' fund" that always needs replenishing.

My mission in Buenos Aires was to consult archives and find informers. As Ayala saw it, the murderer on the coast was no novice: he knew exactly what he was doing, and left no clues. He also made sure each time that somebody else would be the first person the police looked for.

"You're the most pathetic case," Ayala said, to encourage me. "It's normal for the dummy to be some poor fool, a travelling salesman or a businessman having an affair. But for them to use an ex-federal police officer just goes to show how low public regard for our institutions has fallen."

I did not react to his insults. My face was still smarting from his attentions in the police cell, and though I had half a mind to pay him back in kind, I decided enough was enough for one day.

We agreed to meet up again five days later on Mediomundo beach.

"That way I can stretch out and get some sun," Ayala said.

"Count me out, boss. Putting all this blubber on display would be too much like sexual perversion," Rodríguez said, gripping the rolls of his stomach fat.

Burgos drove me back to the Imperio Hotel. He parked half a block away, told me to wait, then went to recover Isabel's car. When he returned, he said that the day-time receptionist, who knew him as well as his night-time colleague, had asked what kind of a mess he had got himself into: the hotel is crawling with detectives, he said. They found a girl dead in a room where a guy from Buenos Aires was staying. He left without paying or taking his things, and he was the one who was supposed to come and collect the car.

"You owe me a hundred dollars," Burgos said. "The night porter didn't share the tip you gave him with his colleague. It's getting more and more expensive to keep people quiet."

I had to hand over the hundred before he let me into Isabel's car, a Renault Mondino that was as impeccable and silent as a cat on the prowl. When I pressed gently on the accelerator, it positively purred.

"Don't get lost," the doctor said. "Buenos Aires is a city full of temptation."

He was standing by the driver's window, enviously stroking the smooth paintwork.

"Don't start with that nonsense again."

"The owner of a car like this must be a fine woman too. Why not fuck her if you get the chance?" he ventured by way of farewell.

11

What is a clairvoyant? Someone who foresees the future, or someone who determines it by suggesting what is going to happen?

I put my foot down. I was keen to get away as swiftly as possible from Burgos and his going on about my sleeping with whichever women I might bump into. I had not had much luck in that area. The last woman in my bed had been murdered, and I had not so much as touched her, apart from our hug at Edmundo's place when she had turned up in such apparent distress.

So she was not Lorena. Then again, Mireya was not Mireya, although with her I did get a bit further than a filling station lost in the desert.

"What else could you call me but Mireya like the tango, Gotán?"

I had laughed that night as we were leaving the Dos Por Cuatro tango bar half a block up from Boedo on the way to Puente Alsina, a dark, cobbled street from bygone days lit by old-fashioned street lamps you would expect to see in a warehouse or in a San Telmo antique shop window. Dos Por Cuatro was once owned by a Basque dairyman but had now been converted by his grandchildren into a tango bar. It still had its carriage entrance, and there was an old milk cart in the yard, shafts pointing to the sky. Nobody uses horses in Buenos Aires nowadays, but at weekends they harness some old nag to it and take Yankee and European tourists out for a ride. They cannot go far because they do not want to get into the busy avenues, but the driver and his attendants are glad of the tips in dollars.

"But you're not blonde, like Mireya was."

I was not very keen on calling her Mireya, which made me wonder if it was because I did not really want to name her at all. We lose what we put a name to. It's like shining a bright light on a flower so we can examine it more closely. Love fades, for this and many other reasons, but always, always too soon.

*

I left Bahía Blanca and sped along the highway at 140. I paid more attention to my rear-view mirror than to the road ahead. I am always afraid that the shot will come from behind, or the push into the ravine when we are standing at the top admiring the view.

It may no fun *being* a policeman, but it is worse to *have been* one. The memories weigh too heavily: there is too much past you cannot return to. And yet nothing is dead and buried. Not even the corpses.

*

Isabel and Mónica were not waiting for me at the Cabildo Hotel in Tres Arroyos. In fact, they had not checked in.

For a brief moment I tried to convince myself they must have headed straight for Buenos Aires. It made sense: what would they have gained by waiting for me? It simply meant they were caught up in an affair that had nothing to do with them, only hours after Edmundo's death.

I called the hotel in Bahía Blanca. According to the receptionist, the two women had left early that morning, in the midst of all the turmoil over the discovery of the dead body. He obviously fancied his chances as an informer for the yellow press. "They took a taxi to the bus station," he said.

When I called the bus station they told me there was no morning bus to Buenos Aires, but one to Tres Arroyos. I had told Mónica and Isabel to rent a car, but they must have preferred the bus: Isabel could console her mother while keeping quiet about the mess they were in that was not of their making, and did not really seem to have anything very much to do with Edmundo either.

I went to Tres Arroyos bus station. The bus from Bahía Blanca had arrived on time. "Not many people got off," the driver told me. He was a lanky, pallid individual who looked as though he had either slept very badly or had just been dumped by a consumptive girlfriend. I found him at the bar of a fast-food stall, tucking into a hotdog with a glass of white table wine.

"Let's see if I can remember," he said when I asked him if he had seen an older woman and a tall, pretty young woman with good breasts, a nice backside and long dark hair. "Let's see if I can remember," he repeated, digging into a decayed tooth with a toothpick and gently belching the smell of hotdog and cheap wine all over me. His memory improved when I slipped a ten-dollar bill into his open left hand, resting as if by coincidence on the counter in front of me.

"Yes, they got off here, with a gentleman."

"A gentleman?"

He shifted uneasily on his stool. The surprise in my voice must have made him realise his information was worth more than I had paid him.

"What was he like?"

"Let's see if I can remember."

I took out another ten-dollar bill, but this time laid it on top of the paper napkin where the half-eaten hotdog was.

"Either you remember or you don't."

As I slammed down the banknote, the half-eaten hotdog rolled onto the floor. I ordered another one and more white wine, but something drinkable this time.

"I have to leave for Tandil in fifteen minutes."

"The wine's for me. What did this 'gentleman' look like?"

He licked his lips as though cleaning the rim of a glass, ready to try the chilled Torrontes wine the barman was busy opening.

"There were two of them," he said, as though he had just remembered.

"Two gentlemen?"

"Yes, and two ladies. What's so strange about that? Are you a policeman?"

I filled his glass and poured a half for myself. He tossed the wine down in one gulp and held out the empty glass for more.

"It's nice and cool."

I refilled it. This time he drank only half of it. The wine seemed to refresh his memory.

"Those two were policemen as well. I can smell them," he said, wrinkling his hooked sommelier's nose. "Built like tanks. Not very tall, about my height. But built like tanks. Lots of gym and steroids."

He sat there staring at the counter, pretending to be lost in thought. I knew that if I seemed anxious, he would want more money. I said I was leaving.

"They all got into a car that was waiting for them," he said in a rush.

"What kind of car?"

"One of those 4×4s they have in the country. Tyres as fat as aeroplane wheels. Red. A Chevrolet, I reckon."

"Did you see anything unusual or threatening? Did they push the women into the vehicle for example?"

He fixed his cloudy eyes on me. They were as cold as the wine.

"Gentlemen, I said. Not killers. All muscle, but polite."

I paid for the wine and the second hotdog, which he had not touched. I commended him to get a relief driver for the Tandil run.

"I like people who try to help," he said, patting me on the back. "Tandil is just up the road. It's all dead straight, and there isn't much traffic. Thanks, though."

With that he swallowed another glass of wine, wiped his mouth on his sleeve, and winked at me as he left.

All muscle but polite, two gentlemen had kidnapped Isabel and Mónica.

Some time later I heard on the radio that a bus on its way to Tandil had left the road on one of the few bends on the highway from Tres Arroyos, had sailed over the roadside ditch and come to a halt in a soya field.

12

All I had was someone else's car and a fake I.D. card. There had been a beautiful blonde waiting in bed for me, but she was dead. And the friend who had kindly invited me into all this mess had been dropped from the catalogue too.

Tres Arroyos is one of those hundreds of Argentine country towns that are pretty enough to the people living there but have nothing to tempt a visitor to spend so much as a night there. The inhabitants know their charms, and try hard to conceal the sheer boredom of the clean, deserted streets, the grid of avenues round the main square, where town hall and church silently confront each other.

If the vehicle that Isabel and Mónica were taken away in was a 4×4, that probably meant they were being kept on a nearby *estancia*, in some shack in the middle of the countryside that would be difficult to locate and hard to get to.

I decided to give Tres Arroyos a chance by staying there a night. I registered at the Cabildo Hotel with my brand-new identity: Edgardo Leiva, married, commercial traveller. The plan I had hastily arranged with Don Quixote, his sidekick and the fat forensic specialist, fell apart if Isabel and Mónica had disappeared. The idea had been to take them back to Buenos Aires so they could quickly get back to their normal lives and not become involved in something none of us knew the true dimensions of.

A pair of muscular but polite gentlemen had pushed in before me.

I visited half a dozen estate agents, and found out all about farms, market gardens, and dairy outfits for sale or rent in the region. Everything was as I had expected: the pampas around Buenos Aires are the last redoubt of that rich Argentina that in the early years of the twentieth century our leaders used to dazzle millions of European immigrants with. They did not, of course, tell them that the really fertile land was already owned by others, most of them descendants of the soldiers who had robbed the Indians of it in the first place. All that was left to distribute was rough, parched land that needed a lot of brute strength and a great deal of money to make anything of.

The immigrants, driven out of Europe because imperial wars had left them starving, supplied the brute strength. The rewards for all their hard work were waiting for them in their graves.

"What exactly are you looking for?" the man in one of the last agencies I visited asked me exasperatedly.

I told him my interest was not strictly commercial, for the moment at least. It could be a farm that had not been worked for a while, with a rundown or abandoned shack on it. I did not care because I was not going to live there. I wanted to buy something cheap.

"You're not going to find anything cheap around here," he warned me.

He got out some maps and spread them across his desk. There were three properties that might interest me: farms of less than a hundred hectares. On two of them there had been a building of some kind or other. One was in ruins; the other was very run-down, with the roof missing over half of its six or so rooms.

"I'm interested in that one."

"The owners live in Buenos Aires. I'm sure there's no-one there. We could go now, it's not far."

I asked him to tell me how to get there. We could go early the next morning, I suggested.

"No, the morning's impossible for me," he said. "Give me a call and we'll arrange a time."

I shook his hand, looking as pleased as if we had just done a fantastic deal. He was obviously interested in selling something; I was more concerned about getting him off my back. I had the information I was looking for. If the two polite gentlemen had taken Isabel and Mónica to some out-of-the-way place, it could be the half-ruined ranch on a neglected farm. There would be no witnesses. On any working *estancia*, market garden or dairy farm there are farmhands, cows. If the estate agent was right, on this one there would be nothing more than thistles and a ramshackle wind-pump.

I climbed back into the Renault and switched on the radio. As I did so I remembered I had left Bahía Blanca without checking to see if the car's papers were in the glove compartment. As I opened it, the snub-nosed .38 fell onto the passenger seat like a cat escaping from a cupboard. On the radio they were forecasting a storm for that night.

*

Debora, I wrote on the steamed-up glass of the bathroom mirror. As I was combing my hair after the shower, the letters gradually faded, leaving only my face in view. If memory is a window on the past, I give up. All the glimpses of it I get are snatches of events seen through shutters. I hear footsteps but have no idea whose they are, whether they are coming towards me or leaving me for ever.

"Call me Mireya if you like, Gotán. You're really pathetic, but call me Mireya if it makes you feel good."

She had no idea I was a policeman when she allowed me to call her that, to talk to her as if we were in some cheap melodrama, exaggerating my lines, making fun of my own autumnal passion. I was in no hurry to tell her what I had once been, and anyway, she was delighted at my current occupation as a salesman of bathroom furniture, washbasins, bidets and toilets, together with all the fittings and pipes . . . "I don't suppose you carry samples with you, do you?" she asked, laughing. "No, just leaflets. Don't laugh, sweetheart," I said. "Somebody has to make sure that people can perform their ablutions in modern, well-designed surroundings."

She liked my voice and the way I looked at her. "There's something so old-fashioned about everything you do," she told me. "You're like one of those old 78s transferred to a C.D.," she insisted, clinging to me, incredulous and fearful.

I did not have to wipe her name from the mirror. The draught between the bathroom door and the window saved me the trouble.

*

I called Buenos Aires. When I heard Isabel's voice on the answering machine I caught my breath. While I was enjoying the happy hour in Cabildo Hotel, she might be dead, and Mónica with her.

My next call was to my own apartment. I do not like calling when I'm not at home, out of respect for Félix Jesús's feelings, because every time the telephone rings he arches his back and spits as if he is being threatened by an Alsatian. But it was night already, so he had probably already slipped off through the cat-flap I had made for him in the basement.

After two rings, the recorded messages kicked in. I heard a voice saying: "The girls are fine, but don't even think of looking for them or they're dead meat. Wait for news." There were no insults, and the tone was like an astronaut resigned to the idea he would never get back to earth. I hung up and had to go and sit at the bar until I stopped sweating.

I ordered a mineral water and while the storm they had forecast began to make its presence felt, I thought things over.

Edmundo was dead, so there was nothing I could do for him. Nor could I help the three murdered young women. But Isabel and Mónica were still alive, if I was to believe the emotionless bulletin of the person who had called me in Buenos Aires. I was determined to head back there at first light. I had the suspicion that somebody had deliberately dismantled a jigsaw puzzle, but that all the pieces were still there. Of course, the universe is a whole, but as we thread our way through it between lucidity and madness we all have to fit the pieces back together as best we can.

I could not allow myself the luxury of going to sleep that night, even though I was tempted by the freshly made bed, the T.V. in my room, a film I could watch until I fell asleep halfway through, and outside my window the rain, lightning, and perhaps even hailstones crashed against the streets of the town like the horses' hooves of an army of occupation.

It seemed a pity to take Isabel's new Renault out of the hotel garage where I had left it and expose it to the rain that was lashing the roofs of Tres Arroyos. If there are hailstones it could ruin the paintwork, I thought. It is normal to exaggerate the danger when you are about to face the unknown, to think, for example, how silly it would be to catch a cold, when in all likelihood the night was going to end with bullets flying.

Two and a half kilometres up the highway, turn left onto the side road until you reach a fork, then left again. Another nineteen hundred metres down what is little more than a track you come to a gate, and beyond that is the property, the estate agent's map told me.

If the storm carried on much longer, it would soon be impossible to reach the place. I drove out onto the highway. It was easier to see into my conscience than through the windscreen. I drove slowly, aware I could be hit by a truck or a bus travelling at more than a hundred driven by someone who loved hotdogs and cheap wine. A flash of lightning showed me where to turn off to the left.

At least I was safe from the insomniac madmen on Argentina's main roads. I speeded up along the deserted side road until I reached the fork. I bore left again, and suddenly had to slam on the brakes to avoid colliding with the farm gate.

This was not a good time and an even worse situation in which to go visiting a farm of less than a hundred uncultivated hectares. I switched off the engine and the lights. I could only see my hands when I lit the cigarette I decided to smoke before getting out. The condemned man's last moment of pleasure.

13

My last puff on the cigarette coincided with an easing of the storm. The rain fell more gently now. Crickets began to strike up their music.

I got out of the car and clambered through the wire fence onto the property. The torch and the .38 in my hand belonged to Isabel. I could not imagine her with a weapon, and wondered if she knew how to use it, where she had learned to shoot and who had taught her. Edmundo was not someone who favoured guns: he was an old-school type, said they were the devil's work. I am not a great fan of them, either; that is why I have not used one for years. Besides, you do not need a .45 to sell toilets to the middle classes.

I walked towards the only light I could see. I had to watch my feet on the uneven, slippery ground. Despite the darkness it was obvious the land had not been worked for years, like so many small farms on the fertile pampas that were created by the subdivision of big estates, generations of inheritances wasted by the descendants of decadent oligarchs, then dismembered by the miserable ambitions of bureaucrats who had never smelled damp earth or cow dung in their lives.

By the time I arrived at the source of the light I was covered in mud and exhausted. Before me stood a big, square old house with a veranda. It was here that my guiding star was hanging. A 4×4 was backed onto the veranda. There was not enough light for me to be able to tell whether or not it was red.

The estate agent would have been surprised if we had gone out there that afternoon, because lights were on inside the house and there was the steady hum of a generator from the back.

I felt for the snub-nosed .38 in my jacket pocket. I was not even sure the gun worked: women who carry weapons never seem to bother to maintain them, and see no reason to dismantle them from time to time to clean them. I also guessed that whoever was inside would probably have as much firepower as the Israeli army. I was not going to survive a shoot-out; my only chance was to remain unnoticed until I could learn something of what was going on.

The mud plastered all over me was useful camouflage. Besides, they say it does wonders for old, dry skin. It nutrifies all the molecules, and for a while at least you are as soft as a baby's bottom. I crawled along like a lizard, going past a drinking trough and finally stopping to get my breath back next to the wind-pump tank.

Bank employees moan because policemen can retire ten years before they do, but I would like to see *them* up to their ears in mud, on either side of their fiftieth birthday, or being bashed on the head or shot from behind by an accomplice of the thug they have just caught red-handed. When I left the Buenos Aires police I swore that I had done my last of these pentathlon events, and yet here I was. And the rain was pouring down again.

*

I sheltered under the eaves, next to a small window that turned out to be the bathroom vent. The electrical storm lit the vast empty pampas once more. I peered round the corner of the house and confirmed what I had suspected: the 4×4 was red.

There was no sound from inside the house, not even voices. They were probably asleep, or sitting there in silence because they had nothing to say to each other. I crouched down and was backing away from the wall when I felt hot breath on my right cheek. I froze, expecting a blow or a challenge, but all I heard was a low growl. Cautiously, I turned my face as slowly as possible. I found myself staring into the muzzle of an enormous farmyard dog.

How can I describe what I mean by a farmyard dog? They have all kinds of genes, from the most aggressive to the most docile. They have pedigree or mongrel blood, and can, of course, be of any size. The only thing they all have in common is that they hang around farmhouses, which they are never allowed to enter, hoping to snaffle a few scraps and perhaps even a friendly look from some human being – although only very rarely a pat or a stroke.

I decided to sit down and relax, to allow the dog to sniff my clothes and stick its nose into all parts of my muddy body. He cannot have found anything untoward, because at the end of his inspection he began to wag his tail and nuzzle me. I started stroking him, at first apprehensively and then determined to make sure he would be on my side. The dog soon rolled over and waved his legs in the air like an upturned cockroach. I tickled his belly. I could feel the warmth of his affection, and this made me happy in a way I had not felt for a long time. If I had been taken by surprise and killed there and then, I would have died with a silly grin on my face.

A blinding flash followed a few moments later by a crack of thunder jolted me out of my beatific state, and brought an abrupt end to the dog's pleasure. We were both back on the alert. I went up to the only proper window in the house, followed closely by the dog, by now my firm friend.

The light on the veranda which had been my guide suddenly began to flicker. The generator was on the blink or was running out of fuel. Inside the house, a voice asked what the fuck was going on, so I sneaked back as best I could to my hiding place next to the wind-pump. I was just in time to see two men emerge from the house, presumably the muscular but polite gentlemen the bus driver had told me about. Surprised by my retreat into the shadows, the dog hesitated midway between me and the house, staring towards my hiding place.

"What's wrong with that dog?" one of the men said.

"How the fuck should I know!" the other said gruffly. He set off round the back of the house, cursing the generator: "I told you to buy a decent one, not some cheap Oriental crap."

They had a brief argument, with one of them defending his decision because it had saved them a stack of money, the other one still going on about Chinese products: "This heap of shit is going to leave us in the dark any moment now," he said. His words proved prophetic. The generator suddenly died without so much as a sigh.

The weak, flickering light from the bulb was replaced by intermittent blinding flashes of lightning. The dog took advantage of all the confusion to come over to the wind-pump and sprawl at my feet. He wanted more stroking: he must have been autistic.

"Can you see anything?" the man who had been concerned about the dog asked his companion.

"That's why I brought the torch, asshole," replied the other.

The first man, who must have had some mastiff in his blood, still seemed more interested in the dog's behaviour than the electricity problem. He started towards me. He might not have a torch, but I was willing to bet he had a gun on him. The dog must have recognised him because when he was only two metres away from me, he roused himself and set off to greet him, wagging his tail.

Two or three seconds at most must have passed between the flash and roar of the gun and the brief, heartrending yelp of pain. I flattened myself against the ground as the second man came running frantically towards where his colleague had fired the shot. The circle of light from his torch illuminated the massacre.

"You killed the dog, you idiot."

"Something moved in the darkness and came for me," the other man said.

"You killed the dog . . . you bought that Chinese crap, and now you killed a dog whose only fault was to wag its tail at everyone."

"What did you expect me to do? You had the torch. I thought someone was attacking me."

"Who's going to attack you? Who else is out here? We're in the middle of nowhere. You're just paranoid, and I don't want someone who's trigger-happy alongside me. Next time you'll take a pop at me. Get a transfer to headquarters, find a desk job and run the numbers game. Poor dog, look what you did to it!"

The dog-killer tried to defend himself: "Don't insult me like that or I'll beat your brains out. I'm going back to town tomorrow, you can stay here doing this crappy job, and see where it gets you." He was still protesting as the two of them headed back towards the darkened house.

I lay flat on the ground for a while longer, covered in mud and with the rain beating down. If I stayed like that, in a couple of hours I would be putting down roots. As soon as I thought the danger was over, I stood up stiffly.

At least I had learned something. The muscular but polite gentlemen were either police or army, and they did not seem to be on an official mission. And one of them was so jumpy he was ready to fire on anything that moved without identifying itself.

I edged back towards the house, this time heading straight for the small bathroom window. It was big enough for me to wriggle through if I could remember the Houdini tricks I learned long ago in the circus run by my uncle, a wandering artist and unforgettable magician. For me he was like a human porthole who allowed me a glimpse of other worlds, even though I did not choose to explore them when I grew up.

I jumped up at the window and hung from the sill for what seemed like an endless minute. My muscles were no longer used to this kind of exercise, and I was afraid I would slide off, but instead I discovered that inside each one of us there exist, like veins of mineral in a gold mine, reserves of energy that we only need sufficient conviction to summon up.

At the age of seventy, my uncle could not only still free himself from a mass of chains in under five minutes, to the delight and applause of his public, but was also capable of making love twice in a fortnight, as his fourth wife told me. She was thirty years younger than him and a trapeze artist.

I thought of my uncle and hauled myself silently and easily into the bathroom.

*

It would be simpler getting out – unless I was discovered, that is. The floor of the bathroom was higher than the ground outside, so jumping out in an emergency would not take so much effort, especially as I would probably be impelled by the desire to save my skin.

I opened the bathroom door stealthily, and slipped into a corridor. The only light was a feeble glow at the far end of the passageway. I edged my way down until I came to a small living-room where the gentleman who had killed the dog was yawning like a hippopotamus and scratching at his crotch ostentatiously. Perhaps he had crab lice. There was not much light, but even if there had been, I was sure his face would have shown no sign of remorse for his stupid, senseless act.

I crept back halfway down the corridor, where another, wider passage led to more rooms. I finally decided to switch on the torch.

The first room I went into had no roof. A fine drizzle fell onto a sideboard that was the only piece of furniture. Portraits of somebody or other's ancestors hung on the walls. I looked in the sideboard drawers, but they were empty. The next room I went into was similarly run-down, but had more furniture: a bed with the frame leaning against the headboard, a bedside table, another, smaller sideboard. It was raining in here, too, and the sideboard was also empty.

I thought I could hear voices, so switched the torch off before making my way towards the third room. I held my breath as I stepped inside, worried that one of the floorboards might creak and give me away. This room did have a roof over it, so there was no drizzle inside. I could not hear voices now, only two people breathing at a steadily increasing rhythm.

I stepped back out of the room. I hate being a peeping Tom, even if in this case I could not see a thing. Pornographic spectacles have never excited me. Pathetic exhibitionists, if you ask me.

Instead, I went down the corridor and into the last room. This was another living-room, bigger than the others, with an oval table and chairs, and a glass-fronted dresser with enough crockery for a decent dinner service. What a strange place, I thought: half the roof missing, some of it tumbled down, and yet with plates and cutlery to hold a dinner party and stage a pleasant social occasion.

The light from my torch, which I was shading with my hand, showed there were papers spread out on the table. They looked like maps: somebody must have been studying them when the lights went out.

I could not make them out clearly because I did not have my glasses with me. Besides, it was so dark. They seemed to be diagrams of a military barracks. There were blockhouses and big open spaces; it could also have been a hospital, if an arsenal had some medical purpose, as there was an arrow pointing to one of the oblongs with a list of weapons written in the margin. These were not weapons like Isabel's .38. They were the latest rifles with infra-red sights, and helmets with cameras built into them, like the ones the Yanks and the Israelis use when they go on their tourist trips to the Arab world. Each category had its own column listing the technical details and quantities – hundreds in the case of the rifles, tens when it came to missiles, which were also listed.

I was startled by what I took to be a cry of terror. It was like being at the local flea-pit as a child when the vampire appeared and, before sinking his teeth into the damsel in distress, turned to the camera licking his lips as if to say: watch out, kids, you're next.

The cry, which had nothing to do with terror, came from the bedroom with the roof. It was a woman, but almost at the same time a man's groan raised the noise level to that of an operatic soprano's *vibrato*. A thunderclap outside was like a roll of drums, and the crockery in the sideboard crashed like cymbals.

I never discovered whether what shook the house to its foundations was the storm or the orgasm.

PART TWO

Paradises and Plots

1

So, on one side there was arms trafficking. On the other, a serial killer of women who, if not exactly of loose morals, were not of very tight ones either. This seemed like two worlds from completely different systems, like Pluto and Ganymede. No way the two of them could meet. Even the existence of one of them was questionable, as if it had not yet swum into the astronomers' ken.

I left the ruined or half-built house the same way I had got in. I felt angry with myself for not having the courage or the lack of scruples to avenge the dog. The killer was sleeping peacefully while his colleague was enjoying himself in bed.

I was still squirming out of the bathroom vent when someone opened the door. If I had waited a second to see the face of the person coming in, holding a candle stuck in the top of a beer bottle, I could have saved myself a lot of time and trouble.

I sell bathroom furniture. I am not a detective. When I was in the police force I was not one either, and I hate speculating over things I know nothing about. There are detectives with diplomas, philosophers, people trained at university to sniff out the unknown. The National Shame has its homicide and scientific experts; it is not Sherlock Holmes we need in Argentina, it is the will to investigate. If the greatest living criminals in our history are walking around freely, it is because somebody right at the top has decided they should not be punished.

I strolled calmly away from the house beneath a heavy, steady rain, which helped dissolve and wash away the mud I was covered in. I drove back to the hotel in Isabel's car. It was not a four-wheel drive, but coped splendidly with the mud-bath of the track, and when we reached the asphalted road it wanted more speed than I could risk because the town was so close.

As soon as I woke the next morning I rang Mónica and Isabel's number in Buenos Aires. Something told me that if anyone answered it would not be Isabel.

"Pablo, thank God! Where did you get to?"

"Where am I, you mean. I'm at the Cabildo Hotel in Tres Arroyos. We were supposed to meet here."

Mónica fell silent, then a few seconds later started to sob. She had no idea I knew something of what had happened to her, and could guess the rest. Still sobbing, she began telling me about their ordeal: she and her daughter had been intercepted on the bus they had decided to take from Bahía Blanca to Tres Arroyos. Two men – "polite but all muscle" I was tempted to say, but did not – got on the bus after swerving in front of it to bring it to a halt. My hotdog driver had forgotten to tell me this particular detail.

"There was a woman driving their car."

"A young woman?"

"Yes, and very pretty. She looked like a T.V. presenter."

I wondered whether I was dealing with the illegal arms racket or the white slave trade. Perhaps it was both: after all, they are different markets, and modern marketing gurus tell us we should spread our portfolios.

"Is Isabel with you?"

Mónica broke down again. After a while, choking and spluttering, she tried to explain. No, Isabel was not with her: the men had taken her off somewhere else. As soon as they were forced into the car, the two of them had been blindfolded. Then the car sped off along what Mónica thought from the way it lurched and swayed must have been a dirt road. Finally they came to a halt and Isabel was literally yanked from her side. Mónica heard her shouting, desperately calling out to her:

"Mummy," she shouted, "Mummy, help me."

Mónica was still sobbing, but there was no stopping her now.

"'Let go of her,' I screamed, 'if you want someone, take me.' Then somebody hit me on the head: I thought I was going to die, Gotán, but I must have only passed out. I could still hear her shouting, I was begging them to let her go, thrashing to and fro as if it was a nightmare. After that they must have given me a sleeping pill or something, I don't know. When I woke up, I was in the Accident and Emergency department in Haedo."

"In Haedo?"

"Yes, on the outskirts of Buenos Aires. I asked them who had brought me there."

"Let me guess," I said. "The police."

She could not deny it, and did not seem surprised at my magical powers of deduction. She had been taken there in a police patrol car. "We found her by the roadside," the officers had told the duty doctor. "When she's recovered, send her home, if she can remember where she lives." None of the police had stayed to keep an eye on her, but one of the doctors was so concerned that he offered to take her home. Mónica accepted, but did not tell him anything about what had happened.

"I don't trust anyone, Gotán. I don't know what's going on."

To calm her fears, the doctor said he earned less than a housemaid, and so had to keep his mouth shut and get used to seeing very strange goings-on. Mónica timidly asked what kind of strange goings-on. The doctor, who had only been out of medical school for a couple of years, said his parents had told him all about what had happened in Argentina during the '70s dictatorship. He had always found it hard to believe there could be criminals as vile as that in such a beautiful country, with its bountiful land packed with cows and soya, as well as hard-working people like his parents, who had slaved their arses off – he used a more polite term, because he was speaking to a lady – so that he could get to university, become a doctor, take an oath to save lives, all lives, including those that were not worth saving.

But now he did not know what to think.

"It's true the armed forces thought they could bring Nazism to the south of Latin America. But they were thrown out twenty years ago. In the '60s, twenty years after the Second World War, you wouldn't find a single Nazi in either of the two Germanies, not even in a museum. Here they stroll down the streets like lords," said the doctor, trying to navigate a traffic jam on Avenida Rivadavia, heading in towards the centre of Buenos Aires.

I reminded Mónica that one of those two Germanies had been full of prosperous capitalists, while the other was filled with reluctant Communists. In response, Mónica reminded me quite rightly that all she was interested in was finding her daughter alive.

"If you want to discuss politics, go and find the doctor in Accident and Emergency at Haedo," she said.

"Thanks, but no thanks," I said.

When they reached her apartment, the doctor had asked her if she knew what had happened to her.

"I was on the verge of telling him, Gotán. But as I said, I don't trust anyone now. He could have been another policeman in a doctor's gown."

"I'm a policeman," I said.

She sighed wearily. It was all too much for her, only a few hours after she had buried Edmundo, even if he had been such a disappointment to her.

"You *were* one, Gotán."

"You're right. Now I sell bathroom furniture."

"I wouldn't buy anything from you. I'd be worried every time I went to the toilet: 'Where did he hide the microphone?'"

Our shared laughter was forced but necessary. I told Mónica to take care, to make sure she did not open her door to anyone, and that I would see her in Buenos Aires.

*

Before leaving Tres Arroyos I called Burgos' mobile. He must have been busy cutting up the latest corpse, because all I got was his voice telling callers to leave a message. In the thirty seconds I had, I urged him to get somebody to go out and look over the farm in daylight; the estate agent could tell them where it was and how to get there.

I had no problems on the drive back to Buenos Aires. The traffic police stopped me at Las Flores and asked to see my papers. I handed them the I.D. card I had been given in Bahía Blanca in the name of Edgardo Leiva. That was no problem, but they did almost arrest me for not having my registration or any other of the documents required to drive legally.

"I'm sorry, lads," I told them, and flashed my old police badge. They saluted and waved me through.

A couple of kilometres further on, I threw Edgardo Leiva out of the car window.

2

I was right to get rid of my false I.D. I was no fugitive, there had never been any murder at the Imperio Hotel in Bahía Blanca, and nobody had been looking for me or missing me while I was away. Félix Jesús was asleep on my armchair in front of the T.V., and yawned as he grudgingly gave me a welcoming purr.

Had the serial killer claimed another victim? Yes, he had: a body had been found on the verge of the Viedma highway. The victim had been difficult to identify "due to the advanced state of putrefaction" but eventually "it was established that it was the body of Catalina Eloísa Bañados, also known as 'Lorena' in fashion circles", according to the crime reports buried deep in the inside pages. The papers also reported the "regrettable disappearance of a loyal company servant" in a paid announcement from the C.P.F. oil firm.

It was as if Cárcano had died of old age while writing his memoirs. There was even a death notice from his widow and daughter, although Mónica later told me they had not paid for it and had no idea it was going to appear. None of his friends or work colleagues wondered why there had been no laying out of the body or burial, somewhere they could send a wreath or a bunch of flowers to. None of them bothered to call his home and leave their condolences: the only message on Mónica's answering machine was a threat: "Your husband was no innocent, so don't make waves," a hoarse, distorted voice had said.

"Who are they? Who's behind this nightmare? Where is Isabel?"

Mónica had no-one but me to ask these questions of, and I could only guess at the answers in silence, like someone who has seen a flying saucer but cannot tell anyone because they will think he is mad.

I had gone to see Mónica as soon as I reached Buenos Aires. She hugged me tight, repeating the same three questions over and over, then cried until she had run out of tears. After that she made some coffee and we sat together in the charming living-room her husband had abandoned to chase after his blonde.

"We never know when we take the first false step, when we make that first fatal mistake," I said. "Edmundo thought he was finding happiness, but instead it was death that was waiting for him."

"He was a dirty old man," spat Mónica, as angry as she must have been when he left. "You're all the same, young men too: they all lose their heads over whichever Lolita they happen to bump into."

I did not argue: after all, she was only saying what I had.

Love out of season is devastating. It destroys all our certainties: what should be a gentle warm breeze turns into a fierce forest fire driven on by the wind. All our past and the intricacies of our uncertain future are reduced to ashes. And when it is all over, the dirty old man is left grey and hollow, dead without being aware of it if he has survived, or well and truly dead if someone has taken a pot-shot at him from point-blank range, as in Edmundo's case.

If this last love does not help prolong life, what is the point of charging like a horse into the blazing meadow?

*

That same evening I met up with the chief crime correspondent of *La Tarde*, the evening newspaper.

"Nobody's interested in your story, Martelli. People are too busy buying dollars; Argentina is on the skids again."

I had known "Werewolf" Parrondo since he had started as a trainee at *La Nación*. Tall and ungainly, "no good at football and not clever enough for university, the only thing left was journalism" he once told me over a drink, trying to sum up his life. His nickname was an obvious allusion to the thick tufts of hair that shot up like a mane almost from the top of his eyebrows. Over time his colleagues had shortened it to "Wolf".

"Argentina isn't collapsing of its own accord," I said. "It's being taken down by demolition crews."

Disaster was upon us yet again. A government that had lost all authority was not waving but drowning. It had frozen everyone's bank accounts, was busily denouncing plots everybody knew of but nobody would do anything about because, as ever, there was money to be made from catastrophe.

"I don't give a flying fuck about politics," Wolf said, stabbing an olive, biting into it as he talked, and interrupting himself to spit the stone as far as he could. We were at the counter of a dismal bar on Avenida Caseros, round the corner from his newspaper. "I've never understood why people always vote for the same dummies. If we're so set on getting screwed, why do we protest like virgins when we find ourselves in a brothel?"

He spat out the second and third stones together. One was bigger than the other, so the first ended on the floor, while the other landed on a table where an elderly beau was sitting with a crone at least ten years older than himself. She was gazing at him like a lovesick adolescent. The man shot Wolf a glance out of the corner of his eye, but did no more than sweep the stone off the table with the edge of his right hand.

"Look, that cretin is trying to get the old maid to sign over her pension to him. In the olden days, all that crap used to be for an inheritance; now the devil buys souls for loose change. It's the end of the world, Martelli."

"This is the third murder, Wolf. And where should her dead body appear but in my bed. But instead of trying to arrest me, somebody took the body and put it by the roadside. How can you not be interested in that?"

Wolf stared defiantly at the superannuated seducer, then turned his hairy maw in my direction.

"Let's get things straight, Martelli. Of course it's a good story. I can just picture it: a dead blonde in the bed of a former Buenos Aires police officer. I'd buy it with my eyes shut."

"So?"

"So, it's not what it seems. There's something more to it. It's a message from the mafia, Martelli. They remove the body and feed it to the dogs so that we'll understand: 'Don't get involved' is what they're saying. Do I make myself clear?"

"And who are these 'they'?"

Wolf turned away from me.

The antiquated swain was trying to get his wrinkly friend to make up her mind. A couple of sheets of paper lay beside their glasses, and he was talking quickly in a low voice, gesticulating, his hands skimming the table top. Every so often he grabbed the bag of bones that was his companion's hand and stroked it. Whenever he did so, she looked down in embarrassment, although the blush on her cheeks came from the powder she had daubed on her lined, pale skin.

"Go ahead and arrest him, Martelli," said Wolf, without looking at me. "That guy is a son of a bitch."

I finished my warm glass of beer.

"I don't have a badge. I'm a civilian these days."

Wolf turned his attention back to me.

"What do you want me to publish? You don't have a thing. There are no photos, no testimonies. C.P.F. is one of our major advertisers; if they get upset they'll cancel the contract and the paper will kick me straight out of the front door. What other job could I do at my age?"

"Looks like she's going to sign," I said, peering over Wolf's shoulder.

The bag of bones had raised the pen that the decrepit seducer held out to her like a cup of poison.

Just then two youngsters burst into the bar. They could not have been more than fifteen or sixteen, I thought, although one of them tried to make himself look older with a few straggly hairs that barely created a shadow on his chin.

"Attention!" the smaller of the two shouted, as though he were an army officer striding into a military dormitory. "This is a hold-up! Stop what you're doing and put all your money and valuables on the table!"

The pair must have been dazzled by the street lights outside, or by watching too much T.V. They obviously expected the bar to be full, but the only customers were the sad conman and his victim, the Wolf and me. When the two would-be gangsters realised their error, they grew even more hysterical.

"You two, put your money on the counter. And you, the one with the hair dragged over to hide your bald patch, get the rings off that old woman and put everything on the table!"

I was just about to, the sad seducer was trying to say, but he was so frightened he could not get the words out. The taller of the two youngsters, the one who obeyed orders, came to scoop up their disappointing booty.

"I work at the paper round the corner," Wolf told them as they took his five-dollar Chinese watch. "I'll call the photographer if you want your picture in the news."

The two teenage criminals stared transfixed like rabbits in headlights, until finally the shorter one went up to Wolf and kneed him in the groin. Wolf doubled up in agony.

"Two real smart-arses, eh?" said his attacker. "Search the other one," he told his taller colleague. "He looks like a copper."

A hand searched inside my jacket and fished out Isabel's .38.

"Fucking pig," said the smaller one. "You're done for!"

In a second he raised his gun and pulled the trigger. The hammer struck twice, three, then four times. I spun round like a top on my stool with both my arms stretched out, and hit the smooth-cheeked kid on the side of the head. I followed this up with a head-butt, then kicked out at the taller one, who had come over to help his friend kill me. I caught the .38 in mid-air and stuffed it into my belt. I carried on kicking the two of them on the floor until I could see from their rolled-up eyes that they had lost consciousness.

The barman stood behind his counter like a waxwork dummy. Still clutching his stomach, Wolf asked if that was how I persuaded my customers to buy toilets and washbasins. The old lady lay face down on her table, either dead or in a faint, clinging to the pen she had been about to use to sign away all her chances of a dignified old age. Her seducer had vanished.

Incredible as it may seem, I was already reproaching myself for almost beating the life out of those two young thugs who, as soon as they left hospital and were released by the magistrate because they were minors, would find somebody else to shoot sooner than I would find Isabel or Edmundo's killers.

Wolf straightened up and poured himself another whisky. I called the real police to come and take care of things. When I hung up, Wolf and I stared at each other like two police frogmen at the bottom of a sewer.

"The country is on the skids, Martelli," he said. "Buy dollars."

3

La Tarde was a free sheet published by Argentina's biggest-selling daily. It was handed out at rail and underground stations throughout Buenos Aires. Thousands of worker bees read this and similar publications while they clung on for dear life to the straps in the crowded carriages transporting them back home every evening. The fortunate few who managed to find a seat probably fell asleep by page two or three; those who had to stand perhaps got as far as page eleven, where Wolf had published under a banner headline:

BLONDE MODEL IS COASTAL KILLER'S THIRD VICTIM. BODY FOUND IN IMPERIO HOTEL BAHÍA BLANCA.

Beneath, in smaller type:

DOUBLE KIDNAPPING IN SAME REGION: MOTHER RELEASED; DAUGHTER STILL MISSING.

Wolf had taken a chance linking the two events. I called the paper to thank him. Distorted by a cheap synthesizer, Beethoven's "Ode to Joy" kept me entertained while the operator searched for their chief crime correspondent. Without success.

"Parrondo isn't in," I eventually heard a woman's voice say.

"Is he sick?"

"Who's asking?"

"A friend."

This time she hesitated before replying.

"You can probably find him at home."

It took some persuading to convince her that although I was Parrondo's friend I did not have his home number. I explained who I was, and what had happened the day before. All the ambulances and patrol cars must have caught the attention of everyone working at the paper: they even took photographs, I said, although none of them were published.

*

"Did you like the splash I gave your story, Martelli?" Wolf said, when finally I tracked him down. "Instead of congratulating me, they sent me on gardening leave. When they fire me and pay me compensation, I'm going to buy myself some love. So far, they've only given me a warning and a suspension, so I'm all alone."

He was in a good mood, which was rare for somebody whose job consisted of interviewing police informers, eating with drug traffickers and talking to victims' relatives demanding justice. More often than not their loved ones had been murdered by the same police whose bosses he was trying to bribe over the meals he bought them.

"It's like one of Dante's circles in Hell," he used to say when he tired of the comedy and was ordering another whisky with no ice in the bar where we had been attacked. "The people giving the orders to steal and kill, who sometimes even carry out the killings themselves, are the very ones protesting at the upsurge of violence here."

That was nothing new in Argentina, I would remind him on the afternoons we used to spend together after he called me – like someone calling a doctor in an emergency. I recalled Perón saying that violence up above creates violence down below.

"That's nonsense, empty words for the young idiots in that antediluvian era you managed to escape from. Just look what happened when they were in power back in '73 – a complete disaster. Don't talk to me about politics, Martelli: all politicians care about is power, they grow fat like leeches on other people's blood."

But this afternoon he was almost happy, or at least relieved, and excited too, because he thought he had got hold of one of the threads of the skein I was trying to disentangle.

I picked him up at his place in Almagro. As he climbed into Isabel's car he looked refreshed and triumphant, as if the assault and being suspended from the paper had been a tonic for him.

"There's always a price to pay," he said, once he had settled in the passenger seat and stroked the dashboard as if he were caressing a woman's body. "I published the story not because I believed you but because I found out a couple of things about your dead friend which didn't match the memories you seem to have of him."

"We don't choose our friends for their good behaviour," I said.

"Alright, but we shouldn't believe myths about them either. Let his widow cry for him if she likes. Talking of which, this car isn't yours."

I pulled up at a corner simply to eye him with astonishment.

"How do you know that?"

Drivers behind me began to sound their horns.

"The light's green," Wolf said. "You'd better move or we'll be lynched."

He waited until we had set off again to talk about his sixth sense, his experienced journalist's nose for seeking precise information rather than letting himself be taken in by appearances.

"You don't earn a lot selling toilets."

"Bathroom furniture."

"Let's face it, not even with your ex-policeman's pension on top would you be able to buy and run a car like this."

"I was thrown out of the force, so I don't get a pension."

"Which only goes to show how right I am. The car must belong to some widow or other, and the only one you've been dealing with recently is your friend's."

"Why does it have to be a widow? It could be a rich heiress, a businesswoman – a princess."

"Sure, Cinderella."

Wolf lounged back in his seat, and would have put his feet on the dashboard if his arthritis had let him.

"So what have you found out, apart from the fact that the car could belong to the widow?"

"Let's go to the National Library," he said, to my surprise, when he saw the outline of the massive building by the park off Avenida Figueroa Alcorta.

*

The National Library is a futuristic palace that grew old before its time because they never finished building it. Now it has computers but no programmes, and employees paid next to nothing. Wolf asked for a book by William Faulkner, and we went to sit in a corner of the reading room.

"This Yankee revived literature and won the Nobel Prize, back in the days when it was still a prize they gave to outstanding writers and not those in a particular clique. Nowadays the only people who read Faulkner are students like my son, Martelli."

"We didn't come here to read *Light in August*," I said, whispering the words as Wolf had done to avoid us being thrown out. "Tell me once and for all what on earth you found out about Edmundo Cárcano's secret life."

"Don't you realise you'll never understand anything about the complexities of the human soul if you haven't read writers like Faulkner? What do you read, Martelli?"

"When I was in the force I read forensic reports. Now the brochures from bathroom-furniture makers are wonderful, they're full of colour photographs. I take one to bed with me and fall asleep peacefully."

"That's a lie. Nobody who was a police officer during the dictatorship sleeps peacefully."

Our whispers had grown gradually louder, and threatened to end in a slanging match. Other readers started shushing us, and an assistant came over to tell us to be quiet or leave. We promised to behave. I took a deep breath, sat in silence for a full minute, then stood up to go. Wolf caught up with me in the corridor.

"I didn't mean to offend you," he said, panting. He still had the book in his hand.

"I sleep peacefully, Parrondo."

"My friends call me Wolf," he said, trying to smooth things over.

"And mine call me Gotán. But for now, it's Martelli and Parrondo. And it's time we got a few things straight. I wasn't thrown out of the force because I was a rotten policeman, and nor did I win promotion by killing guerrillas."

"O.K., Martelli, I'm not interested in your past. It was a stupid thing to say, but I didn't really bring you in here to read Faulkner either. He bores the pants off me, just as he does my son. I brought you here because we were being followed."

I studied Wolf for a moment, then turned to have a good look round. We were halfway down a long, wide corridor that ended in a flight of stairs. There was no-one else there apart from a scattering of people in the reading room, and a few bored library assistants waiting for their shift to end. Nothing out of the ordinary.

Not a muscle of Wolf's face moved. Either he was telling the truth or he was a very good liar. He asked me to wait while he returned the book, then came straight back, feeling his pockets for a pack of cigarettes.

"A red car," he said, lighting up as we left the library.

"Buenos Aires is full of red cars."

"But this one was following us. I always make sure I adjust the wing mirror so I can see behind."

"Paranoia."

"Or an instinct for self-preservation, Martelli. Apart from getting me suspended, what I wrote has obviously upset some big fish, and they're rude enough to want to remind me I'm not immortal."

We went out into the park. The spring night was cool and heavy with scents. There were a few couples promising each other heaven on earth or explaining why it would never work. No different from any other evening in the squares of Buenos Aires.

Wolf told me not to get back in the car.

"Unlock it and leave one door not shut properly," he said. "Then let's sit for a while and have a smoke."

"If you're going to propose, you've got the wrong man."

Wolf came to a halt, looked up at the sky as if to make sure it was not clouding over, then stepped over the low wire round the edge of the grass and started to pee behind one of the bushes.

While he was thus engaged, I went over to the car. I sensed there was something wrong about this perfect spring evening, that I should not be doing what I was doing. It was not my car. It did not even belong to the widow or to Cinderella, but to a dead friend's daughter. She had been kidnapped, and I was doing nothing to discover where she was, assuming they were no longer holding her in the countryside outside Tres Arroyos.

I followed Wolf's instructions. He came over, pointing towards a nearby bench. Instead of asking him what the fuck he thought he was playing at, I accepted a strong, rough cigarette and we sat down.

"From here we can see without being seen," he said, between drags.

I am no angler, but I have been on fishing expeditions with friends addicted to the sport. They can spend an entire day and night just waiting for their float to bob. There is nothing more boring than to watch them waiting: they look like cows chewing their cud. There is no glimmer of human life in their eyes, the hope of catching a fish turns them into fossils – you could find them in exactly the same position in a hundred, a thousand, or a million years.

We did not have to wait that long. Every big city is like a bazaar for car thieves. Although most people do not notice them, you just have to sit still and you soon enough see them at work.

This one was young, wearing a thin blue jacket and tie, with light-coloured trousers. He was carrying a briefcase like a salesman or health visitor. He kept shifting it from hand to hand as though it were heavy. He was walking along slowly, looking for an address, his eyes darting along both sides of the street. As he went past the parked cars he shot a glance inside each of them, then tried the doors of all those where there was no flashing red alarm.

The not-quite-shut door was the apple for our innocent Adam. He crossed the street diagonally from in front of an apartment block, and leapt straight into Isabel's car as if he owned it.

By now it was completely dark. All Wolf and I could make out were the glowing red tips of our cigarettes. The explosion caught us exchanging puzzled looks, but that lasted only a split second, because before we knew what had happened we were flat on our backs on the grass, right next to the bush where Wolf had emptied his bladder.

4

So there I was without a car again. This time it was a real shame. My own was a big old jalopy, a Ford Torino adapted in the '70s to run on natural gas, so they had not stolen anything of value down beyond Bahía Blanca, unless a collector got his hands on it. But Isabel's car was a different matter: it was as beautiful as its owner, though I still found it hard to think of Isabel as a grown woman.

I had to accept the fact there were people who did not want me alive, and that is never pleasant. Until I answered Edmundo's call begging me to come to Mediomundo as quickly as possible, my life had been rolling along without any great dramas, the only excitement the occasional sales convention or trip to the provinces with my samples of toilets and taps for all tastes and budgets. Sales had fallen off considerably in recent months: 2001 grew darker and darker as it went along. Storm clouds were gathering on the horizon, and nobody wanted to spend money on anything but changing Argentine pesos for dollars, and then depositing them or hiding them under their mattresses. But someone who lives alone does not need much, enough for his vices and a bit of food while waiting without much hope for the days to go by, and for the weekends to pass as rapidly and as unnoticed as possible.

As it turned out, answering that call and driving though the night had not saved Edmundo's life, and had put mine at risk. Get rid of that one too, somebody had said, some executive, some boss or other, some *capo*, a police or army officer, a big businessman, any of those shadowy figures who in Argentina press their intercom and give the executioner his instructions without bothering so much as to see the victim's face, or hear about the friends who will miss him, the orphans who sooner or later are going to quarrel over his inheritance, the women who are going to have their hearts broken or heave sighs of relief.

The worst thing about being sentenced to death without being tried, let alone charged, is that you do not have the faintest idea why your car gets stolen in the middle of the Patagonian desert, why you find a dead girl in your hotel bed, why somebody blows up a car lent to you by a beautiful dark-haired young woman – a woman who could be your daughter but is not, and who has been inexplicably kidnapped without any ransom demand. You do not know a thing, just as when you leave childhood behind and find yourself drifting on a sea that adults think they know like the back of their hands, but where they are irredeemably lost, and where all of us end up shipwrecked.

*

The night of the explosion I called Mónica to tell her what had happened. In an outburst of desperate revolt against the inscrutable laws of the God she worshipped in her electronic church, she begged me to forget the whole thing, to leave her in peace. She had decided to trust the police who had proper badges and pensions, not an outcast like me. "Look what happened to Edmundo when he asked for your help," she said. I decided it would be pointless, then at least, to try to defend myself. Besides, it was all true: I had been thrown out of the police and out of the life of the woman I loved.

There must have been something wrong with me for things always to turn out this way. I was never able to form a stable relationship, to be with a woman who dreamed of growing old beside me, if indeed such women exist. A short while after they were with me, they all realised they were on the wrong bus and that if they did not get off quickly they could end up anywhere, in the river or a shanty town, the back of beyond of the beyond, on the planet of the apes, at the opposite pole to happiness.

Lies, of course. Blatant, obvious, despicable lies they told themselves when it was already too late, when they were already clinging to a love that creaked and groaned like a raft on dry land. What seas did they hope to cross, what horizons were they going to discover, when they were stranded, inescapably beached on the bitter sands of disappointment?

But that is my life, or my karma as those charlatans claim, the fraudsters who see God everywhere by gazing endlessly into their own navels. My karma is to be the blind spot, the dead centre of other people's storms, the calm water out of the main current. So many women, so few I really miss, just one in particular, Debora or Mireya, my last tango in Barracas, the damp streets, fog on the River Riachuelo, the worst kind of folklore, like a second-rate watercolour by Quinquela Martín, or one of Borges' knife-fighters from a half a century ago, trapped on his street corner and tossing the inevitable coin for all or nothing.

There are no other choices when you have to confront your faceless enemy, the one who is bound to attack you from behind. The coin decides if it is all or nothing. And if it is nothing, that means nothing.

*

Wolf suggested we walk away from the explosion. It would take some time for them to find out who owned the car. A car being blown up on the streets of Buenos Aires is not such an everyday event as it is in the Middle East or in Hollywood films, but we could watch the fuss on T.V. and avoid all the questions for which we had no answers.

I had arranged to meet the doctor and the Cervantes duo the next day, and I did not want to return to Bahía Blanca empty-handed.

About ten blocks from the National Library we found a bar that looked quiet. Wolf ordered a Gancia, and I asked for a beer, cheese straws, crisps and peanuts. We were celebrating the happy hour of survival, so we drank a silent toast to our immortality and then, slumped back in his chair as he had been in Isabel's unfortunate car, Wolf at last told me what he had found out about Edmundo Cárcano.

"Some reports, whispered comments, lots of speculation," he cautioned me lest I get too enthusiastic. "I want to enjoy my suspension like a well-earned holiday, even if it is unpaid," he said. "Journalism is a trade for educated gossips, just occasionally endowed with a sense of aesthetics that allows them to give shape to their tittle-tattle. But sometimes reality is based on pure fiction, Martelli. You may be the most upright person in the world, but if the atmosphere all round you is corrupted, and the corrupt don't go to jail but are rewarded with the best cars and the best women, sooner or later you will flush your values down the toilet – sorry for the allusion. C.P.F. is a multinational that does business all over the place. It has legitimate employees and employees in the black economy."

"That's because they drill and refine black gold," I said. "Naturally, some of them get splashed."

Wolf took advantage of my interruption to polish off the last handful of crisps. He ordered another Gancia and more crisps. Then he went on:

"If you work as an office boy, you have no choice but to be a saint. If you're a manager in a multinational, you have to give in to sin or you're done for. Edmundo didn't get where he was because of his professional abilities, believe me."

"But he was only a departmental manager. The big bosses at C.P.F. are all imported," I said. A lukewarm defence of my friend's reputation.

"And precisely because of that they don't understand what's going on locally. They earn ten times as much as the home-grown people, so they can even permit themselves the luxury of turning down offers. Listen, I'm not making any moral judgement here. I would have done exactly the same in your friend's shoes."

"And what did he do that you would have done exactly the same?"

"Calm down, all in good time. First clear one thing up for me, Martelli: why did your friend ring you the night he was killed?"

I hesitated about giving the information to a gossip-monger with an aesthetic sensibility, but it might be all he had to go on beyond the speculation of his informers.

"He asked me to come to his beach house as soon as I could."

"Did he say his life was in danger?"

"No. And he didn't sound agitated. 'It's something that will change your life, Gotán,' he said. 'But if you stay tucked up in bed you'll miss out.'"

Wolf made short work of the second dish of crisps. He did not offer me any.

"I don't have any friends in the police," he said, as if resigned to the fact. "And don't thank me for still being alive, I didn't do it on purpose."

"I detest funerals, Wolf."

"Call me Parrondo."

"O.K., Parrondo. I don't want to have to go to any more funerals of people I'm fond of. It's useless suffering. I can't bring them back to life, and I'm terrible about remembering the good times we had together."

We sat in silence for a while, Wolf with his Gancia and me with my warm beer. We were both staring out of the window overlooking the square, in the hope that we would see the outline or face of someone we knew who could shake us out of our gloom and doubts, or help us get back to normal, as though when we parted company Wolf could go straight back to his job at the paper and I could climb into Isabel's car without being blown to smithereens.

At some point, Wolf turned towards me and our eyes met. If the unnamed game he had been playing was Hide and Seek, he had obviously reached a hundred and shouted out in his mind, "Here I come, ready or not." I was home free.

But the sinister game we were caught up in was only just beginning.

5

Against all expectation, and above all apparently against our better judgement, we ended the evening hugging each other and promising to meet again when everything had become clear and justice reigned again on Earth, or at any rate in Argentina. Wolf allowed me to call him Wolf, and I said he could call me Gotán.

I said no to his offer of a taxi home. It was a fine night for walking, and besides, I needed to take my time leaving the place I could have died in.

Halfway there I stopped off at a bar to go to the toilet. On the T.V. screen, watched by two lonely customers, I caught a glimpse of Isabel's car in flames. It was a news flash on *Cronica*, with ticker tape announcing in huge letters that the tank of a car running on liquid gas had exploded. As I had my pee I imagined the debate there would be in the next morning's papers about the risks of using liquid propane gas as fuel. They would probably not even bother to find out who the car belonged to. Once she was free, Isabel could report it stolen, and claim on the insurance.

But who was going to free Isabel, and from whom?

The jigsaw puzzle Wolf had pieced together from the bits of information he had gleaned here and there indicated, or at least suggested, that not only sheltering but operating freely beneath the umbrella of the Argentine subsidiary of C.P.F. was an N.G.O. whose aims were not altogether charitable, even though some of its members were grateful recipients of its donations.

The N.G.O. was called the New Man Foundation. It had a formal structure to help it administer funds and gifts from private and official sources. These were intended to improve the infrastructure of a shanty town on the outskirts of Buenos Aires. According to censuses – preferably ones collected from helicopter gunships – the shanty town was home to thirty thousand souls with not a single credit card among them.

It is moving – at least, it moves me – to see how the state and big business are so concerned about the poorest and most needy in our society. Even though it may not crop up on their balance sheets, there are always organisations appealing for solidarity to help rescue the inhabitants of our infernos. Collections, donations of all kinds, and paragraph seven of point four of the law granting a big international construction firm the right to build a brand-new motorway over the heads of the poor provincial workers crammed into the shanty towns mean that a few coins from the petty cash accounts of businesses and contracts find their way to these worthy organisations.

Nothing wrong with that. The more coins the better, if Uncle Scrooge shakes out his pockets. Donald Duck quack quack can pick them up and dig at least a couple of drains to put sewers in. But sometimes, so many wearisome times, not even this spare change reaches its destination. Sometimes not enough care is taken with a cigarette that has fallen to the ground and bang! everything goes up in the air like Isabel's car. Goodbye soup kitchen.

Because of the position he held in C.P.F. – institutional relations manager or some such title – Edmundo had been asked to join the ranks of the N.G.O. aiming to transform all those workers without any hope of work into the spitting image of the New Man that the followers of Che Guevara had dreamed or hallucinated about in the '70s. The first contacts must have been formal, to sound each other out rather than to listen to worthy humanistic speeches about how, in order to save capitalism and western society, we ought to be paying more attention to the poor before they rise up and eat us raw.

This is exactly what the Roman Catholic Church that supported the military dictators said, as did all those who financed the military adventures that have laid Argentina to waste. Nobody has a problem sounding off like this nowadays, despite the fact that thirty years earlier that kind of idea cost the lives of thousands of humble political and social activists and those who, dazzled by the thought of an armed socialist utopia, declared war on an army whose mission has always been to turn its weapons on its own people whenever called upon.

There was nothing odd, therefore, in the fact that an oil company chose to support those who said they were working on behalf of the dispossessed. Quite the contrary: newspapers, magazines and the T.V. are full of praise for these instances of "good" capitalism, whereas they castigate the ogres of the international lending agencies for coming up with adjustment plans that will steal the bread from the mouths of little orphans.

"Who is going to suspect that C.P.F. sets aside funds for the New Man not to feed the sparrows in the shanty town, but to buy and sell arms on the black market?"

This bald assertion of Wolf's had taken me aback more even than seeing Isabel's car go up in flames. They were only his suspicions after talking to his contacts in the dead of night, but they might at least explain why his bosses at the newspaper had taken such drastic measures against him. Nothing in what Wolf had published even hinted at what he had told me, but even so it had brought out the haemorrhoids on the dirty arses of those in charge at *La Tarde.* Although rumours of this kind are more common in newsrooms than coffee breaks, nobody is willing to print anything that could cause a stink. There is no analysis of what is going on, and still less reporting of it. The journalists are all far too worried about hanging on to their desks in their little compartments, making sure they live to enjoy the benefits and holidays they have worked so hard for.

"Poor guy," I said to myself as I walked down the acacia-lined streets, taking in the intense perfume of jasmine wafting from houses with gardens. Edmundo had spent most of his adult life in C.P.F. He had the classic career of an exemplary employee, from office junior to top manager. Thirty years of getting up at dawn, eating breakfast half asleep, rushing out to catch the 7.15 train, then spending the day between reinforced concrete walls that kept out the sun and rain, buried alive on one of the top floors of a building identical to thousands of others in cities all around the world, surrounded by zombies and transformed into a puppet just intelligent enough to accept the life he was living, an unbroken line drawn between youth and the moment when they gave him a couple of pats on the back and a gold medal for his loyalty to the company.

Nobody, not even Mónica, could have judged him for falling into temptation. Even if the apple he bit into was a shady business, a street with the unavoidable dead end. Not very different from the life he had been leading, except that in this case death caught up with him just when he thought he had found a way out, courtesy of a beautiful young woman.

"If he called you at midnight and asked you to come immediately, it was because he needed to confide in someone," Wolf said, trying to see beyond the obvious. "Things were probably getting out of hand."

"What could I have done?"

"I don't know, maybe he needed a front man, or a bodyguard . . ."

"Give me a break, Parrondo. I'm just a decrepit old animal, like Félix Jesús."

"Who's Félix Jesús?"

"A decrepit old animal."

*

I walked almost forty blocks through the warm spring night spiced with the scent of flowers and police sirens. As I had done so often over the past five years, from a public phone booth I dialled the only number I could not wipe from my memory. I needed to hear a voice, to imagine that by saying a magic word I could recover the past, could retrace my steps like a little boy who runs away from home but as night falls starts to feel afraid and runs back to the maternal embrace.

You said hello, but then perhaps because it was so late or because of some strange music I could not hear but which pierced your soul, you said, yet again, "Please, please don't phone me any more."

I hung up and wandered on, through more blind alleys in my labyrinth. "Don't phone me any more," you said for the first time five years ago. "I don't want anything to do with a policeman."

You had fallen in love with a toilet salesman and woke up when you heard all about my past in the National Shame. It was one night when we were drinking in a bar we used to go to where we could cling to each other for a few well-danced tangos. We were there, roused by the music and heading for bed, when fate, tired of shaking its tumbler, suddenly threw the dice and we lost it all.

The guy dancing with an old crone in a short skirt and red high-heels refused to get the point of me turning away when he lurched towards us and shouted: "Why, if it isn't Inspector Martelli . . . we've put away some crooks in our time, haven't we, eh? Tell her, tell my friend here, who we are." He stopped dancing, leaving his partner to complete her twirls and then rush off, embarrassed, to the toilet, while my tiny world collapsed around me. Without a word, you turned and walked away, Mireya. Since then I have never plucked up the courage to tell you the truth, like a murderer forced to confess his crime before he can begin to explain it, explain why he aimed for the heart of the man or woman he hated, to explain that hatred, to explain why unreason is so much stronger than reason. I felt the same sense of shame as the old tart who had run to hide in the toilet, except that I stood rooted to the spot in the middle of the dance floor, having to listen to the guffaws of my drunken one-time colleague: "Let her go, Martelli, she doesn't deserve you. She'll never understand what we've been through together."

I had handed in my gun when I was kicked out of the force, and never had another one until Isabel's snub-nosed .38 fell into my hands. That was the only thing that saved that idiot's life, defying me from the stinking bog he was drowning in, as though wanting me to kill him there and then, to put an end to his ghastly life. I was paralysed by images that flashed through my mind like streaks of lightning in a storm, burning images of bodies tortured to the point of death, with this same man standing there, his whining voice deep in the jungle of desperate cries, complaining about going home late this night of all nights: "My boy's got an exam in the morning and asked me to help him." He was saying this to a policeman who had joined the force because he had been promised the same as Edmundo when he first started at C.P.F.: you'll grow old without having to face death, you'll be protected, it's a life with all the support you need so you won't fall, even if you never learn to walk on your own. Not even that was true: death caught me out, it reached out and embraced me and I could never be free of it again. It had been with me ever since, and still was that night when yet again you hung up on me before I could say a word.

*

When finally I reached my apartment I was exhausted. The explosion, Wolf's revelations, my long walk, the telephone call like a distress flare in the darkness. To make matters worse, it was a full moon, and under its spell Félix Jesús had gone out to prowl on the rooftops.

I did not switch on the light. The silvery splendour of the moon through the living-room window bathed everything in brightness. I opened the fridge and poured myself a glass of milk to get rid of the acidity in my stomach. I drank it in small sips, trying to overcome my distaste. As I stood by the window I could see the silhouette of my cat on the ridge between my building and an old mansion that had been rebuilt and was now the Macedonian consulate. I have no idea whether

Macedonia is a country, a city, or one of those nightmares the world has woken up to after its Cold War sleep. Félix Jesús had no idea either, but he could not give a damn anyway, and perhaps the female he was pursuing was from there, perhaps she had crossed half of Europe and the Atlantic curled up in a diplomatic bag, just to meet him.

I poured the last quarter of my milk into Félix Jesús' bowl so that he could replenish his strength after his amorous adventures. I went to bed and had almost fallen asleep when the telephone rang.

I never answer the phone after midnight because blah, blah, blah. . .

Whoever it was rang off, then insisted a second time. I picked it up apprehensively, holding the receiver as far away as possible between my thumb and first finger, as if the call might not only be a threat, but be capable of carrying out that threat there and then. There was no sound at the other end, so I said hello.

"If you'd told me you had problems with wax in your ears, I could have syringed them for you."

The music in the background suggested the doctor was out drinking, possibly in Pro Nobis. A woman's laughter confirmed my suspicions. The redhead, and the Swedish barman, too, no doubt.

"What are you doing up so late, Burgos – and with women?"

"I'm on duty, Don Gotán."

"Why on earth does a forensic doctor have to be on duty? Are corpses in such a hurry to be cut up?"

"Nobody is really dead until they have their death certificate. Bureaucracy has spread so far it occupies spaces previously reserved for metaphysics, religious speculation, or any other science of uncertainty you care to mention."

He lowered his voice, and it sounded muffled as he protected the mouthpiece with the palm of his hand, even though the techno music was so loud not even he could hear himself speak.

"I'm calling to tell you not to come. We're travelling instead."

"Travelling where? And who is 'we'?"

"Don't be dense, Don Gotán. Who did you meet in Bahía Blanca?"

I reeled off the names:

"A blonde who doesn't travel any more, two police officers, one of whom owes me something for the going over he gave me in jail, and a forensic doctor who saved me from being locked up for something I didn't do."

"The day after you left, another girl was found dead in one of those cheap motels on the outskirts of Bahía Blanca."

"So why are you coming to Buenos Aires?"

"I'll explain tomorrow. Get some sleep now. I'm going to round up my passengers at first light and we'll set off then."

He sounded as jolly about his journey as if he were going on holiday or to a picnic. I could just see him negotiating his sky-blue V.W. as fast as he could up Route 3, eyes half-closed against the bright sunlight and nursing the hangover he would have from the drinking he was doing in Pro Nobis.

"Take care," I managed to say. "Not too fast, and take turns at the wheel."

The doctor laughed at my concerns.

"Don't worry about us, Don Gotán. And polish up the obelisk for me."

6

Provincials dream of finding an excuse to visit the city they hate the most: Buenos Aires.

This Goliath's head on a puny body is the favourite reason given for Argentina's eternal frustrations – when it is a provincial providing the explanation. All the lifeblood, from the neck down, goes to feeding this megacephalic monster. This has been the case since the nineteenth century, when the Unitarians won the civil war against the Federalists. Then, as in every other war, it was not the good fighting the bad, but powerful leaders on one side confronting powerful leaders on the other, and using as their emissaries half-starving soldiers who, blinded since childhood by an enmity towards anyone who was different, had become warriors ready to lay down their lives for the fatherland, the flag, traditions, any of the symbols dragged out every time a people is called upon to tear itself to pieces.

The Unitarians won, and Buenos Aires started to grow. At the beginning of the twentieth century it took in poor European immigrants, and in the '40s equally poor Argentine migrants arrived from the provinces. The blood-letting continued, fed by even poorer immigrants from neighbouring countries. At first there was work – if not for all, then for a good many of them. Afterwards there came Perón, *compañeros*, the great unwashed, all the Peronist folklore, Peronist trade unions, Peronist jobs. Perón was thrown out by the same military who had put him there, supported by the middle class, priests and communists indignant at seeing so many dark-skinned people from the interior swarming to Goliath's head. Ciao, Perón, but the transfusion of golliwogs, nig-nogs and the lumpen continued. They would arrive at Retiro with their goats and their strange dialects, and build (that's one way of putting it) their tin shacks: whole neighbourhoods of cardboard and tin shacks, post-war ghettos in the land of wheat and cows.

Eighteen years later, and Perón was back. This time he died before they could throw him out again, but all the same the military, and of course the middle classes, who were exasperated that so many Peronists had become political activists, third-world priests, or guerrillas, took it upon themselves to kick out his widow and all her court. The massacre, which had already started with Perón's return, became a silent, bitter struggle, but the riff-raff still kept flocking to Goliath's head. There were even "civilian–military" expeditions in Buenos Aires, and straightforward military ones in Tucumán province, to make sure these dregs of society vanished without trace.

*

"What a shit-hole this city is!" was Inspector Ayala's first greeting to Buenos Aires, as the three of them shot along Avenida General Paz at 120, dodging the buses.

He had just woken up, shaken to life, no doubt, by the manoeuvres Burgos made to stay on the road. After a night out drinking and six hundred kilometres of driving, he was like a jittery phantom beyond all sense of danger.

"Couldn't you go a bit slower, doctor? We're almost at the centre," Rodríguez protested. He was wide awake, and had been preparing *mate* for Burgos for the past hundred kilometres.

"What would you know about the centre of any big city?" Burgos grunted. Apart from being a roly-poly doctor he was originally from Buenos Aires.

The trio turned up at my front door at 11.15 in the morning, looking like the living dead.

Burgos, insomniac and ashen, "Though I did get some sleep on the straight bits," he said proudly; Rodríguez, who had done his best to keep him awake, and barely acknowledged me; and Ayala, the most alert of the three: "I swallowed a bottle of sleeping pills and half a tumbler of gin before we left," he said. He asked if I had any idea where they could stay in this shit-hole of a city, gazing disdainfully at my few sticks of furniture and at Félix Jesús who, as exhausted as our visitors, lay fast asleep on the dining-room sideboard.

Thinking ahead, I had made a reservation for them in a hotel near Retiro. Not the Sheraton, of course, but not some dingy boarding house with only half a star either. It was a hotel for provincial tourists who come to Buenos Aires and want to spend the night out eating, going to the cinema, window-shopping, taking their photographs in front of the obelisk, gaping open-mouthed on a tour of Puerto Madero, crawling like ants along the streets and small squares swarming with other country cousins in a decrepit neighbourhood known by the name of "Palermo Hollywood", full of walking mentally-wounded and transvestites.

Ayala's protestations that all three of them were broke led me to wave goodbye to any hope I had that I could free myself of their unwelcome visit.

"We're on a secret mission," Ayala declared solemnly.

"A clandestine one," the doctor corrected him.

Like the slaughter of cows by moonlight out in the countryside, I recalled: the ones that provided the juicy steaks with no hygiene controls, but at half the normal price, the ones that kept the doctor in such rotund shape.

"We don't have official backing for this," the inspector said. "We're using the weekend and two days' overdue leave. That means we've got four days to clear up this affair."

"Of course, it also means we have to pay our own expenses," Rodríguez said. "And if we get ourselves killed, they'll throw us out of the police for being so stupid." He did not seem to be as keen on the expedition as the other two.

"They'll know what they are doing," I suggested. Then with a sigh I uttered the fatal words: "I guess it doesn't matter if it's only for four measly days."

*

I prayed it would not occur to my daughter Cecilia, a single mother with two children who has been living in Australia for the past ten years, to make a surprise visit to Argentina to see her father. In a few minutes

I transformed the pretty bedroom I kept spick and span for her into a tiny refugee camp. The three countrymen soon spread their tent over the floor – they had obviously supposed that in a city as big as Buenos Aires they were bound to find somewhere to camp. I pushed the few pieces of Cecilia's furniture against the walls so they could enjoy the three by four metres of floor space, shut the door on them, and sat down to have a martini and watch T.V.

The main news item was the hysterical reaction of customers when told that the amount of cash they could withdraw from the banks was restricted. Argentina was about to go into a nosedive yet again, but the poor bastards were being told to tighten their belts and not say a word.

"Good idea not to let them get their hands on the money," Ayala said, coming in to sit beside me. He took a sip of my martini. "If they did, they'd only take it abroad."

I explained as gently as I could that the people who had real money had already been taking it abroad for ages, while those caught in this latest trap were the same old victims, the ones in families where everyone including the dog went out to work, or those who had inherited their parents' house and had sold it and were trying to live off their savings.

"I couldn't give a fuck about the suffering middle classes," Ayala said, adding for good measure that he was no leftie, not even a Peronist. "They think they're the country's moral backbone, but they're pathetic. They get us to do their dirty work, then go round clucking like hens that we're torturers. Tell me, what the fuck do they want? You used to be a policeman, didn't you?"

I did not answer, but instead asked about the other two. I wanted to know what had brought them to Buenos Aires when the four young women had been murdered around Bahía Blanca.

Ayala said Burgos and Rodríguez were sleeping it off like addicts, snoring like wild cats, and we had to give them time to recover.

Their journey had been a middle-of-the-night, spur-of-the-moment decision. By first light they were already underway, with the lunatic doctor driving. He had such a regular and intimate contact with death, the inspector said, that he never believed he could die at the wheel.

"He thinks he's immortal," I said.

"Something like that."

Ayala polished off my martini and, while I was preparing another, told me what they had found out thanks to the skill and energy of the gut-ripper, as he called Burgos.

Of the four dead women, three had appeared in the open air: one by the roadside, another in a field, and the third in an abandoned warehouse in the port area of Bahía Blanca. The only one found indoors was Lorena, and yet the police report said she had also been found by a highway.

"Who put her in my room, and why? And why did they take her out again?"

Ayala waited until I had passed him the martini before he went on.

On the T.V. screen I could see the puffy face of a fifty-year-old man declaring that this was a country of swindlers. "They won't let me withdraw more than 250 pesos a week. How can I live on that? Does the minister live on that?" he howled. Earlier, the minister, a bald man who had been president of the Central Bank during the dictatorship and had cancelled the debts of the top businessmen who had paid for the massacres, the same bald fellow who the democratically elected president prior to the one now being pilloried had brought in as his saviour, the same man who the current imbecile had called on to save his skin, had appeared on every T.V. channel insisting as cool as a cucumber that Argentina was not in crisis, that if the government was preventing people from withdrawing their money, it was so that they would use their credit cards: "In which other modern country do people still use cash rather than cards?" proclaimed old baldy, the jack-in-the-box for our dictatorships and lily-livered democracy.

"Are we watching T.V. or talking about what happened?" Ayala scolded me.

*

Burgos found that his everyday bread and butter was snatched from him before it could even reach his mouth. Lorena's body was sent straight to La Plata to be examined by the federal forensic pathologist who had taken an interest in the case. But before this expert could even put on his rubber gloves and pick up his scalpel, the official autopsy report had been released to the national press. According to this report, the same maniac who had taken the lives of the other women was responsible for the death of Catalina Eloísa Bañados, in the circle of aspiring models known as Lorena.

Infuriated by the cynical way in which public opinion was being manipulated, the La Plata pathologist had telephoned Burgos.

"They were colleagues at university," Ayala said. "Burgos doesn't quite see eye-to-eye with him because he's Jewish, but he's not religious. He's married to a Christian and hasn't set foot in a synagogue since they clipped his foreskin."

Ecumenicism is a great thing, especially if it means that the half-converted Jew trusted Burgos sufficiently to confide in him that the weapon which had inflicted Lorena's mortal wound was not the one used on the other three girls.

"Very similar, but not the same. About a tenth of an inch thicker than the other stiletto. Besides, that one was a vulgar bit of steel. This one is a finely crafted dagger. Finely crafted from fine steel," so Ayala reported the La Plata pathologist as saying.

"A professional job."

"The man who killed the others is an amateur."

"But a killer nonetheless," I said, holding up my martini glass and peering into it like a clairvoyant into a crystal ball.

"That poor blonde was as dead as the others," Ayala admitted.

I stood up and paced around the living-room. Now that the T.V. was off I could hear the doctor's loud snores and incoherent swearing from Rodríguez.

"He talks in his sleep," Ayala said. "Sometimes he even gets up. Don't be alarmed if he comes in at night and tries to hug you. He says his father pays him visits at dawn, which is odd because he never knew who his father was. He and his mother abandoned him on the front steps of Bahía Blanca hospital hours after he was born."

"I'm not interested in the reasons for your friend's sleepwalking. Sooner or later, they'll find the man who killed those other three girls. Even if it takes ten years, people like him always get caught. They don't want to die without the world knowing who they are. Our problem is Lorena."

"She's dead too."

There is not much point trying to discuss things with someone who is already half-drunk, but the other two were out for the count, so there was nothing else for it.

"The fact that the body was moved, and the way the forensic report was suppressed, means that it was not that maniac, or any other one, who killed her. She was planted on me – first alive, then dead – because I was Cárcano's friend."

"And who was Cárcano? A two-bit employee who stuck his hand into the petty cash so he could show his bit of fluff a good time."

I poured more martini into Ayala's glass. He knocked it back like medicine. His eyes glazed over, and he called to Félix Jesús. He even tried to stroke him, but the cat sneaked behind the curtains that shaded the room from the harsh midday sun.

"Cats are bad luck anyway," Ayala muttered. Then he leaned back on the sofa, and he too fell fast asleep.

I wondered what I would find when I returned if I left the three of them sleeping off their journey and their excesses. But I could not hang about for them to come to life. I had to go out and check on a few things.

I scribbled a note saying that I would be back soon, then left without locking the front door, hoping that no robber would dream of burgling an apartment where two policeman and a forensic expert were sleeping like dormice.

The city looked marvellous. It positively glowed in the sunlight. The streets were full and all the stores were packed with people buying T.V.s, fridges, even cars, as if they had just popped out to buy a packet of biscuits at the corner shop. The ones with cash were buying dollars or high-priced items. Nobody knew when the fire alarm would go off, but they were not waiting to hear the sound of sirens before they began rushing for the exits.

I called Wolf from a public telephone, but all I got was his answer machine: "Take to the rafts, the ship is sinking." Then there was a peep . . . and a silence where I could record a message.

I hung up, annoyed, then called Mónica. She was one of the few people in Buenos Aires who had not rushed out to buy dollars. Just for a change, she started sobbing over the phone.

"I'm sorry I spoke to you like that last night. I know you're the only one who can help me, but I'm very confused. My whole life has been turned upside down, Gotán."

There was the familiar sound of her trying to choke back her tears, then the request:

"Come round now. I've got something to tell you."

7

My taxi dropped me off forty minutes later outside the apartment block where Mónica lived. We could have got there in ten had we not run into striking workers who had cut off the avenue and forced us, with much blaring of horns and swearing, into a long detour. The urban pressure cooker was building up steam. It was only a matter of days, or maybe hours, before everything hit the ceiling.

I told Mónica I could not stay long, because my place had been taken over by a bizarre trio from the Bahía Blanca police.

"I've no idea what's brought them here. Must be a sense of pride. No policeman likes having somebody else's problem dumped on them."

"What kind of problem?" Mónica said distractedly.

"Dead bodies."

Her next comment took me by surprise.

"Including Edmundo's."

Mónica did not keep cats. What she did have was a pair of canaries. Crazed by being shut in their tiny cage, they sang at all hours of the day and night. Isabel called them "my political prisoners" because they had been locked away without a trial. She would have liked to set them free, but her mother insisted they brought moments of joy to her sad existence.

She stared at them as she talked, perhaps to avoid having to look at the way my face fell as she made her confession.

"Edmundo was not what he seemed," she began.

"I'm beginning to discover that."

She took such a deep breath it was as if she were about to dive underwater.

"Nor am I, and nor is Isabel. Nobody is who they seem, Gotán."

"Bingo! Why do you think I like the tango so much?"

"Don't hate us for what I'm about to tell you."

*

The problem with confessions is that they always come at the wrong time. A president tells us how his life in office was made impossible. But he does this when he has been ousted and is powerless to prevent people being fooled by the next democratically elected fraud. If only he had come clean the day after his inauguration, with the applause and shouts of "Long live the president!" still ringing in his ears, then the people could for once have taken justice into their own hands and rampaged through the main square to string up all those white-gloved crooks who shamelessly passed the milch cow of the state from one to the next. But of course he did nothing of the sort. He kept his mouth shut, because he liked hearing the applause (who doesn't?) and because he dreamed of getting his hands on the udders too.

If Mónica had spoken out earlier, then Edmundo would still perhaps have been alive. Poorer, but alive.

"I never believed the stories about him getting promotion and bonuses," she said. "What bonuses, if he was not selling anything, or involved in any of their so-called strategic plans? Besides, the oil is there underground. You extract it, refine it, and use it to prop up the whole economy. By selling it abroad."

"I know a bit about economics and politics. That's why I prefer to read thrillers."

"Edmundo was never a team player. 'One of these days I'm going to screw them,' he used to say. 'And I'm not going to let them screw me. Then you and I can go on a world tour, starting with Italy. I owe you that.'"

"And the 'New Man Foundation' gave him that opportunity."

"How do you know that?"

I told her.

"Journalists. Always digging dirt. Just like the police. The dirty work is not so much gathering all the stuff, but deciding what to do with it. 'This one should be locked up, that one should stay out because he's up to his neck in it and could be useful as an informer, that other one is no use to us, throw him off a bridge and make it look like an accident.'"

"You make it sound disgusting."

"That's why I sell bathrooms and am on my own. I have a daughter in Australia, two grandchildren I don't know, even from photographs. The bedroom I was keeping for her has been invaded by a bunch of deadbeats. There's not much room left for disgust, Mónica. Tell me more – I don't know everything."

*

I'm not crying for you, Mireya. Nor for anyone else: I hate pity, and self-pity is even worse. It is like stabbing yourself in the stomach to impress other people by spilling your guts rather than really trying to kill yourself. And it's nothing short of a scandal for a sixty-year-old who has had the power of life and death over the defenceless. I was even given a medal for shooting a teenager who had stabbed his own grandmother and cut up his younger brother with a broken beer bottle.

The kid ran out of a shack in the Villa Diamante shanty town, hands high in the air. "Don't shoot," he shouted, "I'm innocent." He was too young even to shave, and was crying like my daughter when she failed her first exam or when she broke up with her childhood sweetheart.

I knocked him to the ground with a blow from my gun-butt and charged inside the shack. After I saw the bodies, I spun round like a turnstile and cut him in two with a burst of fire. My police partner came over, picked up a kitchen knife, and forced it into his hand. There was an official enquiry. The prosecutor accused me of using excessive force, my defence lawyer argued it had been self-defence, and my companion said he did not see exactly what had happened, that by the time he had run over from the patrol car the kid was already dead. I was on the T.V. news and in all the papers. Next to that of the smooth-cheeked victim, my portrait looked like Frankenstein's monster after its third operation. "Another itchy trigger-finger: How long must this go on?" screamed the tabloids.

No, I'm not crying for you, Mireya. You didn't even take the trouble to find out what had happened in my life. For you it was enough to learn that before I sold toilets I had killed people. "What kind of justice are you talking about?" you asked, the first and last time we talked about it. "I'm sure if you were a policeman during the dictatorship you must have been a torturer. You ought to have died, Gotán. You're dead to me."

I ought to have explained. If only explaining were as easy as raising a weapon and firing when rage rises in your throat as though the soul were leaving a dead body through the mouth. I'm not crying for you, I never have done, but I did not put up a fight either.

You did like me calling you Mireya though. "It sounds kitsch," you would say, "but in your arms I'm swept away by the music, the lights, the show you're putting on, Gotán. Take me away from here, anywhere out of this world."

Who would ask a shipwrecked sailor to quit his island, his palm tree, his coconut? The ocean is dark, deep, and cold. From out on the waves you shouted "Murderer!" You never called "Goodbye".

*

Mónica's version was not all that different from Wolf's. A few details, a million pesos here, a million there; the number of people involved, some of them well known, others the anonymous worker bees of corruption. Edmundo came somewhere between the two. He was busy on the telephone at his office in C.P.F. headquarters. Occasionally he went to a meeting either at a posh restaurant in Puerto Madero or a few blocks closer to the port, among the dark rows of containers.

Mónica found out when the institutional relations manager's earnings could no longer be concealed, at least from his wife, because they had joint accounts. "Although he also opened one in the islands," she said, meaning the Cayman Islands, one of the many safe havens for the savings of the good, the bad and the ugly in the parallel economy.

Edmundo did not trust his bosses, either as employers or as partners in this siphoning-off of funds. "They drop you in it at the first opportunity," he would say to Mónica whenever the situation depressed him, whenever he realised what a huge betrayal of business ethics he was caught up in. "They're always cutting each other's throats, they pursue the person they want to get rid of until he has a heart attack and dies. Then they send the biggest wreath to the funeral, give his wife medals, and even grant her a pension. It's spare cash to them." And if there was no heart attack? "Plan B," Edmundo told Mónica, predicting his own fate.

While Edmundo was diverting the small change from these shady deals into his joint account, the honest gentlemen of New Man turned a blind eye to everything. Just about everyone was getting their hands dirty. And if they formed a brotherhood of traitors, they could hardly expect some sucker with a halo and wings to come down and offer them redemption like Jesus at the Last Supper.

But the account Edmundo opened in the name of Catalina Eloísa Bañados was the last straw for the organisers of the fraud. A tribunal of dinosaurs in old-fashioned waistcoats and gold watch chains gave him the thumbs down. Lorena was right to get in my car and tell me to take her as far away as I could from Mediomundo; she was hoping that by losing herself in the depths of Patagonia she would have time to think. But she did not even have time for a pee in the service station before they caught up with us.

"Your bladder saved your skin," Mónica said. "They can be cautious when they need to, but they're not afraid of spilling blood if their business looks as though it will suffer."

"They would have forgotten all about me if they hadn't seen me with Isabel in that Bahía Blanca restaurant. Worse still, instead of keeping my head down I tried to tackle the guy who came in looking so full of himself with Lorena."

Poor Lorena had already been their hostage. I had been intoxicated with her scent the one time I had embraced her, but Edmundo had staked everything on her. Their joint account was opened, and the money deposited. They told her that if she signed, she could go free. But they killed her anyway, after screwing her.

"They were waiting for you that night at the Imperio Hotel," Mónica said. "The receptionist told me. He's a parrot trained to talk if offered money, Argentine pesos or dollars. 'A couple came and asked for Señor Martelli,' he told me. 'A portly gentleman and a very pretty young woman.' If you had returned from your night-time adventure a little sooner, you wouldn't be here now."

"I was in a police cell. A provincial inspector slapped me around. I was rescued by a forensic doctor who eats steaks from cattle butchered out in the countryside by the light of the moon. They're juicier and cheaper that way, he says."

While he was waiting, the portly gentleman screwed Lorena, and instead of the conventional cigarette and glass of whisky afterwards, he stuck a stiletto under her breast. The finest steel, though.

"Did nobody see him leave?" I asked Mónica.

Apparently from that moment the parrot had stopped squawking.

I could imagine the police's hurried discussions, nervous phone calls, a mobile phone ringing in the overcoat of the man in charge. Instructions to the maids to leave everything clean and tidy once the girl's dead body had been carried out on a stretcher. Nothing ever happened here. The mobile rang again, and the man in the overcoat said "Yes, sir" half a dozen times or more, then went to talk to the hotel manager and reminded him that if any of this got out to the press, he would personally be checking the hotel's fire safety status that very afternoon.

"But why did they kidnap Isabel?"

Distraught, Mónica looked at me and shook her head as though trying to rid herself of the images of her daughter's abduction. She could still hear her cries: "They dragged her away from me," she said, struggling to staunch the tears welling up yet again in her eyes, and to stop shuddering at the memory of the terror so that she could tell me clearly:

"I have no idea, Gotán. No-one has contacted me. I thought they would demand a ransom, or some information they thought I must have, but I swear I don't know anything more. All I have is a dreadful feeling about this."

I gave her a hug. I was becoming an expert in comforting women, although all I could offer were empty words and gestures, a little bodily warmth.

I asked Mónica to move out of her apartment. I promised to talk to a friend of hers who lived on her own not far away.

"Make sure you go," I told her. "You're in danger here."

*

You need to stay out of it as long as you can, I told myself as I left her. You cannot always be on the front line, exposed to the crossfire of those scrabbling for power in this country full of people resigned to their destiny, the sheep who flock to electronic or established churches, the believers in paradises that have been brought crashing down by capitalism's hypnotic charms.

The only paradises left in Buenos Aires are those you find in its streets. Trees that President Sarmiento had brought over from Japan in the nineteenth century. Proletarian sparrows sing in their branches, sharing airspace with pigeons used to being fed in the public squares. They nest up in the cornices of the tall buildings where they are born, eat, shit on people, and die. The zoology at ground level is not much more diverse: dogs, cats and rats fight over streets and wasteland, although it is the rats that come out way ahead in the basements of the grandiose mansions in the smart neighbourhoods and in supermarket storerooms.

Then there are the murderers. People trained to kill if hired to do so, crack shots who no longer bother to blacken their faces or wear balaclavas, but are clean-shaven and wear cologne bought in Paris. But not even the documentaries on the Discovery Channel or Animal Planet show them at work.

We feel sad when a lion tears a deer to pieces. That is the law of the jungle. It is a natural law. The one we are governed by was invented by us. And there is no rational or aesthetic explanation for terror.

8

It is so nice to come home and find your family all waiting for you.

Even before I opened the door, the smell of spices and fried food reminded me that I rarely cook, but usually eat in canteens, and then survive by taking antacids to put out the flames of heartburn. I went straight in without knocking and headed for the kitchen. Burgos was there, putting the final touches to a lentil stew. He was wearing an apron he had found in a wardrobe, probably belonging to one of the women who very occasionally invade my solitude.

As befitted those of their persuasion, the two policemen were doing nothing useful. Rodríguez was sprawled on the sofa watching T.V. Ayala was going through my sparse library, apprehensively examining novels and a few philosophical treatises bought by my ex-wife in her student days, which I sometimes browse when I am fed up with T.V., although I invariably come to the conclusion that I am impervious to anyone else's thoughts.

We ate in the kitchen, enveloped in the smell of garlic and watched over by Félix Jesús, who was observing the spectacle from the blue cushion on top of the washing-machine that served as his bachelor bed.

"Let's talk business while we eat," Burgos said. "Heaven knows what we might run into, and it's always best to meet destiny with a full stomach."

"The Last Supper," Rodríguez said, with a rumbling laugh that had the same effect on us as a reheated meatball.

Yet we did not really get round to talking about what was worrying us until we had finished eating. Instead we talked football. Ayala told us he would have liked to become a professional footballer rather than a policeman, but had never got beyond the youth team of a Bahía Blanca club playing in the provincial championships. Even in those tournaments, he said, the results were fixed. The skilful players were offered a few dollars so they would all of a sudden become paralysed when it looked as though they were about to score, leaving the team that had been backed to come out on top to win the game.

"If anyone did not accept the rules, they made sure his leg was broken in the next game," Ayala said. "While the referee was attending to the bunion on his left foot."

Ayala gulped down a glass of table wine that he had filled to the brim, wiped his mouth on his sleeve, and said:

"That's why I joined the police. If there are bones to be broken, I prefer them not to be mine."

Burgos had encountered something similar in his profession. When he was a student he discovered that the top doctors used the public hospital as a shop-window for their talents. They would appear as experts on T.V. and then the next day parade along the corridors and operating theatres like national heroes. The transfer of patients and even hospital supplies to their private consulting rooms and clinics, not to mention the use of public facilities for experiments the medical council would never have approved of, was common currency in the anthropomorphic trade where they earned their fortunes.

"I prefer to practise medicine on the dead," Burgos concluded, stacking the plates and carrying them to the sink like a good housewife. "I don't have to compete with any social climbers who use the Hippocratic oath to conceal the dirty business they're involved in, and I don't run any risk of being sued for malpractice."

Rodríguez did not seem to want to add to this stock of confessions. He preferred to dig out scraps of food with a toothpick and the help of his little finger, spitting whatever he found onto the floor. He was a true provincial policeman, someone who had never had anything like an ambition. He earned enough to allow him to live in a small house on the outskirts of Bahía Blanca that he had never finished building. According to Ayala, it was the only house within a 200-metre radius, and was regularly lashed by freezing Antarctic winds.

"To make matters worse, he built the bedroom facing south, so in winter he never has enough blankets or ponchos to wrap around him when he's trying to get to sleep in the deep freeze."

"Anyone can make a mistake," Rodríguez said grimly. "That's why I bought a weathervane, one of those tin cockerels that turns with the wind. When his backside faces south, I sleep in the kitchen."

"What about you, Martelli?" Ayala said, emboldened by the cheap wine. "How come you start out as a policeman and end up a toilet salesman?"

I settled in my seat. Félix Jesús threw me a glance of encouragement or compassion. It is hard to tell with cats, although I was pretty sure that the glint in his ever-changing eyes was one of solidarity.

"First of all, I don't sell toilets. I market bathroom furniture. And that's far better than getting my arse shot off in a city full of hypocrites where everybody wants the police to be teachers and social workers rather than to put crooks where they belong. And secondly, I'm still a policeman, even if I don't have the badge or the gun any more. People are born policemen, it's not something you choose, like becoming a dentist. The only thing that happened when I was thrown out was that I lost my pension."

"And why did they throw you out, if you don't mind my asking?"

Félix Jesús arched his back on the blue cushion. One look from me would have been enough for him to launch himself at Ayala. I turned my back so that he would calm down.

"I do mind," I said calmly. "You didn't come six hundred kilometres with a mad doctor at the wheel to hear my confession."

Burgos greeted my reply with a guffaw from the kitchen, where now he was washing the dishes.

"You're right, Don Gotán. You'll have to excuse the inspector, he's as curious as that cat of yours, who's staring at us trying to understand why we've invaded his territory."

Ayala did not like being compared to a cat. "They're disloyal creatures," he said, clearly unaware of the true feline character. Then he said he was about to pee himself, got up and shut himself in the bathroom. His subordinate focused on me as if he had only just discovered I was there. This was how these two functioned. If one of them switched off, the other came into play, suddenly alert to any possible threat from outside.

I was definitely outside. They accepted Burgos, to a certain extent, because his skill had little to do with police work, which consists of bringing brute force to bear on a specific object. But I was cut from the same cloth as them, even if I was slightly different. That made me dangerous. Worse still, I was from the federal force, which was hated and feared from Ushuaia in the south to La Quiaca in the far north. Even though I had been thrown out, I remained for them a stuck-up enemy from Buenos Aires, the police's police, someone who could never accept them as equals. And were they right!

I met Rodríguez's stare without flinching until Ayala sat down again and he looked away. I had the uncomfortable feeling that if there was a shoot-out in the four crazy days we were going to spend together, I would have to keep my eyes peeled to see from which direction the bullets were coming.

"Let's talk turkey," Burgos said.

"What have we got?" I said, as if this was a card game.

Accustomed as he was to being a teacher – he was, it transpired, qualified to teach in schools in Bahía Blanca and Carmen de Patagones – Burgos led off with what we knew and what we were guessing.

*

A police car from Tres Arroyos had been out to inspect the farm I had visited that dark and stormy night. They had gone because Ayala, who was a friend of the local inspector, had asked them to do him a favour.

"I was left looking a fool," said Ayala.

The inspector laughed: "Your friend must have seen ghosts. The farmhouse is abandoned. Two of the rooms have no roof, not even a cigarette smuggler would use it as a hiding-place."

"Didn't they at least find the corpse of the dog that was shot?" I protested.

"Don't go out alone at night," Rodríguez scoffed, playing the big man. "Least of all if there's a storm."

"There were three of them," I insisted. "Two men and a woman. They might have spent the night there and then moved on. The hotels in the region might not be up to much, but nobody would stay in a place like that without good reason. And there were diagrams spread out on a table."

"You should have taken them," Ayala said. "We've got no proof now."

I had to admit he was right. We always think that what is obvious to us cannot be flatly denied the next day. Yet this happens all the time and all over the world.

"But Burgos has some news," Ayala said. "Go ahead, Doctor."

"Lorena did not have sex the night she was killed," Burgos vouchsafed. "At least not with a man."

He explained that according to the unofficial autopsy his friend had carried out in La Plata, there were no traces of semen in Lorena's vagina or anywhere else on her body. "Not one single damn spermatozoid," were the words Burgos said his colleague had employed.

"The receptionist told Cárcano's widow he saw her go in with a man. Perhaps the murderer did not penetrate her, but there could have been some foreplay to get her to relax with him."

"Perhaps he couldn't get it up," Rodríguez said. "These depraved types often fire blanks."

"That's possible, but not very likely," Burgos mused.

After that there was such a prolonged silence that even Félix Jesús stirred, accustomed as he was to the grating sound of our voices provoking all kinds of possibilities. When I asked if that was all the news, none of them spoke, but they all looked at each other as if they were still deciding whether to include me in the game or leave me out.

I tried to calm my provincial colleagues' fears.

"You've stumbled on something important. You don't know what it is exactly, but you know it's serious stuff. I'm not looking for a promotion. I was thrown out of the National Shame and I'm not trying to get back in. All I want is to save the life of my friend's daughter. I've no intention of ever using a gun again either. I'm a civilian now, and besides, I've lost my reflexes. Somebody put a bomb under my car and I didn't even realise it."

"How did you escape then?" Rodríguez said.

"Pure intuition, and not even mine – a journalist's."

"We're screwed if the press are in on this," Ayala protested.

"We shouldn't turn our noses up at alliances," Burgos corrected him, playing the strategist.

Ayala sighed, breathing fumes of garlic and cheap wine all over us. He respected Burgos even though he was not a policeman. His bloodhound's nose told him that anyone who could read dead bodies as if they were sacred scrolls must possess some mysterious power. The doctor did not boast about his talents, but he was the one who had decided to make the trip to Buenos Aires. The other two had enthusiastically latched on to the idea, partly so they could have an unexpected holiday, and partly in the hope it might lead to promotion and medals for bravery.

My clarification seemed to have had the desired effect. Ayala raised his eyebrows as though to tell his cards partner he was holding all the aces, and Burgos took this as a signal to continue.

"My taste for meat slaughtered out in the open, preferably under a starry sky, may give me hallucinations, but at least it's meat I'm eating, and not ground glass."

He explained that, fed up with being looked down upon by the "serious" scientific community, forensic scientists like him had got together via the internet and formed local, regional, even international groups. They were even hoping eventually to establish an international society.

"But it's nothing like a sect or a Masonic brotherhood," he said. "We are not promoting any system of values. What ethical code could we glean from dead bodies when while they were alive most of them were conformists, cynics, or dyed-in-the wool bastards?"

I settled back in my chair to hear the rest. Félix Jesús did the same on his bed.

"Drug traffickers are the lords and masters of half of Colombia," Burgos said, as though giving a lecture. "They kill not simply to make money; they even claim they want to change the world. In the areas they control they pursue social policies that would be the envy of Sweden. They have created a perfect synthesis of feudalism and socialism. The poorest of the poor both fear and love them, and don't expect a thing from their bourgeois governments."

"There's nothing new under the sun," I said.

Burgos scowled at me for interrupting.

"For years now the *favelas* in Brazil have been liberated territory. The drug traffickers have taken them over with guns and violence, love and cocaine."

I thought of butting in again to argue that Lenin was not Maradona, that Marx had not denounced capitalist surplus value so that states could justify imposing more V.A.T., that the revolutionary dreams of many generations should not be confused with the struggle of worms in garbage. But this was not about me, it was about saving Isabel's life, and perhaps the tainted meat that swelled the fat doctor's stomach contained an ounce or two of proteinic lucidity.

Burgos unfolded a large map of Argentina. Félix Jesús licked his front paws then began to rub his eyes, as if he could not believe what he was seeing.

"In Argentina, the last few forest jungles are being devastated by the multinationals," Burgos pronounced in apocalyptic tones. "But even if there were more of them, back in the '60s the guerrillas in Tucuman had to eat the roots of the Peronist revolution raw."

Burgos seemed to be giving his disenchanted, idiosyncratic version of what had happened to the guerrilla struggle in Argentina. "Nobody lifted a finger to create a different society from the sewer we're all living in," he declared. "Then again, although there are hardly any jungles left for demented revolutionaries to hide away in, we don't have shanty towns like they do in Brazil either."

Ayala and Rodríguez seemed to have nodded off – they had probably heard it all in Bahía Blanca. I said nothing. I did not want to be dismissed with another withering look. I wanted to see where the gut-ripper was heading, and decide whether I wanted to go with him.

"No, what we have are 'emergency zones', 'marginal neighbourhoods', houses full of squatters, drunks and male whores under our urban flyovers. Most of them are the underclass. They aren't organised in any way, and their principal objective is to rip somebody off to get a joint, a fix, or a hotdog and a coke. But in some places this situation is gradually changing."

He paused again to ask for water. I pointed to the cabinet behind his bald head and to the sink in the kitchen. He blew out his cheeks: he did not want to drink tap water, but as I don't believe in mineral water he was forced to continue, however dry his throat.

"A forensic scientist, also a hacker and a member of the society we are creating, hacked into the intelligence services' computer system and downloaded this report."

"It could be a fake," Ayala said. "As far as I know, spies don't publish their work on the internet."

"Inspector Ayala isn't a fan of technology," Burgos said, winking at me. "But the web was invented by the secret services, so it's reasonable to suppose that they use it."

As he said this, he handed me two printed sheets. I told him I didn't have my glasses, and asked him to tell me what they said.

"The report mentions two big marginal neighbourhoods, both on the outskirts of Buenos Aires. One to the west and the other to the north of the capital. It talks of trucks moving freely halfway across the country to unload their suspicious cargoes in these hotbeds of delinquency."

"Drugs?"

"And arms! Tens or hundreds of weapons a time. Who knows how many over a period of weeks, months . . . even years?"

I went to fetch my spare pair of glasses and glanced at the sheets of paper.

They had been printed on an old machine with a dot printer that was almost out of ink. I told Burgos that if he was thinking of fighting organised crime he ought to buy himself a new one.

"I'm not fighting anyone, Don Gotán. I don't even know how to use a pistol. You have retired from the force, and not even the pickpockets in Bahía Blanca are scared of these two."

The pair he was referring to shifted uneasily in their seats, but did not quarrel with him.

"Why all those weapons?" I asked. "What those people need is food, work, health centres, a sense of dignity."

"So our National Shame here is a romantic at heart," Ayala mocked. Burgos laughed too.

"Don't make us laugh, Don Gotán. You know better than any politician in the country that half of the people in Argentina are lost causes."

I took a deep breath, held it in, then blew out the air and tried not to think.

In Argentina, there are more supporters of the final solution than there are of Boca Juniors football club. After the last attempt to achieve it by those in power, our economic and social ruin has been so plain for all to see that preachers forecasting the end of the world have sprouted like mushrooms. Even Mónica was a member of an electronic church which saw no hope of changing reality and suggested death as the only path to redemption – after signing over all her worldly goods to the pastors of the church, of course.

But I had not allowed the three musketeers over my threshold to discuss theology or politics. What I wanted was their help to find a lead that would give me at least a vague idea of who had killed my friend and abducted his daughter.

"A couple of the leaders or co-ordinators of the organisation must have been meeting in that 'country house' you so rashly visited to the other night," Burgos surmised. "We don't really know whether Ayala's inspector friend was telling the truth. They undoubtedly left some traces."

"Condoms in the room with the roof," I suggested.

"He said there was nothing, not even a cigarette butt. Either you were imagining things or he's lying."

As Burgos resigned himself to having to drink tap water, I told them what "Wolf" Parrondo had discovered. I explained that despite his profession he was a decent sort who had saved my life (as well as his own) and had taken a risk publishing the story.

When I went on to tell them that Mónica had been released in Haedo, the fat doctor clenched his fists and pursed his lips. The few hairs on his head stood on end, as if he were Einstein lighting on the theory of relativity.

"They didn't go far to release her."

It was all in the report. Burgos asked me to read it out loud, so I would know what it said and to refresh his companions' memory.

Badly written and with spelling mistakes suggestive of a not-too-bright adolescent, the report contained the results of six months of the alleged tracking of well-known dealers in Haedo and Ramos Mejia, in the Buenos Aires suburbs, including their visits to police stations supposedly under arrest, although this was in fact a sham that allowed them to visit police chiefs in their own offices without witnesses, recorders, or indiscreet C.C.T.V.

About once a fortnight, a container lorry made its way into Villa El Polaco, a continuation of the Carlos Gardel shanty town that had grown like a barnacle on the side of Haedo hospital.

The traffickers were never held for more than twenty-four hours. The police log-books said they were taken in for questioning after anonymous tip-offs which somehow always proved groundless. And oh! what a surprise, this procession through the police stations invariably took place the night before the truck's arrival.

A month earlier, with a copy of this intelligence report in his hands, a public prosecutor by the name of Gorostiza had decided to intercept one of these trucks on Route 8. Two provincial police patrol cars and an armoured vehicle from the capital blocked the road at the exit to Pergamino. This was at the end of a bridge where there were no verges, so the driver had no choice but to stop in the middle of the road. The traffic behind him started to build up. While the lorry was being searched, from 8.15 to 9.30 at night, a queue of cars, other lorries, and buses stretched almost a kilometre back along the road. People got out to protest, but even though the reason given was that there had been an accident, those who walked as far as the lorry were shouted at to get away. Some were shoved and even offered violence by the armed police carrying out the search.

"A magistrate friend of mine got his hands on a copy of the lorry inventory," Burgos said.

There was nothing about it in the intelligence report, but in the container the prosecutor had found sixty-six M.K. 40 rifles, twenty of them equipped with night-sights; some recycled old .45s, sixty 9 mm pistols, and half a dozen mortar shells. All this hardware was carefully stored underneath two dozen Thonet chairs the lorry driver had to deliver to Casa F.O.A., an interior design exhibition held annually in Buenos Aires.

"What happened to the cargo? Whose legal jurisdiction was it? Where was the news published?" I wanted to know.

"At 9.30 Route 8 was cleared, and the lorry headed the procession onwards. The lorry driver was able to deliver his furniture to the exhibition on time."

"And the weapons?" I asked.

"That same night, the prosecutor had a telephone call telling him to be very careful about what he made of his discovery. The next morning, after writing a letter to the investigating magistrate saying he was at his wits' end with depression, Gorostiza hanged himself. The magistrate sent his condolences to the prosecutor's young widow, and after that silence reigned. If family and friends said anything, none of it came out. The fact that a prosecutor in Pergamino had decided to hang himself was not considered newsworthy by the national papers."

*

Of course it was not news. Who cares?

A year earlier, a young T.V. presenter had vaulted without a pole from his apartment balcony. Four floors down, then a splatter of blood on the pavement, which the cameras of his own T.V. channel carefully recorded and showed for days afterwards. The kid, who was barely thirty years old, was a coke addict. "He hallucinated", according to a friend. "He wanted to be free." His photograph, the face of the beautiful and damned, appeared in all the newspapers. Psychologists, priests, even political analysts came out with all kinds of theories and went on and on about how decadent a society must be to throw its most promising youngsters out of windows.

The lorry took its varied cargo to each of its destinations. A week later, when Gorostiza's wife wanted to lay a bunch of flowers on his grave, she could not find the cross marking it. Some anonymous avenger had removed it, some recalcitrant Catholic who had decided to take divine justice into their own hands and punish a suicide.

9

Don Quixote, Sancho Panza and the doctor decided to go out and sample Buenos Aires nightlife. They could not persuade me to join them. I am no good as a tour guide: I know next to nothing about Buenos Aires' nocturnal geography and I am too old to buy affection. I wished them luck and as soon as they had left I turned off the light and went to bed.

At 2.30 in the morning the phone rang.

"Don't tell me you were asleep."

"I still am. At this very moment I'm dreaming that a 'p.p.' is telephoning me."

Wolf did not ask what a "p.p." was and I did not give him time to find out for himself.

"A stupid pen-pusher," I said, but without malice. "What are you doing waking people up at this time of night?"

"I was returning your call, Martelli. The country's in flames, and you're snoring."

I got out of bed and looked out of the window.

"Where's the fire?"

"Tomorrow a whole neighbourhood is going to go up."

I sat on the bed and fumbled for the bedside light. Yet again I had broken my sacred rule of not answering the telephone after midnight, and yet again I was in trouble.

Thanks to the contacts in the police whose palms Wolf had greased and to legions of informers who lived in among the dust of the legal cases sleeping the eternal sleep of Argentine justice, he had discovered that in less than twenty-four hours, federal and provincial police would be sharing a picnic, presumably by moonlight, in Villa El Polaco, in Haedo.

"Bingo!" I shouted, suddenly wide awake as though somebody had thrown a bucket of cold water over me.

"Don't tell me you play the lottery."

"Life is chance, Parrondo. A series of coincidences, manipulated by remote control in the hands of a madman."

"Does that mean you're coming or not?"

"Where?"

"I already told you. To the picnic. I've got room for you in a patrol car with a uniform who owes me a favour."

"Count me in. What shall I bring?"

"A notebook. But whatever you do, don't bring a weapon. You won't be a policeman or a toilet salesman. Tomorrow night you'll have your first assignment as a journalist."

*

The provincial dummies slept until noon. Félix Jesús preferred not to return to the invaded apartment, but sat out on the rooftop opposite until the sun forced him to seek shelter under the sink in the laundry.

The first of the three to appear – with a hangover – was Burgos.

"I dreamed about the living dead," he said, sipping the weak *mate* I reluctantly shared with him. "They cornered me at the end of a street and wanted revenge for my autopsy reports. 'I was stabbed to death and you wrote that I died of a heart attack,' said one cadaver who must have been at least two metres tall, with a forty-day-old beard on a face eaten away by formaldehyde. 'A train cut me to shreds and you wrote I died of cirrhosis,' said what remained of another one, a man as fat as me with huge green bags under his empty eye sockets."

"They're only nightmares," I said, shocked all the same by his story.

Burgos dismissed my uninformed comment.

"It's normal. The dead use the half-open doors of our subconscious to make their complaints. But nobody listens to them. I've had to live with this kind of thing ever since I chose forensic medicine."

All of a sudden I did not feel like sharing the *mate* with him. I put some fresh leaves in the gourd and told him to carry on drinking on his own. At that moment, Ayala and his assistant surfaced and wanted to join in.

I took advantage of the fact that the team was all together again to tell them my news. Ayala was sure it was no coincidence.

"They're going to put on a show. The next day it'll be all over the front pages. It's a chance for your journalist friend to make amends with his bosses."

Burgos said Ayala was probably right, but that I should not turn down the invitation.

"I didn't. I said I would go. What about you three?"

"We'll follow the caravan," Burgos said. "I'm not going to stay in and go to bed. Buenos Aires by night isn't so bad."

"Tourists generally make for San Telmo."

"But we're not Japanese tourists. I know Haedo. I was assistant to a famous abortionist in Ramos Mejía, and when I was young I worked for two years as a volunteer in the Santiago Cuneo hospital."

"This man is one big surprise," Rodríguez said proudly, as if the roly-poly doctor were his invention.

"Going into one of those shanty towns is like doing an autopsy of the city," Burgos said. "All its guts are on display in front of you: the foulest but also occasionally what is most sublime about our society."

"You mean you've met the Virgin in a shanty town?" Ayala laughed at him.

"The Virgin and all the saints live there," Burgos said solemnly. "Not that I've ever seen them. I don't believe in that kind of meeting on earth, even though the churches get rich promising them. I'm not religious. Poking around in intestines spilled by a knife, or hearts sliced in two by bullets means the only possible communion is with horror."

He drank the rest of his *mate*, then handed the gourd back to Rodríguez, who, being the junior, had been given the job of handing round the drink.

Burgos said that if things had not changed since his day, the hospital was a no-man's-land.

"The thugs used to come in shot to pieces. They either came out as good as new or they died, but no records were ever kept. At night you could hear shooting all round the hospital, sometimes even in the grounds themselves, where there was also a scrapyard. On the pediatric ward they had to replace the wooden shutters with lead ones after a bullet ricocheted off the ceiling and nearly killed a three-year-old boy.

One day the oxygen cylinders were stolen. The next they were sold back to the hospital at half price. How could they refuse a bargain?"

"The hospital is right next to Villa Carlos Gardel," Burgos went on. "Villa El Polaco must be one of those blisters that appear on the surface of the city, a place for gangs to hide out in when they're at war with another gang. That's why there are all those weapons involved; something big is cooking. And Inspector Ayala is right: if the police force is venturing there, it's because the script has already been written."

We sat in stunned silence. The only sound was the slurping of the *mate* as we passed the gourd from one to the other.

*

Wolf had discovered that the New Man Foundation had set itself up in Villa El Polaco. Sometime before Edmundo's death, they had built a health clinic and a ward for abandoned children under the age of six. They had also been building a chapel, but that work had been suspended when an undercover T.V. crew filmed the priest having sex with the boys he was catechising.

I wondered if Edmundo had ever been to the shanty town to see how the money provided by C.P.F.'s godfathers was being spent. I doubted it. At the end of the '80s, by which time he was solidly ensconced in the oil company, my friend brought the curtain down on his social conscience. He never went so far as to say that the shanty towns were full of the dregs of society, of those who preferred to live on benefits and theft rather than do any work. I knew he had signed petitions of solidarity with the poor who had hitched a ride on President Menem's panjandrum and were dragged along alive until they lost every last shred of dignity. But I knew he was disillusioned, and sick of it all.

"You're a policeman," he would say to me. "You don't have any great dilemma, because the police are there to protect bourgeois property. But I used to believe in something different, in a new order. 'The people are never wrong,' Perón used to claim. And look what happened: the people elected his executioners and have carried on doing so ever since. If the British had not yomped all over us in the Falklands, Admiral Massera would have been president now. And I even suspect things might have been better that way. Many more dead, but better."

Edmundo was probably right. Instead of boycotting or corrupting politicians, the money men who propped up Massera and the rest of the dictatorship would have been enthusiastic supporters of a democracy in jackboots, marching in double file like Pinochet's victorious armies in Chile. But Edmundo's killers did not give him time to reconcile himself with his conscience.

10

Burgos planned to go and see the colleague who had whispered the real information about Lorena over the telephone. While they were at it, they could reminisce about university days at La Plata, girlfriends they had shared or fought over like dogs, ideas that had put them at loggerheads and realities that had re-united them in the fragile truce with our regrets that characterises life for anyone over fifty.

Ayala and Rodríguez said they were going to visit "a museum", without admitting they did not mean the Art Gallery but the police museum in Central Headquarters. This consisted of gruesome weapons and bits of murder victims once famous for some reason or other but long since forgotten by the tabloid press.

They had agreed a rendezvous with Burgos later on so that all three of them could climb into the sky-blue V.W. and wait somewhere near the Lugano police station, the starting point for the punitive expedition to Villa El Polaco due to kick off at midnight.

I spent the afternoon and evening writing to you, struggling to order my thoughts and pin them to the page like dead butterflies. You would probably read my letter with apprehension rather than nostalgia. Nothing is the way I said it was; everything is in such chaos in this windowless, doorless room where I keep my memories of you.

Nobody, least of all you, will bother to follow these tracks to see where they started out from, who it was that tiptoed through the life of the woman he loved the most, to glean some idea of how he could possibly be the same man who kicked down doors, smashed furniture, and held his gun to the head of the people whose homes he had burst into.

"The violence is the same," you said when I tried to explain in order to keep you with me. "There's no difference between blowing a crook's brains out or a student of sociology's. You're a killing machine and you don't realise it."

How could I accept what you said without losing you? How could I spill my heart out without you feeling so disgusted that you shut your eyes, turned on your heel, and left?

I spent the whole evening trying to find a way to explain what a mess I had made of my life, to convince you that we do not live in Disneyland, that Donald Duck went quack quack quack when you were a little girl, but you never understood a thing, that there is no such thing as a society where the police spend the entire day helping old ladies and blind people across the road.

You were never going to read all that nonsense, Mireya. It was nothing more than a way of filling the evening, just like going to see an old friend from university to talk about the clandestine struggle against fake autopsy reports or sordid prostitute murders. Or going to the police museum to get kicks out of the smell of formaldehyde that bits of bodies were floating in. Nightmares that become routine for forensic doctors or policemen who have done more than direct the traffic or give directions.

Vain dreams; moments when every horizon looks black and every breath leaves you gasping for air. I tore up all the sheets of paper I had struggled with for hours.

*

At 9.30 I met Wolf in a bar on Avenida del Trabajo and Tellier. The whole neighbourhood stank of abattoirs. Nothing unusual in that: if the roly-poly doctor had been around he would have been as emotional as a country boy in the city when the smell on the breeze took him back to his childhood down on the farm.

"Did you bring your reporter's notebook?"

"If a diary where I write all my heartaches will do instead, here it is."

I showed him a blank book, missing the pages I had thrown away.

"If anybody asks, you work on the paper with me. I do the crime reporting, you cover the social side of things."

"What happens if there's shooting? Where do I hide?"

"Don't play the fool with me, Martelli. If you've brought a weapon, you can stay here."

I undid my jacket and lifted my arms. Wolf shrugged as if to say "come off it" and looked away. There were just the two of us in the bar, apart from the waiter watching the football on T.V. The street outside was deserted.

"This isn't the Normandy landings," Wolf said eventually, leaning across the table towards me. "This kind of operation is planned in advance. It doesn't come from some headstrong magistrate – the police have taken their precautions. They have informers all over the shanty town. They would never move in otherwise."

"What are you trying to tell me, Parrondo? I'm a toilet salesman, remember."

"Times have changed. Fundamentalism is for the Arabs. In Argentina nowadays everything is up for grabs."

We walked three blocks to the local police station. Nobody stopped us at the entrance. Wolf introduced me to the officer who owed him a favour. As he had promised, there were spaces for each of us in a patrol car that had the insignia, searchlight, and sirens to prove it was working on behalf of us all. I felt a tug of nostalgia, although Wolf was right that times had changed. The car was nothing like the ones I had known so well: the dashboard was as full of instruments as a jet plane. A keyboard and a small screen made the interior look yet more futuristic. Over the radio I could hear the control-room voice above those of police patrolling the streets. The city was calm, apart from some insignificant demonstrations in Palermo and Belgrano. "Middle-class assholes protesting that they can't get at their money," said one of the cops. "They're more hysterical than a bunch of transvestites."

*

"This is going to be a walk in the park," said the man Wolf had latched on to. "But just in case, don't take any risks, and don't run off to the first layabout who calls you over to complain about police brutality. You might get taken hostage, and if anything happens to you, I'm the one who'll get it in the neck. Understood?"

Yes. If Ayala's suspicions proved correct, we would not be the only real or fake journalists taking part in the raid. The government was trying to convince public opinion that it was fighting crime without massacring anyone, showing respect for thugs and criminals as though they were tender young schoolgirls – even though the greater part of that public opinion (family heads, practising Catholics, orthodox Jews, rich businessmen or mediocre public- or private-sector employees) were in fact calling for tougher measures: "That's enough taking people into custody and allowing them their rights, they need to be shown what's what," these people said. "Tear out their fingernails, grab them by the balls. I'm against the death penalty, but I don't mind seeing them get blown away," they said, say, will always say every time they face the prospect of being mugged in a dark alleyway, hear a noise at midnight in the charming houses they are sweating blood to pay for, or feel a drug addict's knife pressed against their neck.

The police caravan – eight patrol cars, three armoured vehicles and at least a dozen motorcyclists – set off with no lights on across the city. We barely paused crossing Avenida General Paz and met up with the provincial police also participating in the raid. There were at least three times as many of them, and they made no attempt to conceal who they were or where they were going.

They took the lead, roaring down General Paz with sirens blaring, forcing the few vehicles on the highway at that time of night onto the kerb. We roared down Rivadavia at the same speed, slowing only slightly to avoid any of the vehicles tipping over and providing the press and the T.V. with headlines about an embarrassing police pile-up.

When we reached Haedo the signs announcing QUIET – HOSPITAL seemed to excite everyone still further. We were in enemy territory now, there was no going back and getting home for a good night's sleep.

Out of nothing, or rather out of the fog caused by smoke drifting over from the rubbish tips in Villa Soldatti, three helicopters joined the party. I could feel a sense of patriotic duty stirring within. When I left the police force, I swore to myself I would never again allow this demon to possess me, the strange excitement you feel when you know you are about to wreak violence on the weak and defenceless, those who are different from you, those who in the name of ideology or religion spit on the hand that feeds them, reject their masters, want absurdly to be free.

*

I must admit that rather than identifying with what was going on like a veteran, I felt more like a kid at the local cinema sucking chocolate peanuts and cheering on the Palefaces in their bitter struggle against the savage Red Indians.

"We've been laying the trap for days," the officer told us like a tour guide. "Keeping a discreet eye on things. We were just waiting for the merchandise to arrive."

The truck with the merchandise had arrived the previous evening. The routine worked as smoothly as a Swiss watch: two days later, after the cargo had been sorted, it would be handed out to local distributors and neighbourhood leaders, closely watched by the police, as if it all belonged to them. Which it did, to a certain extent, although not exclusively. Taking part in the trade was the only way to try to control the army of outcasts the drug traffickers depended on to win and keep hold of their markets.

Wolf's man was merely repeating his lines: the only reason the police were going in shooting was to reassure the public, to surprise middle-class public opinion with a frontal assault on the shanty towns they so hated. "At last something is being done," opinion-formers in the media would bleat. "Respecting the rights and guarantees set out in our national constitution, unlike during dark periods now happily put behind us, last night a surprise operation was carried out against Villa El Polaco, the headquarters of antisocial gangs bringing terror to Buenos Aires."

While the policeman was busy responding to his superiors' commands on the radio, I told Wolf I could not care less about the motives for this farce, or what the results might be. Clamping his hand over my mouth, he growled that if I was sorry I had come I could get out there and then, but no way was I going to ruin his story for him now that he was out on the pitch with the game about to start.

As though performing aerial acrobatics, the helicopters converged on the same point in the sky. There was a loud bang, and the night sky suddenly became as bright as day. The assault vehicles fanned out: some of them screeched to a halt, while others roared round the edge of the shanty town, careering over the potholed roads and dirt tracks. Armed men wearing helmets and bullet-proof vests leapt out with their rifles and tear-gas launchers. A few seconds earlier, when the flare had lit up the central area that was meant to be deserted at that time of night anyway, motorcycle patrolmen had ridden down the narrow alleyways between the shacks, shouting: "Everybody inside! Those with honest jobs have nothing to fear, but we'll blow the heads off anyone who comes out."

When the action started, Wolf's policeman told us to "cover your backs", then jumped out of the car as the driver steered it into one of the entrances to the slum. Instead of getting out to back up his boss, the driver lit a cigarette and sat calmly smoking at the wheel, like a taxi driver waiting for his client.

I thanked Wolf because without his contacts I could never have got into the shanty town, then I too jumped out of the car, ignoring his shouts of "Where the fuck are you going, you idiot?" Inside the slum, bullets slammed into the walls and the dirt alleys like beetles on a hot summer's evening. Women were screaming, and I could imagine them rushing to protect their kids in the shacks' promiscuous bedrooms, praying to the Virgins of their home provinces to protect them, while their husbands flung themselves to the floor.

I ran bent double, my hands covering my head as though they were a steel helmet. I reached a corner that was no more than a gap between two rows of shacks, and flattened myself against a wall. I pulled out the .38 Ayala had lent me when he heard I was going in armed with nothing more than a notebook. "Don't get yourself killed," he had said. "If you do, the union of journalists will wash its hands of all responsibility. They'll say you weren't one of them, and the police will spit on your still-warm corpse when they learn you were thrown out of the National Shame."

I checked the gun was loaded. I could not quite see why somebody who had slapped me around in the Bahía Blanca police station should be so keen to see me stay alive now. It was anyway too late to change my mind because the gunfire was tracing red and white lines to and fro in the darkness. The police must have been ordered to fire at will down the alleyways. There would be time enough to justify the police actions as self-defence by putting weapons in the hands of all those who died.

I saw a motorcyclist racing towards me. Before he could shoot, I held up my old police badge (a relic I keep for nostalgic reasons, and which I had polished that very afternoon). I made sure my hands were in the air, and pointed the .38 skywards. I gestured to him to cover me. He looked perplexed, but just managed to manoeuvre his bike around me, then pull up at the far side of the alley and leave the engine racing in neutral. I took this to mean he was going to cover my back, so I moved forward, staying close to the walls. I pushed my way into some shacks shouting "Federal Police". The terrified occupants received me like actors in a well-rehearsed performance, entire families in a heap like puppies in a litter, as accustomed to this kind of police circus as they were to the everyday violence the drug traffickers and gang leaders subjected them to.

"You're out of your mind if you thought you were going to find the girl in one of those stinking holes," Ayala said later, when we met up to assess the meagre results of the farce.

Of course, that was what I had been trying to do. Unsubtly, shouting, threatening anyone I thought might be hiding information, as well as anyone who dared to challenge me even though they were defenceless faced with this madman who burst in, kicking down balsa-wood doors and ripping down curtains intended to offer some privacy in these miserable hovels. I did the same for several streets, even after the motorcyclist without warning turned tail, leaving me to my fate. By now, though, the stream of bullets was steadily diminishing and coming from only one side. I was lit up by the helicopter searchlights, like a suburban Rambo left without any budget for his all-action heroics. At one point I found myself a split-second away from emptying my pistol into a doped-up teenager I ran into. He was cradling a 9 mm revolver he had apparently just stolen from a policeman I'm sure he shot for the pleasure of seeing him writhing in pain and bleeding to death.

I could have killed him. Nobody would have called me to account for it. Yet I could feel you looking at me: you were still too close, peering at me like a tropical fish swimming in artificially clear and warm waters, far from paradise, behind glass walls where I saw nothing and your eyes in the middle of nothing. "You're a killing machine and you don't realise it, Gotán," you would have said if I had finished off this smooth-cheeked thug. It is all the same, he's a crook, but he could be a worker, a left-wing café intellectual, a *guerrillero* or one of those youngsters studying to be a chef who still believe the world could be a little less of a cesspit. "Kill him and carry on dancing, you're good at that," I would have heard you say in some hidden corner of my head or in the empty wastes of my sleepless nights. "They're lost causes, if I don't kill them, they'll kill us," you'll say when you're out of earshot of others like you, boasting beneath your penitent's mask.

I stuck my gun between his eyes and took the 9 mm from him. I would probably need it if I got out of the slum alive. I whispered to him like a paramedic to a dying crash victim that I would be back to deal with him when I had finished my search. My threat did not seem to worry him. He stared at me blankly, and hardly seemed to notice the barrel of the .38 pressed against his forehead. Then he closed his eyes and smiled, which made him look still younger, no more than a kid.

I lowered my gun and left the shack.

Outside, the gunfire had ceased. Loudspeakers from the helicopters were warning people to stay quietly indoors. "Your identities will be checked, and those of you who have nothing to hide have nothing to fear," said someone who sounded like a radio presenter hired to make a special programme on his night off.

I walked steadily back to the entrance to the shanty town, wearing my old police badge on my chest. Nobody tried to stop me, although occasionally a guard gave me a suspicious look. Anyone with borrowed I.D. could have walked out of that make-believe raid. Nobody really wanted a gunfight: everybody was following their script, and I must have been the only nutcase who was improvising.

The next morning there were photographs in all the newspapers and extensive T.V. coverage of Operation Run Rabbit, as an imaginative interior ministry official christened it when he pushed in front of the police chiefs to be interviewed. Figures were given, the quantities of drugs and weapons seized, promises that a thorough investigation would be carried out into where it had all come from, those responsible would be caught. "This government has set itself the mission of rooting out organised crime, with the penal code in one hand, and with an absolute respect for the rights of the thousands of honest citizens who live in poor neighbourhoods such as El Polaco."

Wolf did his best to disguise his relief at seeing me emerge in one piece.

"That's the first and last time I invite you along, Martelli," he growled. "You're nothing but a bastard policeman. They could easily be carrying you out on a stretcher with a blanket over your face."

"Yes, but I'm walking out, and empty-handed," I said, suddenly exhausted and wondering what I had been looking for, why I had gone out on a limb like that, whether I really thought I was Sylvester Stallone at a beginners' audition. "If they knew the people they were looking for weren't here, why didn't they leave the others in peace to get on with things?"

"Nobody wants people in shanty towns to get on with things in peace," Wolf said. "Your honest taxpayers want them to vanish, to have them disappear from the map. If they could agree on the political costs, they would build a Berlin Wall to protect the city of Buenos Aires from all these lumpen. Anyway, come with me, this is when the show really starts."

*

Wolf dragged me back inside the shanty town. We walked straight ahead, following the path the police car had taken, and soon came out into the central square above which the helicopters had dropped their flares.

Smoke still hung over the open space, reeking of cordite. More than a hundred young men and women were squatting in the middle, leaning on each other for support. They were all silent, and hardly glanced at each other, still stunned by the attack and cowed by an equal number of police surrounding them.

There were fewer journalists, although it seemed there were more because they were scurrying all over the place, excited by the war scene they were covering live. Every single T.V. channel was there; photographers were shooting roll after roll of film, while the reporters waited for permission from the man in charge of the operation to ask their questions. As soon as they were given it over a loudhailer, they rushed to interview police and officials, but ignored the empty gazes of all those under arrest.

At the far end of the open space, far from the T.V. lights and flashbulbs, lay half a dozen corpses. All of them still brandishing weapons in death. Nobody would ever know whether any of them had actually resisted the police attack, or how many had been picked off to prove that this midnight raid had not been a mere stroll in the park.

The policeman who owed Wolf a favour came up and asked if he was alright. He deliberately turned his back on me, as if he knew what kind of journalist I really was. Wolf did his job, asking him for his assessment of Operation Run Rabbit.

"It seems they moved everything out just before we got here," the policeman said. "We found only a couple of rifles in an informer's house. The traffickers must have planted them there so we would shoot him."

"Where is the informer now?" Wolf wanted to know.

The policeman pointed to the heap of bodies.

"All this is off the record," he insisted, lowering his voice. "If you publish any of it, you can forget your friends in the force."

The police had not found anything, but the T.V. cameras were filming hundreds of packets of marihuana and crack, several plastic bags full of a white substance, dozens of rifles, shotguns and automatic pistols, baseball bats, flick-knives and chains. It was like sale day at a department store, with all the merchandise laid out for the lenses of the local and foreign press.

All those arrested were ordered to stand up and file past the press. Frightened, stiff from having to crouch for half an hour, aching from all the blows they had received, they nevertheless got to their feet and formed a long line that snaked round the empty square.

"We have the whole of Mercosur here," scoffed the policeman, whom Wolf identified as Inspector Quijano. "Chileans, Paraguayans, Bolivian Indians, Brazilians. Plus a couple of lost Ecuadoreans, and even three Venezuelans who arrived not long ago from Caracas with a mission to brainwash the poor and open a branch of President Chavez's Socialist party in Argentina."

Wolf was listening to Quijano like a priest hearing confession. Despite the warning, he had switched on his tiny recorder.

The Chavez supporters identified by the National Shame were three poor devils who had probably pitched up in Argentina hypnotised by the mirage of being able to buy one U.S. dollar for one Argentine peso. This chimera had attracted Latin American immigrants by the thousand: Argentina is closer than Europe, and it is a promised land, a crucible of races, destined to be great. Any South American outcast could save dollars here then go home and buy themselves a new car they could drive along their motorways instead of having to sleep underneath them.

Now the party in Argentina was coming to an end. As so often in the past, the batteries were running low, there was no way to go on blindly borrowing, and it was time to pay up or spend years washing the dishes. We already knew which of the two options it was likely to be, and who was going to have to roll their sleeves up. The middle classes were banging saucepans and shouting that they wanted their money from the banks. The poor were casting wistful glances back at the places they had left behind for the dream of making money in the big city. Only the crooks went on celebrating. In the boardrooms of the big companies busy repatriating their capital and speculating on an imminent devaluation of the Argentine peso, or in slums like El Polaco or Carlos Gardel, where they were preparing for the fiesta of riots and looting the political opposition had been planning for months.

This D-day landing in the Buenos Aires slums was one of the government's last despairing attempts to show it had a strong grip on crime. No-one believed them. The journalists invited to the spectacle laughed in the faces of the police spokesmen, who as soon as the cameras and recorders had been switched off admitted that this was another sham. They said they were sick of being used to deliver a double message: they were supposed to get tough with criminals on the one hand; on the other, they were meant to treat all the lumpen like blood brothers, even if they would not think twice about murdering a policeman.

*

I was beginning to think I had wasted my time going on the picnic when I suddenly saw my Bahía Blanca friends among the swarm of journalists. Like all true provincials, they were drawn to lights, and the only ones still shining in the shanty town were those of the T.V. crews.

Burgos saw me and came over.

"I thought you were dead, Don Gotán, but I'm glad you're not. I don't like to have to rummage around in the bodies of people I've grown attached to."

"It was all a waste of time," I said by way of a greeting.

"Well, better to be out partying here than sleeping like sardines at your place," he said. "But don't give up yet, let's take a look behind the scenes."

We walked over to the place where those who had been killed in action were laid out. We did not need a forensic scalpel to see that none of them had died fighting off the police attack. The bodies had been rotting for hours.

"They finished them off a while ago, probably nowhere near here."

I do not get any pleasure from firing point-blank at someone and seeing them crumple under the impact, peering sightlessly at me as they stare into the abyss. Burgos was not impressed by the sight of death either. But we could not help staring at each other, horrified at what we were witnessing.

"They're travelling corpses," he said. "The logistics of this farce have become so sophisticated that if we had a military dictatorship now, throwing prisoners alive into the sea from planes would seem the work of amateurs."

It was not only Lorena who had travelled after death. What Burgos told me, with all the calm authority of his profession, was that there were people who specialised in this kind of macabre transport. As police investigations usually ended at the graveside, few questions were asked about the specifics of this final journey, unless there was some reason to wonder why healthy, rich and happy young people had suddenly perished of a heart attack.

"But we've still got nothing," I insisted. "I haven't been threatened again, my friend's daughter is still in limbo. Perhaps she's become another travelling corpse."

Burgos puffed out his cheeks. He seemed to hesitate, as if pondering the value of the information he had uncovered. He lit a cigarette and inhaled the smoke like someone waking up and going out in the early-morning mountain sunlight.

"I talked with my colleague in La Plata for a good while," he said.

"Apart from recalling the old days, and the good times that are harder to reconstruct in memory than the most complex crimes, he told me there was blood on the blonde model's body."

"Naturally: she was murdered."

"There's no 'naturally' about it: the blood wasn't hers."

I said nothing and waited for him to elaborate.

"Don't expect me to tell you whose it was," he said. "I don't have a portable laboratory with me, and however influential my friend may be, he can't determine who it came from. He could only say it was a different blood group."

"And the same sex . . ."

"You're the one saying that," he cut in. "I only know what my friend said: there was no semen found on the body."

"But there was on the other victims," we suddenly heard Ayala say. He had crept up on us like a mischievous boy.

"So we do have something," Burgos said, trying to dispel my pessimism. "Where's Rodríguez?" he asked the inspector.

"On a date. He hit it off with the attendant at the police museum and they agreed to meet here tonight. She's on overtime, and he's on leave and six hundred kilometres from home."

He pointed to the rapidly dispersing group of journalists. We could see Rodríguez and his date talking and laughing in the midst of them. Another wartime romance, inevitable now that both sexes take part in police raids and massacres. Unforgettable love stories that will some day be sung by the lyreless poets of the internet age.

We laughed at Rodríguez, whose new companion looked about the same size and weight as him. "A perfect couple," Ayala muttered, envious that his subordinate had managed to find happiness in such an improbable spot as the police museum.

However spectacular the show had been, I still thought that it was a wasted night. Sometimes suspicion sticks to things like moss to a stone, and prevents us picking up on small details.

The detail here was the man I had spotted with Lorena the last time I had seen her alive, in the Bahía Blanca restaurant. When I had first inspected the heap of bodies with Burgos, I had not noticed him. Now it was as though he was whistling from beyond the grave to attract my attention. I recognised his features, although his face was frozen in the grimace with which he had hoped somehow to evade death. Just another body in the first light of day, the sixth in the silent row laid out on the ground. Who could say how far this corpse had travelled?

PART THREE

Butterflies in an Album

1

At 6.00 the next morning we had a working breakfast at my apartment. Burgos, Ayala and me, with pastries and more *mate.* Rodríguez was absent with permission. "That police museum attendant is hot, and I'm not going to miss out on a night of free sex in Buenos Aires, chief," he told Ayala, who replied saying he should not expect to win any medals or stripes for heroism in action.

Ayala told us he had left the police caravan when it crossed the Sarmiento railtracks, and had headed for the Santiago Cuneo hospital with his trusty companion.

"I was just following a hunch," he said.

Burgos explained that in its early days the Santiago Cuneo had been a model hospital, but with the passage of time, and above all of governments, it had become what it was now: a vast ruin which devoured taxpayers' money to pay the salaries of hundreds of employees, only a quarter of whom had a real position. In other words, the other three-quarters sat on their backsides doing nothing or did not even bother to turn up for their supposed jobs. Yet at the same time the hospital could not cope with the huge numbers of poor and very poor patients who flooded there from all over Buenos Aires province, then waited for hours to be told in five minutes whether they had a cold or cancer. After that, they were sent home with a next appointment three or four months later.

"There's a genocide going on right in front of our noses," I said, refusing the *mate* Ayala was offering. "Liberals rend their garments over what happened in the former Yugoslavia, or those Afghan women buried alive, or the abuses the Yanks commit in Iraq, but they can't see what's going on under their noses."

Ayala dismissed my social conscience with a scornful look. Burgos did not deign to pay me any attention. I could see that there was no prospect of setting up a revolutionary cell with those two.

*

Ayala continued with his account of the visit he and Rodríguez had made to the hospital.

"We went in through Admissions. It was deserted. At that time of night, the whole hospital was a tomb-in-waiting, inhabited only by patients and rats."

Nobody stopped them, asked where they were going, or why they were there. Perhaps this was because of the bulges under their left arms, or because anyone could see they were policemen: Ayala with his slicked-back hair, Rodríguez with his razor cut. The pair of them wearing dark glasses in the middle of the night, and the lofty, disdainful way they looked down on anyone they met. Despite this, they are human, and Ayala was shocked at the state of abandonment in the hospital.

"Palestinian refugees live like kings compared to the patients wandering up and down the corridors in there," he said. "Or the people lying in bed waiting for death as though on a street corner for a bus."

"Lots of doctors work for free in public hospitals," Burgos said in defence of his profession. "And lots of patients are cured. It's also true that sometimes their relatives just dump them and never reappear. There are men and women who after a couple of general anaesthetics and a few weeks lying there all alone cannot even remember who they are or where they are from. They cry like babies when they're turfed out so that somebody else can occupy their beds."

As if drawn on by some secret current, the provincial bloodhounds found themselves in a corridor lit only by two 25-watt bulbs. The spectacle in the wards had been grim enough, but now they felt they were in some passageway to hell. "The dead who have no relatives to pay for their funeral must be sent down here," Rodríguez had apparently told Ayala. Like the good Sancho Panza he was, he had a word for each occasion.

"I must say I was shit scared," Ayala said. "My service revolver is useless for shooting corpses. They've already bought it, so they have nothing to lose."

"But dead people don't kill," Burgos said, either to reassure him or in a fit of spontaneous metaphysical enquiry. "I dream of them the whole time. They reproach me for my autopsy reports. They ask me why I open them up when worms are perfectly capable of disposing of them, and eternity is there to bleach their bones. But their condition is not contagious. Death is not a virus, it does not make you ill or threaten your health. It's the end, that's all it is."

Ayala did not seem convinced.

"That doesn't matter. I'd prefer to face a whole gang of drug traffickers than a corpse on the move."

"Talking of corpses on the move, my journalist friend is trying to track down the one I recognised in the line of bodies at the shanty town. He said he'd call as soon as he found something."

"I wouldn't expect too much," Ayala said. "Witnesses or curious onlookers are never going to get to the bottom of this."

Perfectly true, but I had no option at that moment other than to "outsource" the investigation.

Halfway down the gloomy corridor, the two policemen had come across a ward that seemed to house neither men nor women. Nor were there any doctors or nurses: the only people in view were a couple of bad-tempered giants who raised their rifles as soon as they saw the pair approaching.

"I think you're lost, the bathroom is upstairs," one of the guards said.

"Who the fuck are you, anyway?" the other said.

Ayala raised his hands so that the jacket he was wearing would fall open to reveal his gun and his provincial police badge – which in that gloom shone like an F.B.I. agent's credential.

"One of our colleagues has been shot. He's bleeding to death up in Admissions. Where are all the doctors in this hospital?" he said, sounding as indignant as he knew how. The two giants stared at each other, then the one who seemed to be in charge spoke into his walkie-talkie. Nobody responded.

"Where the fuck have they all gone?"

Telling his companion to keep an eye on the two intruders, the first guard said he would go up and find out what was going on. Despite his foul temper he must have believed Ayala, because he left his rifle with his companion. Perhaps he wanted to avoid frightening the patients who were wandering along the corridors thinking they were in a hospital.

"Who wounded him?" the second giant wanted to know.

"Some shanty-town dweller he stopped and asked for his documents only a couple of blocks from here."

"He got what he deserved. The shanty-town people around here all have state-of-the-art firepower. Why did he stop him?"

"Because he looked like a man with something to hide."

"If your friend doesn't die, tell him not to stick his nose in where it's not wanted. This area is run by demons. No priests or police from other areas can get in. It's the guys from Fuerte Apache who run the show here."

Fuerte Apache is a neighbourhood of tall grey buildings built to house working-class families from greater Buenos Aires. The buildings are interconnected by high walkways – the architects who designed them must have been off their head on coke, just like the workers who moved there imagining they would be starting a new life.

Everything in Fuerte Apache was half-finished. The money to complete the job went elsewhere, and the dream soon turned to a nightmare. By now it had virtually become a kingdom of darkness, where different tribes fought for influence, drugs, and territory. They fought for each corridor, each inch of space, and the blood of these warriors of nothingness ran like sewage down the drains.

The giant who had gone up to Admissions came back in an even fouler mood.

"It's true there's no-one there, but there's no injured officer either. Who are you two?"

He did not have long to wait for an answer. Rodríguez hit him over the head with his gun and sent him to sleep before he had even closed his eyes. Before the other giant could react, Ayala had stuck his .38 in his ribs, and snatched his rifle from him so cleanly that if it had been a bullfight the entire audience would have been waving their handkerchiefs in approval.

"Their weapons were duly confiscated," Ayala said with the language of someone used to filing reports. "We locked the sorry pair of them in a broom cupboard. Then we went into the ward."

*

There, in the basement of the Cuneo hospital, was the arsenal that the combined police forces had raided Villa El Polaco for in vain. There were neat rows of explosives, handguns and rifles, together with spare parts, all waiting to be despatched to their intended destinations.

Ayala and his assistant surveyed the weaponry with the same delight as they had shown earlier in the police museum. Never in their Bahía Blanca police station, or anywhere else in the provinces for that matter, would they see such a collection of light and heavy arms.

"There are two more rooms," Ayala concluded his report. "They're connected to the first ward, but they're empty. They're newly built, but I'm sure they're not for patients."

"Medicine is a sacred mission," Burgos snorted. He was fed up with the weak *mate* that was loosening his stomach, but even more so with the society we had created in Argentina, where the most disgusting, corrupt events reflected us back at ourselves more clearly than any mirror.

2

Nobody in Argentina could be surprised that a hospital was being used to stockpile weapons. In the past, union headquarters and ministries have become arsenals. Of course, when gunpowder, gelamon and trotyl replace alcohol, gauze and antibiotics, that means something is about to happen. But at the end of 2001 we were not at war – or so we thought.

Burgos went off in search of more information. At noon he had an appointment at the Faculty of Medicine with the professor of pathological anatomy, another former university colleague. The two had not met for some time because on his way back from a training course in Europe, Burgos had fallen in love with a beautiful young woman in Portugal and had heeded her pleas to go with her to Bahía Blanca to visit her family. Their passionate romance had been short-lived: she soon grew tired of the smell of formaldehyde and flew the nest, setting off in pursuit of a Swedish anthropologist who had pitched up in the deserts of Patagonia.

As though entering a monastery, Burgos – who at that time was not yet roly-poly – buried himself in Bahía Blanca, becoming a convinced bachelor and steadily putting on weight. He also became convinced that the medical profession was anything but a way to win respect "in a country full of cows and wheat where hundreds of thousands of kids go without bread or milk," he said, not to justify his personal sense of failure, but to explain that "solitude is a good hiding place. At least it keeps us out of harm's way. I don't have to kill anyone, Don Gotán, because the patients I get to see are already dead."

That morning, Mónica rang to say that she had received a strange telephone call.

A muffled voice told her that Isabel was well, that she should not worry about her: "You'll get more news at the appropriate moment," the voice told her, giving her no time to ask questions, but adding briefly before hanging up: "Make sure that defrocked policeman friend of yours stops stirring things up."

"Did you record the call?" I asked.

"The answering machine was on. I've also got a call tracer, but they used a public telephone somewhere in the street. The noise of buses makes the voice almost inaudible."

As soon as I had finished talking to her, Ayala and I went out for some air. The idea was to meet up with Wolf, who had promised to use his contacts to try to find out where the dead bodies we had seen in Villa El Polaco had come from. Particularly the one I had identified.

The centre of Buenos Aires creates its own microclimate. The early summer sun was baking the walls of the tall buildings, while the financial measures the government was trying to put in place were frying the brains of the middle classes. They could not get their money out of the banks, and were rushing into the streets like ants when someone pours kerosene on their nest.

Unemployed strikers who usually blocked roads and highways demanding bags of food and money now happily if somewhat warily welcomed the rowdy columns of office workers and housewives shouting slogans protesting against the finance minister and the banks, shrieking that the time for revolution had come. Some of the more outraged were even suggesting it was time to hang in public the politicians they themselves had voted for. These politicians were trying half-heartedly to convince them of something every banker knows: that the money was not in the banks where the naive customers had deposited it, that it had wings or extraterrestrial powers, and somehow vanished into thin air as soon as it passed over the counter.

On the outskirts of the capital, political activists and gang leaders were handing out money in the shanty towns to encourage people to go to supermarkets and help themselves to whatever they could find. The provincial police were under orders to do what they do best anyway: stand there and do nothing. They looked on impassively, secretly rejoicing at the breakdown of the law and order they had sworn to uphold.

Ayala was amazed at the hive of activity in the city centre, although he claimed to hate people from Buenos Aires. The fact was that during those days the whole city was like a gigantic mime artist, gesticulating and grimacing in an extraordinary way. Not even contaminating the water supply with a massive drugs cocktail could have produced an effect as spectacular as the manoeuvres of capitalism in flight.

We met Wolf in a cafe where everybody was shouting at the tops of their voices. Signs of the crisis were immediately obvious. Chairs and tables had been removed from the bar area, presumably to avoid them being thrown around if arguments between defenders and critics of the government got out of hand.

"Did you buy dollars?" Wolf said. "That's what everyone's doing. The banks are not selling them any more; all the bureaux de change closed half an hour ago. There's looting in Boulogne and Laferrere, and rumours that they're distributing arms out at La Cava."

It was only after he had given me all this latest news that he seemed to notice Ayala.

"So now you have a bodyguard?"

"Inspector Ayala is from Bahía Blanca. He came to Buenos Aires for a bit of a rest. Wolf, I'm not interested in the national crisis: tell me what you found out about the bodies at Villa El Polaco."

Wolf snorted and said nothing, muttering what sounded like the rosary under his breath. In fact, he was doing his sums. He was calculating how much the few pesos he had with him would be worth in dollars, and wondering whether it might not be better to spend them on a ham and cheese sandwich and a soft drink.

Ayala had not watched him come in, and had not reacted in any way to his comments. He was too busy trying to interpret the mood of the crowds outside, to work out where they were heading, or what was going on whenever a small group or a couple came to a halt. Their voices reached us like a distant choir or the sound of animals in the jungle, fusing in a lava of sound flowing from the crater of a volcano and destroying all possibility of human communication as it poured inexorably on.

My journalist friend opted for the sandwich, and this seemed to calm his nerves.

"They were all fake," he said, biting into it. "I don't mean they weren't dead, but they were all brought to the shanty town from the morgue. Corpses get lent out like that more often than you want to know. The police raid had nothing to do with trying to find drugs or arrest crooks. It was all a publicity stunt: 'Your police are working for your safety', or 'We are here to protect you'; all that crap."

"And my corpse?"

"His surname was Cordero. I don't know his first name. He was a fixer."

Wolf's contacts had told him Cordero had been an official who worked in procurement for the Ministry of Defence. Cordero's power came from the independence he enjoyed, because the minister was far more interested in climbing aboard the presidential jet to tour the world than in dealing with everyday affairs of state. That meant he delegated everything to bureaucrats he had not even spoken to since his appointment.

Cordero was responsible for small-scale purchases, although these usually consisted of at least a hundred heavy weapons and missile components for low-intensity warfare. The illicit buyers were not plotting to overthrow puppet governments in Asia or doing the dirty work for corrupt Latin American democracies: they were small- and medium-sized drug trafficking organisations in Bolivia and Colombia, who always needed the most up-to-date equipment for their gangs. The arms were sold anonymously and without any guarantee apart from the assumption that if the rifles jammed, or the missiles returned like boomerangs to their launchers, then future contracts would be cancelled.

Our Cordero was not the only one involved in the business, Wolf went on after he had finished his sandwich. He was but a link in the network. All you had to do was click in the right place, and you could find a huge selection of arms for sale. Devotees of the free market, the arms dealers competed fiercely with each other, offering seasonal bargains and all kinds of novelties, including weapons not produced in Argentina but easily obtainable elsewhere. The merchandise was stored in containers broiling in the sun at the port of Buenos Aires while the customers sorted out payment.

Cordero must have got the thumbs down from God or the Devil when a surreal brigade of Argentine policemen arrested one of the customers from the border town of Ciudad del Este in possession of a recently arrived container. Instead of accepting their cut in the deal, they handcuffed the businessman and promptly despatched him to appear in court in Argentina, not bothering with any diplomatic formalities. The Paraguayan consul in Iguazú called his Argentine counterpart in Ciudad del Este (for once not to arrange a date for a game of golf followed by a couple of joints in the residence of one or other of them) to protest at what he called "the violation of Paraguayan sovereignty by a gang of uniformed pirates from your country, which could cause an international incident of unforeseen consequences, dear fellow."

*

The traffickers in these sensitive border regions employ informers to listen in on all judicial, police and diplomatic communications. They soon informed the frustrated purchasers what had happened. The would-be buyers were a newly formed Islamic group which genuinely or just for the sake of it claimed to be behind all the explosions that the sons of Allah inflicted on the enemies of the Koran throughout the world. Cordero's name was noted and passed on to other even more shadowy figures. A week later, he came to the kind of end that Wolf was now telling me about, with a mixture of admiration and disgust, in a bar crammed with savers who had suddenly found their savings all seized by the government.

"They found Cordero in the same Bahía Blanca hotel you stayed in."

This piece of news immediately brought Ayala to life. He pushed a sweaty office worker on his lunchbreak out of the way, drank the rest of Wolf's Coca Cola, and asked him where the fuck he had heard that. Wolf did not blink or even look in his direction. "I never reveal my sources," he said to me. Ayala put a hand round the back of Wolf's neck, yanked him forward, and kneed him as hard as he could in the groin. Wolf collapsed against the counter, gasping for breath. It was his second such assault in a very few days.

If anyone near us noticed what had happened, they gave no sign of it. Wolf's eyes rolled up and he went white as a sheet. I gestured to Ayala to let him go, then made sure Wolf did not fall to the floor. I offered him a glass of water, and a dry cough suggested he was managing to breathe again. A little colour seeped back into his cheeks.

"If this bastard is a friend of yours, I'm out," he said furiously.

"This is his first trip to Buenos Aires," I whispered in his ear. "He doesn't know how to behave in big cities."

"When we left Bahía Blanca a day and a half ago, everything was quiet," Ayala grumbled. "Now there's yet another body. Normally years go by before we have any stiffs at all. And this when I'm away from my post."

Wolf paid his bill and left without saying goodbye. I followed him, signalling to Ayala to stay where he was.

"You're surrounding yourself with garbage again, Martelli," Wolf shouted at me when I finally caught up with him. "I understand that once a policeman, always a policeman, but I'm a journalist and I'm collaborating with you because at the bottom of all this mess is a dead man who happened to be your friend."

"And his daughter is still missing."

Wolf stopped and looked round to see if Ayala was following us.

"He's a bit rough and ready, but he's an honest policeman," I said, not entirely convinced.

Wolf set off again, pushing his way through the streams of people wandering aimlessly along the road as if there had been a mass escape from a lunatic asylum. No-one knew where they were heading, but they were too scared to stop and rest.

"They found the body of the man you saw with the blonde model at the Imperio Hotel in Bahía Blanca. Strangely enough, in the room you had been in two nights earlier, Martelli."

"He made a quick journey to Buenos Aires, then."

"Quicker than if he had been alive. But what is strangest of all, and something tells me I should take advantage of being suspended from the paper to go on a long holiday and not get mixed up in this any further, is how he was killed and what state he was in."

He came to a halt, and made me do the same. The people behind bumped into us, then went on their way without apologising. They were all completely bound up in their visions of the imminent apocalypse, counting the coins they could take home to buy food and medicine.

Wolf had become my mirror. Looking at him, I saw my own face. My own testicles began to ache. I could see he was afraid, and felt the fear as my own.

"When they found him he was wearing women's clothes. Miniskirt and a skimpy top. High heels, and made up as if he was going to a party."

"Was he a queer?"

I was taken aback that I was asking such a stupid question, but Wolf seemed as much at a loss as me.

"Not that I know of. It's a message, Martelli. They dressed him up as a whore either before or after killing him."

"How did they kill him?"

"With a stiletto. Somebody stuck it under his left nipple and plunged it into his heart. The maid who found him fainted on the spot. In less than half an hour, the transvestite corpse was loaded into an unmarked ambulance, a van with tinted windows that set off at full gallop for Buenos Aires, flying through police controls without even slowing down, as if it had a critically ill patient on board. But there is no record of the body being listed in any morgue. It was taken straight to Villa El Polaco, and by the time it was laid out there he was dressed as a man again."

"So the criminals we're up against are conjurers," I said, with grudging admiration.

"I'm not up against anyone, Martelli. This is as far as I go. I'm off on holiday. I don't have a single peso in any Argentine bank. I've managed to get it all out of the country. It's not a lot, but it will guarantee me a couple of carefree months in a neighbouring country. I'll be back once the mushroom cloud has receded. There's bound to be a devaluation, so I'll be a rich man in a country where everyone's been fleeced."

He shook hands, but before I could say goodbye properly, he was swallowed up by the anxious crowd. I did not have the chance to tell him to be careful, although I knew that his usual plan of escape was to take the boat across to Carmelo in Uruguay, then travel overland to Canelones, where a rancher's widow who raised Aberdeen Angus cattle would be waiting for him. They had been seeing each other once a month for at least fifteen years. The widow had children in France and Germany who did not like the idea of their rich mother seeing a gold-digging pen-pusher, so the two always met in secret, far from prying eyes and gossip.

It was a long time before I saw Parrondo again. His byline vanished from *La Tarde*. Whenever I rang I was coldly informed he had quit his job. For two years, the only response from his bachelor apartment was from his answering machine, which parroted the same old message: "Take to the rafts, the ship is sinking."

3

You would think that someone who switches their sexual orientation after death and who has been a public functionary, if not a minister or secretary of state, must be newsworthy. Yet nobody had recorded Cordero's death. I searched through the crime pages in the papers, trawled the internet: nothing. Cordero had never existed and, given the circumstances, was not likely to now. If I had not seen him in that Bahía Blanca restaurant and recognised his face among the "criminals" laid out in Villa El Polaco, I might have doubted his existence myself.

The death sentence on Edmundo that Isabel had referred to must have come from Cordero's office or somewhere else where he did overtime as a fixer in the illegal arms trade. Lorena or whatever her name was must have been his secretary and lover, positions which often overlap to such an extent it is hard to tell when the secretary stops admiring and starts fondling, or whether the secretarial candidate's vital statistics were more important than her professional abilities.

I wondered if Edmundo had betrayed his masters as Mónica had suggested, or had discovered something that made him a target. If the order to kill him had come from Cordero, who then had decided that he, as well as his secretary, had also to be removed from the board?

I had to admit that this bloody game of chess was being played with some skill. The fact that no traces of semen were found in Lorena's body, and that Cordero had been despatched while dressed as a woman meant there were sensitive souls involved in this sinister affair, people who loved opera or the decorative arts, defenders of the conservative order, by all means, but willing to see social conventions evolve a little, provided this presented no threat to power. A kind of moral compromise, allowing things to change so that nothing would change. The eldest son of an aristocratic family, like the unfortunate Cordero, for example, could make an unnatural sexual choice and be supported by his relatives at social gatherings, but woe betide the perverted queer if he imagined he could claim his share of the inheritance. In that case he would very soon turn up in a ditch with a stake up his arse.

According to Wolf, Cordero's death had been a message. The mafias operating at every level of society love messages. The bourgeoisie, members of that supreme mafia consecrated by capitalism and protected either by robust arguments or blood and thunder, demand that the artists it buys should offer a message in their works. They have to be positive even when they are portraying hell. There has to be a chink of light suggesting that good will triumph in the end, that evil will be forced back into the darkness and those who threaten the right to property will burn at the stake.

That wild morning, when Buenos Aires was a volcano of unbridled corruption and millions of petits bourgeois looked on helplessly as infamy erupted on all sides, I felt afraid. Not for the future of society, which I don't believe in, and whose famous stock of values was as volatile as the central bank reserves. No, I was afraid that if I came out of all this alive, I would have to face some unpleasant revelations. Until that moment I had firmly believed that my departure from the police force had been based on a sense of disgust, on my rejection of any kind of complicity with the Argentine dictatorship's barbaric genocide. The system's steamroller could not find any values left to crush out of me. Being a policeman embalmed my spirit – if such a thing exists, and if it is not an illusion to argue that man is anything more than his body.

There is no difference between shooting a criminal who killed an old woman to steal her pension and murdering a school teacher just in case he had left-wing notions. Death does not make ethical distinctions. It claws at everyone in the same way. It is a tiger living inside us, just waiting for the chance to escape and fulfil its destiny. Some people give it the opportunity only once in their life, in a moment of passion, a fit of anger, or for economic gain. Others choose to become policemen. Patrolling the streets of a city like Buenos Aires is to live side by side with the tiger, to let it loose in return for getting paid, to think the beast was really someone else when it mauled and then watched the dying groans impassively, refusing the hand held out for us at the last. To be a policeman is to shut your eyes, stuff your hands in your pockets, and let people die.

*

That warm night in December 2001 the roly-poly doctor looked pleased with himself.

The president had just announced a state of emergency. That evening, supermarkets and stores had been looted in Buenos Aires suburbs. On T.V. you could see the looters parading triumphantly while local store owners wandered disconsolately amongst overturned counters, scattered food, smashed electrical appliances. The police had done nothing because there was no way they were going to open fire on the people: they were their heroic defenders against every kind of abuse.

"It was so nice in there. It brought back so many memories," Burgos said, almost in a trance. "While they floated in their tanks filled with formaldehyde, the dead bodies seemed to be listening to us recalling the olden days. 'Thanks to my profession, I've travelled all over the world,' said my former colleague, who is now a university professor and a member of the academy of medicine. 'I met and socialised with top-notch people in the most refined environments. I was treated like royalty, and even honoured for my contributions to pathological anatomy by countries like France and the United Kingdom. Luxury hotels, receptions, expensive women who offered themselves to me simply to share my prestige. But I don't enjoy any of that as much as I do being here, surrounded by my corpses and now with you, my dear colleague. I thought you were lost forever in those southern wastes.' We ate lunch in there too," said Burgos. "Not much of a meal though, because the professor is vegetarian."

"I hope you didn't share with him your taste for rustled meat."

"You're right, I would have been embarrassed, although when it comes to meat I don't think a man of principle like Miralles approves of eating it at all, however it is raised. A cow is still a cow, and it doesn't really matter if it has a stamp on it from some vet or other – besides, vets are a long way further down the ladder of our profession than forensic experts."

Even though their trip down memory lane had taken up most of lunch, the two of them had spent a few minutes talking about the topic which had in fact brought them together again: the misadventures of an ordinary serial killer who suddenly finds he has other people's crimes laid at his door.

"I wouldn't like to be in that poor man's shoes," Burgos said Miralles had told him. "To pick your victims like he does takes a long time. You have to study all the possibilities, and avoid leaving any traces, because forensic medicine has made great strides in recent years. To be made responsible for somebody else's handiwork must be really tough."

"It's a typical trick of those in power, professor," Burgos told Miralles. "It's like a fugitive crossing a river to throw a pursuing pack of hounds off the scent. Before and during the last dictatorship, the paramilitaries claimed their outrages had been perpetrated by left-wing guerrillas. Ordinary people do not discriminate; they condemn without a second thought. Evil is always lurking somewhere."

"But if we're governed by the Devil, who put him there?"

Miralles was not as convinced as the La Plata pathologist or Burgos that the lack of semen in Lorena's body was significant. If she had not been killed at the hotel, her body could have been thoroughly cleaned before it was taken there. In fact, the time of death did not coincide with when the body was found in my hotel room, although the crime had occurred not more than twelve hours earlier. Miralles did not rule out the possibility that the killer might have been a woman, although he said we should not be carried away by anything we discovered. We should proceed with scientific caution, use trial and error, and above all, be patient.

This professor who had been so acclaimed in Europe and who only found peace among his dead bodies could not know and did not have to worry that while he and his colleague exiled in Bahía Blanca chatted about the good old days, when the worst pain they felt were the pangs of love, a young woman had been abducted and might already be dead.

"Be patient? That's impossible," I grumbled.

Inspector Ayala was busy preparing his weak *mate.* Rodríguez had called to say we should count him out. The police museum attendant had turned out to be a tarantula disguised as a dragonfly. She was sucking him dry, but "I feel so good," he told his superior. To top all this, she had suggested he leave the police down in the southern deserts and transfer to the capital. She said she had good contacts in personnel, who would sign him up as a corporal with a salary twice as high as the pittance he earned in Bahía Blanca.

"But to do that, he would have to live with her in Buenos Aires," Ayala complained.

"Nothing comes for free," Burgos said.

"Perhaps, but Rodríguez hasn't got the faintest idea of what it means to live with a policewoman."

Ayala told us he knew what he was talking about. All his pay went on satisfying the whims of his wife's femininity, which was distorted from the day she chose to join the police. The sexuality of a woman who gets her kicks beating men over the head with a baton is not dealt with in any of the manuals. Who are they arresting when they handcuff a crook? Their father, who always betrayed them with their mother? Their older brother, who dominated them? The man they live with, who beats them?

"The police and psychoanalysis make strange bedfellows," I said, remembering how authoritarian governments had persecuted analysts, and how the mental health services in public hospitals had been decimated when the military napalmed the already sparse forests of analytical thinking in Argentina.

But perhaps the police museum attendant was the perfect partner for a brutish lout like Rodríguez, and the federal police force the ideal place for his petty perversions to go unnoticed in the anonymity of the rosters. Ayala was hurt: he felt betrayed, but he had only himself to blame: he was the one who had brought Rodríguez to Buenos Aires in the first place. His guard-dog loyalty had not even lasted two days. Ayala would have to return to Bahía Blanca alone, empty-handed. He had no proper leads to help catch the serial killer, and no suspects.

I confess I did not feel sorry for him.

*

So often the solution is staring us in the face, but we just cannot see it. Or it is itching at our backside and we scratch and scratch but cannot ease the itch.

That same morning Mónica received a letter registered in Madrid. It was the bank statement for an account in her name. She was positive she had never opened an account in Spain "or anywhere else, Gotán. I've never been one to put money in banks, it was always Edmundo who took care of that." According to the statement, she had $250,000 to her name. The money had been deposited on the day of Edmundo's murder.

"It's a sick joke," she said when I went to see her at her friend's apartment.

"More than that, it's a way of buying your silence."

"By someone who thinks I won't say anything because Edmundo was unfaithful to me, who thinks I'm secretly glad he's dead."

The account had been opened by a complete stranger, probably with fake documents, although he must have had all of Mónica's personal details, her social security and national insurance numbers.

"Only the state has access to all that information," I said, staring time and again at the statement and the letter of welcome from the Spanish bank.

Whoever it was had not bothered to go to Switzerland, the Cayman Islands, or Panama. They wanted the account to be legal and above board, something Mónica would have to justify if she withdrew the money and wanted to transfer it to Buenos Aires. The people making the deposit must have known that in Argentina the banks gobble up their client's money. The idea must have been for Mónica to go and get it herself at the cashier's window in Madrid.

"Help me, Gotán. I don't know what to do or where to begin. The money is like the gravedigger's first spadeful of earth on my back. They want to bury me alive, but why choose such a perverse way to do it? They could have killed me when they kidnapped Isabel . . ."

Mónica's voice failed as she remembered the moment when they pulled her daughter out of the car and dragged her away. She was crying desperately, begging her mother to save her.

"If they didn't kill you, that means they want you alive. Whoever it is, they want you on their side. A quarter of a million dollars waiting for you back in the home country. Not bad for a resentful widow."

"I'm not resentful, Gotán. I loved Edmundo a great deal. I'll spend the rest of my life trying to understand what happened between us."

The evening was airless. In the apartment of her friend, who had left us alone together as soon as she had shown me in, and in the rest of the city too.

Through the open windows we could hear the distant rumble of people beating on pots and pans, lamp posts, anything that would make a noise. They were singing and chanting, unable to sleep because they were so angry and so hot, all making for Plaza de Mayo as they always do when Argentina falls apart.

I told Mónica to trust me. Nobody in their right mind could find any reason to trust an ex-policeman, but they were the words Mónica wanted to hear. She was safe where she was. Her friend took care of everything, even going to meetings to bring news of the electronic church they both belonged to, news of cures and miracles: paralysed people who rose from their wheelchairs or cast aside their crutches and started to walk, blind men and women who suddenly saw the light, deaf mutes who became talkative thanks to the power of prayer.

And the biggest, most unbelievable miracle of all: loves that come back.

4

It is no coincidence that in a country on the verge of imploding, some individual cases follow the same logic. Fragmentation is a threat to any power that boasts it is eternal. In the midst of any shipwreck there is someone on the bridge watching the spectacle in comfort with his life jacket on.

Lorena's death must have upset the serial killer in Bahía Blanca so much it was understandable he might want to withdraw, to distance himself and look for a new patch that would not unscrupulously be taken over by any mafia organisation. It is one thing to commit a crime for personal reasons; crime for profit is quite different. And it is just as awkward to be famous and even celebrated for something you did not do as it is to be accused of something you were not responsible for. Like any artist, a serial killer has no wish to steal anyone else's thunder, and does not seek easy applause. It is not a passing fame he is after, but to become a classic, so that he can escape the cruellest revenge, that of vanishing into oblivion.

The fourth call after midnight made me realise that something was changing in my life. A week earlier, I would not have answered the telephone. Félix Jesús would have looked at me pityingly while it was ringing, then set off on his night-time tour even more convinced that whereas a lack of curiosity can save a cat, it condemns humans to lonely, sleepless nights.

"Martelli . . . ?"

The woman's voice sounded wary and hesitant. I did not reply.

"As I understand it, you live on your own," she said, after a pause of at least ten seconds. "Unless your cat also answers the phone."

This made me sit up. Until now, Félix Jesús had been left out of this.

"Who is that?"

"You don't know me. And I don't know you either."

Again, I said nothing, resisting the temptation to ask how she knew I had a cat. It might just have been a guess – anybody can have a cat. Or rather, not anybody. And my cat is not any cat.

"I was given your number by a journalist," she said, sounding less tense. "Parrondo, from *La Tarde*. He's the one I send my announcements to."

I coughed awkwardly.

"You've got it wrong. You or Parrondo. I don't write reviews."

"You're not a journalist, you're a policeman," she said, growing irritated.

I took a deep breath. I was about to tell her I was no longer a policeman, but I had no idea who I was talking to. I preferred to listen.

"Don't expect him to turn himself in."

She waited for me to make some kind of comment. But far from being put off by my silence, it seemed to provide her with the oxygen I was lacking.

"He's going to stop," she said. "For two or three months, whatever it takes. He doesn't want to be blamed for murders he didn't commit. They tried to frame him for a girl and a transvestite who worked for the government. They're unscrupulous fraudsters, like those people who make photocopies of hundred-dollar bills."

I was beginning to understand, though I could not quite believe a woman would speak on his behalf. When I said as much, she grew even more annoyed.

"You say you understand, but you don't understand a thing. You think that just because you're a policeman, you know about human nature."

"I suppose you're protecting him because you love him," I ventured.

"Of course, he's the love of my life. There at least you're right. He's my man, my partner. Even if he does have that failing."

"It's quite a failing though, isn't it?"

"What about those in power? They've had lots of people killed, haven't they? Didn't they have wives, children, grandchildren? Or shouldn't a criminal have feelings, or need a home, a family to protect him?"

"Do you have children?" I said. I thought she would hang up. Instead, I was surprised to hear her say tenderly:

"Two, a boy of eight and a girl aged six."

She went on replying to my questions as if she were answering a survey. Yes, they went to school, a private one, because you know what state schools are like these days, and besides, they let anyone in, whereas in this school the atmosphere is excellent. No, we don't have any money worries, he earns well. No, I'm not going to tell you where he works, do you think I'm a complete nincompoop?

"Parrondo told me he's leaving the paper."

"Thanks for telling me, I had no idea," I admitted. "What can I do for you two?"

"Tell people. I send my announcements, but nobody prints them. Parrondo said you had influential friends."

She would have hung up if I had contradicted her.

"There's something strange going on here, Martelli, something really serious. He doesn't want to get mixed up in it."

"Is he going to stop killing?"

"For a while at least. He needs to kill, but he's promised me he'll be careful. I'm forever reminding him he has a family to think of."

"Aren't you afraid?"

"He wouldn't harm a hair on my head, poor thing. To him, the family is sacred. The kids and I, we're the apples of his eye."

*

Ayala was not convinced, preferring to put my midnight telephone call down to a need to make him look a fool. It took him a long while to accept what my call tracer told me, but eventually he agreed to go with me to what turned out to be a flea-ridden boarding house out in Liniers. According to the grouchy landlord, a married couple with two children had been staying there until a few hours earlier.

"They stayed in all day, arguing at the tops of their voices. The kids were crying, and my other tenants complained. But they had paid a fortnight in advance, which nobody does round here, least of all the scumbags who were protesting. In the end they stopped fighting, the woman made a telephone call, and they left as suddenly as they had arrived. I wanted to give them back their money, but they refused. They didn't bring any luggage."

In the register, the family head and presumed woman-butcher had written: *Sebastián Gómez, profession – administrative assistant, home address – Bahía Blanca.*

"That could be false information," the landlord said, "I don't ask anyone for their documents, just the money up front. But they seemed decent enough – they made a lot of noise, but seemed decent."

Like the doctor they drove a V.W., but theirs was a normal colour, white. Apart from crying when their parents were arguing, the two children had not said a word the whole time they were there. The landlord's description fitted at least half a million people in Argentina: the man was of average height, skinny, and bald. His only distinguishing feature was that he had no body hair at all, "Not even on his arms – he was as hairless as a chihuahua," the landlord said.

Based on this description, the killer did not seem the kind of man to seduce women by his appearance. Instead, I had a chilling image of the shock his victims must have got when they discovered his smooth, slippery snake's skin. Yet somehow he persuaded them to go to bed with him; there were no marks of violence before he drove the stiletto into them.

Ayala left the boarding house shaking his head. His belief that he was on the trail of a mythomaniac was faltering. Even though it was so early, he called Bahía Blanca and told the officer on duty to send out patrols: "Try to intercept him on the road," he said. "He's travelling with his family, although he'd have to be really dumb to head back south."

The lines on Ayala's face showed his disappointment that the case would be resolved by the murderer yielding to family pressure and calling a halt. If he stopped killing of his own accord, what did Ayala stand to gain as a policeman? He had not even been the one who had taken the call.

"Nobody need know the details," I said, generously. "All I'm interested in is finding my friend's daughter alive."

But Inspector Ayala was not someone who rewarded altruistic gestures. He said he planned to return to Bahía Blanca at first light, with or without his assistant, and by bus if Burgos wanted to stay on in Buenos Aires.

*

But that long, hot Buenos Aires night had one more surprise in store for me.

Burgos had gone out with his professor friend and what he described as "two little orphan girls". He said the girls had been longing for a night in the care of two old fogies with plenty of money. Just as there are volunteers in hospitals to give emotional support to patients who have no relatives, so there are brotherhoods of gentlemen willing to take care of young girls anxious to enjoy the chequebooks of their aged, addle-brained sugar daddies. The professor belonged to one of these brotherhoods – as Burgos later explained – and indulged in this vice because he needed to compensate for his close contact with bodies preserved in formaldehyde by enjoying firm flesh and smooth skin. Burgos himself thought it might be a good way to seek refuge from the bedlam on the city streets.

What he did not foresee was that he would spend most of the night in a crowded common cell in a Santos Lugares police station, where ten dirty old men caught in acts of sodomy or paedophilia had been taken after a police raid. All the details were being typed out by a clerk who barely raised his eyes from the prehistoric typewriter to inform us that the prisoners would stay where they were until the magistrate assigned to the case had taken all their statements.

After we had hung about for two hours, and in recognition of the fact that Ayala was a serving policeman, the inspector who had just come on duty carrying a box of pastries under his arm gave us permission to see Burgos.

"I should have stayed in Bahía Blanca," the doctor wailed as soon as he saw us.

He was slumped in a corner of the cell in which the ten geriatric cases struggled for air, while at least a dozen flustered young virgins crowded together like puppies on a row of teats.

"Ayala was going to leave this morning, with or without you," I said.

"Like rats abandoning a sinking ship," Burgos grunted, avoiding the inspector's dull glare.

"Where's the professor?" Ayala wanted to know.

"They took him straight home. They herded the rest of us into their van like cattle, but they found him a taxi. All he had to do was promise to call the magistrate, who is a friend of his."

While the country was collapsing around our ears, and the roly-poly doctor was licking his wounds in the crammed Santos Lugares jail, the magistrate who was supposed to be taking their statements was too busy on much more important business to come to Santos Lugares. It was the inspector himself who told me this, as he offered me his last croissant and a few sips of sugary *mate*.

"An officer has gone to try to persuade the pain-in-the-arse neighbour to withdraw his complaint. I don't want this garbage in here all day. Who's going to feed them? The courts? And anyway, the complaint is about noise, not about prostitution or the white slave trade . . . A thank you wouldn't go amiss . . ."

His last words referred to the way I grimaced as I handed him back the *mate* gourd. "Thank you," I said through clenched teeth. "Who's the magistrate in charge of the case?"

He looked at me, uncertain whether to tell me.

"That's confidential, part of the proceedings, blah, blah, blah . . . But I've heard you were thrown out of the National Shame, so I'll tell you. His name is Patricio Quesada."

I jotted the name and telephone number on the corner of a newspaper, then tore it off. The front page was filled with photographs of the previous evening's demonstration in Plaza de Mayo.

"In any case, as soon as my man gets back and confirms the neighbour has withdrawn his complaint, I'm letting the lot of them go. I want them out of here by midday. I've got no funds, and I'm not sending any of my men out to beg food for this bunch of old perverts and underage whores."

I decided to keep the magistrate's details anyway. Call it instinct or a hunch, faith in the capricious ways of fate, or the sense of smell of a battered old hound who despite wind and rain picks up the sulphurous odour of his own urine and finds his way home intact.

The officer came back soon afterwards, and by 8.00 in the morning all those rounded up in the raid were thrown out on to the pavement. Ayala and I waited for Burgos, who finally appeared, eyes lowered. He hailed a taxi, and we set off with him in search of his sky-blue V.W., which he had parked outside the brothel.

"There is a God," Burgos said triumphantly as he clambered behind the wheel of his exotic vehicle. "That magistrate friend of the professor is one of the people who ordered the raid on Villa El Polaco. He told me as we were being carted off. That should give you something to chew on, Martelli. Allah is great, but Buenos Aires is greater still: it's a huge bucket full of crooks and traffickers. That's why they needed three magistrates from different jurisdictions to authorise the police to go in shooting."

"And what did they find?" Ayala wanted to know. "I had to go to the Santiago Cuneo on a hospital visit with that horny brute Rodríguez to uncover the weapons."

Ayala was in a bad mood again, and with reason. Rodríguez had been devoured by a policewoman who was turned on by the pickled organs in the police museum. The case he had been pursuing in a city he hated was slipping through his fingers, and nobody seemed to give a damn about a cache of weapons stockpiled in a teaching hospital.

"Do as you see fit, Martelli," Burgos said. "There is a God. It's up to you whether you believe in him or not. I'm heading back down south."

"Me too," Ayala said.

"There's nothing more I can do here," the doctor concluded. All he had done, in fact, in Buenos Aires was to talk to two other medical experts, probably as roly-poly as himself, and spend his nights in bars or brothels. And still he was complaining.

Not long afterwards, once they had taken a shower and bundled up the few clothes they had brought with them, Inspector Ayala and Dr Burgos left for Bahía Blanca. They gave me a final message for Rodríguez.

"If he calls or turns up here, tell him either to come back home and place himself under arrest, or to clear out of Argentina altogether. If I get my hands on him, he's done for," Ayala said, genuinely distressed at his subordinate's desertion.

*

With that, we said goodbye. I needed to be alone. I might not have learned much from the three Patagonian musketeers, but even though we had been stumbling around like three blind men in a minefield the experience had alerted my antennae. I could feel a chill breeze blowing from somewhere, even though in those torrid summer days all Argentina seemed to be gasping for breath, and one or two ancient cadavers were beginning to stink.

Soon after my guests had left, I called Patricio Quesada. When I asked to speak to the master of the house, the maid who answered the telephone went silent. I heard her put down the receiver, then the sound of footsteps coming and going. Finally, a young woman's voice told me this was no time to be making declarations to the press. I was not a journalist, I tried to explain, but she slammed down the receiver. When I called back, the line was busy.

After trying in vain to reach Wolf, I lit a cigarette and switched on the radio.

It was 10.15. Half an hour earlier, at 9.45, the front wheel had come off a car speeding along Avenida General Paz. The car had literally flown over the central barrier and crashed head-on into a bus. The accident had blocked the road, causing a long tailback, so the radio announcer was recommending drivers use alternative routes in and out of the capital. Several people had been hurt, and one killed: the driver of the car, a chauffeur who had been ferrying magistrates around for twenty years. I did not have to wait long to learn the name of his passenger, who was now in a coma at the Fernández hospital. It came as no surprise.

5

Death was shadowing me, either two paces ahead or two behind. It seemed stupid – or suicidal – either to speed up or slow down to meet it.

The shadowing had begun with Edmundo's murder, and I had gone along with it. Reluctantly at first, but Lorena was as persuasive as the Pied Piper of Hamelin. From that moment on, I had simply watched events unfold.

Although Argentina can seem like a no-man's-land, much of it is occupied by warring forces fighting in full view of everyone. This is not 1920s Chicago, with gangsters being shot at the barber's or while they are eating like kings at the most expensive restaurant in town. But there are witnesses who die of viruses that are never identified; people involved in multimillion-dollar scandals who are found hanging from a radio mast the night before they are due to appear in court. There are magistrates who discover at the last minute that they are not competent to judge a case, or suffer strange yet surprisingly frequent accidents such as seeing the front wheel of their car go hurtling across the highway, their car following like a dog chasing a bone.

Patricio Quesada was not in intensive care. He was not even in the Fernández hospital. By the time I got there, the hospital director was explaining to a group of reporters in the main reception area that he had heard about the accident from the press, and had no idea who had released the information, or why. The reporters dispersed, muttering theories: the information had come from the government's official news agency, so you did not have to be very bright to deduce that the magistrate must have been on to something very big indeed. Since there was no hiding the fact that the car had crashed into the bus, and no chance of concealing the identity of the person involved, somebody in some ministerial or corporate office had placed a call to put the pack of journalist hounds off the scent.

I could not think of any other nearby hi-tech hospital where they might have sent a federal magistrate to try to save his life or let him die in peace far from the prying eyes of the press. It seemed to me too soon to leave the hospital and go and chew on my frustration by myself. Every hour that passed could be putting Isabel at greater risk. Perhaps it was too late to save anyone, in which case my only option was to go back to selling bathroom appliances as if nothing had happened. To forget I had ever been a policeman.

But how could I forget, if I could not forget you? If I kept calling you in the night, just to make sure you were still there? Some day I would say something, and that would be it, because you were just waiting for the moment to slam the last door in my face.

In the end I am not sure if I took on this case nobody asked me to get involved in purely because I was a policeman stripped of his badge and his reason for being. Someone who needed to prove to himself he still existed and could still want you, hoping against hope that one day he could meet you again without you turning away, without you being ashamed of having believed for a moment in this shipwreck survivor. Why should you believe, when the only credentials I could show you were my capacity for violence and the hatred with which I slaughtered the hyenas society protected like hothouse plants. Yes, I shot people who abused the fact that they were human to protest their innocence when they were no more than wolves usurping the dignity of their victims. Why should you believe in someone who would not hesitate to say he would do the same again?

*

Curiosity sharpens instincts like the scalpel the doctor uses to dig around in the guts of his dead bodies. A policeman's curiosity is unhealthy because the job of defending the rules of co-existence that nobody respects inevitably relies on that keenness which hypocrites call a lack of scruples. Hungry lions or tigers only study the deer's escape routes or the strengths and weaknesses of its herd. Once they have discovered them, they pursue their quarry and do not stop until they have devoured it. The good citizen by contrast simply points, sometimes with his finger, sometimes without a word. And the policeman or soldier of the day kills, tears apart, shares out the spoils.

I do not think I set off to find Isabel because she was my murdered friend's daughter. I think it was out of curiosity, the desire to feel for myself what until then I had only witnessed in other people: joy, tears, anguish and even fear when the tunnels of the labyrinth finally converge in a great cave, when reaching the centre of the Earth becomes a question simply of accepting the flames, of screaming as they consume us.

I left the Fernández hospital unconvinced by the director's blunt denial that he knew anything. As I walked past a side entrance I was struck by the large number of policeman obstructing the doorway, by the cars blocking access, and people in everyday clothes standing on the pavement outside, smoking and looking as if they were waiting for a bus, although none came past there. I strode inside without slowing down, flashing my out-of-date but shiny police badge. Because I am a policeman – even though I sell bathroom appliances I have a policeman's face – and nobody stopped me. There were too many of them anyway. They were busy chatting with each other, recognising faces from various police stations or from headquarters, where they would never have acknowledged each other if they passed in the corridors. Here it was different, they were simply hanging around, they did not know what all the fuss was about. What possible threat could there be to a magistrate – apart from themselves, it occurred to me.

Once inside the hospital I walked along with my eyes to the floor, like a blind man. They were refurbishing this part of the building so it smelled of fresh cement and paint, and my feet crunched on grains of sand. Halfway down the corridor I passed two labourers discussing Boca Juniors' victory over a Peruvian team the evening before. I was sure they had not gone out to buy dollars: they probably earned just enough to pay off some of the debts they owed the corner shop where they had a slate every month.

I walked along quite calmly. Everything in here seemed very relaxed, as though it were a different Argentina.

The two bear-like figures I came across, blocking access to the only room at the end of the corridor, were not policemen but ex-soldiers. Former commandos now in their fifties, they clearly kept in shape thanks to hours in the gym. They were of an age where more than one death during the last military dictatorship must have weighed on their consciences, if they had such a thing. When I was five metres away from them they gestured roughly for me to come to a halt. In a flash of inspiration, I asked them where the toilets were.

They looked inquiringly at each other, but since, as I said, the atmosphere inside the hospital was relaxed, they nodded towards a dark corridor to my left. Without pausing for a second, I plunged into the darkness. They could have followed and finished me off there and then, but how could they have guessed that someone who not only looked like a policeman but was in fact a policeman might be working on his own account, rowing against the current?

I had a pee as I would in any public urinal, staring up at the freshly painted ceiling. I was the only person there, and it was obvious this was a part of the hospital no member of the public was allowed into. I peered at the recently installed mirror, hoping to find in my reflected face some clue as to what to do when I left the toilet. I was convinced the patient inside the room must be Quesada. I knew I had to get to him somehow, before I was killed or he died. I guessed if he was not in intensive care he must either be dead already or not half as badly injured as had been reported on the news. If that were the case, they must be keeping him in isolation: either because his life was in danger, or because whoever it was wanted to get rid of him on the quiet.

I left the toilet without much idea of what to do next. I set off in the opposite direction to the room the two guards sat outside, thinking I would have to find another way to get to the magistrate. Just then, one of the bears called me. There was no way I could make a run for it, so I decided to play along with them. I walked back towards the man, who was on his own now and seemed friendly, although of course you should never trust anyone's gestures or good intentions.

As I approached him, I was in two minds whether to pull out my .38 or smile. I decided a smile would be more effective.

"You're a policeman, aren't you?" he said. "Could you do me a favour? It's only for a minute. My mate's gone up to the café and left me on my own here. But I need to go as well," he said, trying his best to sound friendly and squeezing his legs together to show how desperate he was.

"Go ahead," I said, "I'll cover for you." I made sure he saw my gun and badge, and tried to ignore the rush of adrenalin coursing through my body.

As soon as the bear rushed off to the toilet, the adrenalin took over. I slipped inside the room. Dressed in shirt and trousers, the magistrate was sitting in a visitor's chair reading *La Nación*. He peered at me coolly over his glasses.

"There's a public toilet halfway down the corridor," he said. He was obviously annoyed at my intrusion, but remained polite.

"We're leaving."

He stared at my .38 and blinked as if someone had blown powder in his face.

"You're not a policeman."

"My contract has run out, that's all. Get up."

The bear who had gone to the toilet or the one on his coffee break could reappear at any moment, and neither of them would have any compunction about shooting me. I could not rely on the slow, tortuous course of Argentine justice forcing the magistrate to obey my orders. I twisted his arm behind his back, shoved my gun against his neck, and pushed him out into the corridor. By some miracle, it was still deserted.

Quesada did not protest. Either he was resigned to whatever might happen to him, or he had been promised it was all a game, and that nothing would happen if he obeyed the rules. I frogmarched him towards the exit, though for most of the way I had to prop him up under his arms. As we walked past the toilet door, the strong smell of shit reassured me: the ex-commando was obviously giving me a couple of minutes' head start.

Our corridor led into another, then on to a poorly lit staircase and the closed door of a goods lift.

"Are you going to kill me?" the magistrate enquired, as if offering me a cigarette.

"It's not part of my plan," I said. "I simply need to talk to you in private."

"Lawyers always ask for an appointment."

"I'm no lawyer. Keep walking or we're both done for."

I decided it was better to go up than down, and we soon found ourselves in the gynaecology and obstetrics waiting room. It was crowded with pregnant women of all ages. I had never seen so many in all my life: some with huge stomachs, others with small bumps, and still more without any visible signs of pregnancy except for their placid, bovine eyes, warm as the milk they would feed their young with. All of them were accustomed to waiting for hours to be seen: most of them were standing, or sitting on long, narrow wooden benches; others were stretched out on the floor, their stomachs spread on the tiles beside them as they dozed. Those who had arrived later still kept up lively conversations, although they would probably not be seen that day and would have to get a number to come back another time.

"What a disaster," the magistrate said. "What a disaster."

He could have got away from me then, but either it did not occur to him or he had some vague notion that I was saving his skin, or perhaps it was because I was sticking so close to him I was almost his Siamese twin, and the butt of my revolver was pressed gently but convincingly against the rolls of his waist.

"The state has no money to spend on looking after the poor," I said, to finish off Quesada's remark. I looked towards the door, where another inscrutable corridor awaited us.

"It spends a fortune," the magistrate corrected me. "The health budget is enormous, but the money disappears along the way. Straight into the pockets of the mafia that governs us."

So Patricio Quesada was critical of the system. That reassured me: it probably meant he was not on the same side as his guards or those who had put on the farce of his hospitalisation. But my optimism was short-lived, because at the far end of the room I suddenly saw two huge figures who made the other guards look like stick insects.

The magistrate stopped in his tracks, forcing me to do the same.

"Put that toy away," he said, meaning the .38 I had inherited from Isabel's car. "Have you got a mobile?"

I did as I was told with the gun, then started patting my pockets, until I realised I had never used a mobile in my life.

"Somebody here must have one," the magistrate said.

"What you're likely to find are lots of merrily growing foetuses, but I don't think they use them . . ."

A ringtone nearby proved how wrong I was. But the call was not for one of the pregnant women, it was for the doctor striding towards us without so much as a glance at the crowd of waiting patients. The magistrate did not hesitate.

"I am a federal magistrate, and I have to make an urgent call."

The doctor gave him a look he must have practised on all his poor patients.

"And I'm a doctor from the Buenos Aires Faculty of Medicine. Can't you see I'm busy?"

With a strength I would never have suspected in him to judge by his slight frame, the magistrate grabbed the doctor's mobile. He spoke with the same sternness he must have used to hand down his sentences.

"I repeat, I am a federal magistrate. And this man here is a policeman who in the past has killed honest citizens, mistaking them for criminals. I'm sure he would have no qualms about doing the same now."

The doctor went white. Although Quesada's comment seemed to me neither wise nor just, I glared at the trembling medic. Not that it mattered: the magistrate was already talking to his secretary.

"The orange file," he said. "We're in the Fernández hospital, with the gynaecological out-patients."

With that, he handed the phone back to the doctor, patted him on the back, and thanked him for collaborating in the work of justice. The doctor wandered off in the opposite direction, utterly bewildered.

The thugs at the entrance seemed to be growing impatient. While one of them received instructions via a walkie-talkie, the others made crude gestures suggesting we were for it. I was afraid that if they got the go-ahead they would not hesitate to advance through this human seedbed, crushing anything in their path.

I suggested to the magistrate that we duck inside a cubicle. A pregnant woman wearing nothing but a hospital gown was sitting on a couch.

"Are you the doctor?" she asked timidly when we burst in.

"Yes, but not the kind you want," the magistrate said to calm her. "The gynaecologist is on his way."

"I've been sitting here for half an hour already," the mother-to-be said, who could not have been more than thirty, although she looked at least forty. "I live outside Buenos Aires in Morón. I got up at three this morning to come for my appointment. I've been at the hospital since five. I was told I would be seen at seven, but now it's almost noon and I haven't even had breakfast."

Even though she spoke in the faintest of voices, this torrent of words had rushed out unstoppably. Her tale was that of any poor, long-suffering woman of the Buenos Aires suburbs.

"What a disaster," the magistrate said again. He seemed more concerned with the social situation than with his own safety. "An absolute disaster."

The gynaecologist came in without knocking, only to find my .38 under his nose.

"Put your gun away," Quesada said sternly. "You're behaving just like them."

He was right. Besides, the gynaecologist was less courageous than the doctor we had met in the corridor. He collapsed to the floor before we could catch him. The pregnant woman on the couch began to scream as though she had gone into labour, so we decided it was best to beat a retreat. As soon as we emerged, we were surrounded by the orang-utans who had obviously decided to invade the waiting room.

The sight of my revolver and their rifles provoked pandemonium among the women. We were engulfed by a rushing flood of bellies of all sizes and consistencies. The orang-utans were swept to one side, but this did not stop them trying to aim at us above the torrent of female heads, even though they could not steady themselves sufficiently to get off a good shot.

We managed to reach the reception area, with the women still screaming and looking desperately for somewhere to hide. We heard a shout for us to stay where we were, and did not need to count to realise that at least a dozen thugs had their guns trained on us.

"Stay close to me," barked the magistrate. "And keep calm, don't do anything rash."

I promised myself that if I got out of this alive, I would go back to selling bathroom appliances. In fact, I would devote myself exclusively to selling toilets: it's a growing market, and these days people with money want a bit of comfort so they can sit and read their Francis Bacon in peace.

"Walk slowly towards us, your Honour," the leader of the group bawled through a megaphone. "And you, scumbag, throw your weapon on the floor and raise your little arms, there's a good boy."

"Don't worry, I'm not going to move," the magistrate said. I was not so much scared as resigned to the fact that I was going to die riddled with bullets. For a policeman, dying at the hands of sharpshooters is the same as receiving absolution *in extremis* for a Christian.

Quesada raised his voice to remind the goons threatening us that he was a federal magistrate.

"I order you to put your weapons down," he said firmly but serenely.

The group broke ranks and surrounded the man with the megaphone. They may have been used to obeying outlandish orders, but even they balked at opening fire in a hospital reception area. Besides, Patricio Quesada was a well-known figure: he was often on T.V. making statements about drug trafficking cases, illegal arms sales, the white slave trade, child prostitution – all the usual.

They hesitated so long it was obvious that the man with the megaphone was awaiting instructions. By now a wall of patients, visitors and curious onlookers had surrounded us, as well as several smartly dressed medical salesmen, their briefcases stuffed with samples. The new arrivals asked those already there what was going on, and the old timers who had seen everything from the start told them what they thought they knew. "It's a kidnapping," I heard one of them say, "that guy over there was trying to abduct a judge, but he didn't realise the hospital was full of police." Another one, not two paces away from me, spat out defiantly: "All kidnappers deserve to be killed. Why don't they just shoot him?" A third onlooker asked why there were so many police in the hospital anyway. "Because the government's about to fall, and they're scared of anarchy. All the doctors are being mobilised for when there's a massacre," explained the one who had already condemned me to death.

At that point the goons must have received their instructions. Without so much as a word of warning the man with the megaphone ordered them to back off. A couple of uniformed policemen went over to break up the crowd. "Move along now, please," they said impatiently, and to us: "You two go home."

"I can't believe it!" I said. "First they want to kill us, now they tell us to go home."

"Let's get out of here," the magistrate said. "But stay close to me."

He knew what he talking about, because as we edged towards the exit I could see the man with the megaphone drawing his hand across his throat to make it plain what he intended to do if he ever caught up with me again. My intervention had spoiled a game that someone had designed and developed on a computer screen. This time it was the magistrate who squeezed my arm to make sure I kept moving. We reached the broad pavement in front of the hospital and dived into a blue limousine with tinted windows. "Poor Martínez," the replacement chauffeur said immediately, referring to his colleague. "What bastards they are." The magistrate nodded in agreement and added, "What a disaster, those sons of bitches will stop at nothing. What a disaster!"

6

Five minutes later, when the car plunged down the ramp into the basement of the Central Law Courts, it became obvious that Patricio Quesada was not someone who liked to file cases away or take his time questioning defendants and witnesses. As soon as the car came to a halt, two federal policemen ordered me to get out with my hands behind my head.

"Take his gun, handcuff him and bring him to my office," ordered the magistrate. Only a few seconds earlier he had been asking me how I was feeling.

"Don't worry," the chauffeur said to reassure me. "These two are real policemen."

Closer in spirit to communism than is generally admitted, "savage capitalism" in the Third World means that there are at least half a dozen lawyers for every bourgeois, whereas ten thousand workers or the same number of unemployed people have to make do with a single under-qualified legal representative. From each according to his need, to each according to his ability to pay: Marx and Lenin would not have believed their eyes if they had lived in today's Argentina.

Handcuffed and stripped of my revolver, I was led in by one of the uniformed policemen, who saluted all the clerks we passed. Two assistants welcomed me into Quesada's chambers. They also offered me coffee, which I could not accept as my hands were still handcuffed behind my back. One of them typed my personal details with two fingers on a Remington, then I was shown a bench and told to wait while the magistrate prepared to see me.

Although I often find it hard to fall asleep in my own bed at home, in this uncomfortable position I soon drifted off, only jerking awake when my head nodded forwards and I found myself staring around me like a newborn babe. It was only just beginning to dawn on me that the person I had forced to abandon his sham internment in the Fernández hospital could easily arrest me for depriving him of his liberty. My predicament was made even worse by the fact that he was God almighty in this legal world.

I have no idea how long I had to wait, but when finally I went into the magistrate's chambers I felt refreshed. The uniformed officer had taken my handcuffs off.

"I had to open a case against you," Quesada apologised, smiling in a way that added the finishing touch to my astonishment. "Technically, you tried to abduct me, and that is a punishable offence."

He gestured for me to sit down in front of an imposing desk piled high with files.

"In fact, you saved my life," he admitted with a sigh. "If, as I believe, your intentions were different to those of the people who put me in the hospital in the first place."

If I demurred in any way, I could almost hear the cell door opening, then slamming shut and the key being thrown away for good.

I explained how I had reached him, the complicated system of perceptions and intuitions that functioned like pulleys operating in a vacuum, usually bringing me nothing, but just occasionally surprising me with an unexpected load.

"Your friend was lucky," the magistrate said, meaning the roly-poly doctor who had been caught with his hands on the flesh of young temptresses. "I'm going to make sure those squalid geriatrics end their days with their bones whitening in the coldest jail in Patagonia."

I did not like to remind him that the medical professor had avoided being taken in by mentioning his name. It is always best to say nothing when magistrates, priests or generals are carried away by fits of puritanical zeal. At any rate, the "grandparents" and their sham "grandchildren" were now not his first concern. The accident he had narrowly survived meant he had either to face his adversaries head-on or to forget them altogether.

He started shifting files on his desk, taking some from the bottom of a pile and putting them on top, then doing the reverse. I soon got the message that he did not think this an appropriate place for us to talk, even if it was his office – or perhaps precisely because of that. He motioned to me to get up and follow him.

We went out through a side door, avoiding the reception area, then walked down the service stairs. Five minutes later, still without having exchanged a word, we were seated at the counter of the noisiest bar in the area.

"Magistrates' offices in Argentina are one big ear," Quesada said, more relaxed now, even though he had to struggle to make himself heard above the hubbub. Most of those making it were lawyers demanding justice not for their clients but for themselves. They too had been caught out by the government's restrictions on withdrawing money. "Everything that's said is picked up by the intelligence services. Or by blabbermouth journalists with their hidden cameras."

"I'm not a journalist," I said. "And I'm no blabbermouth."

"Before I say any more I should check why you were thrown out of the police force, but there's no time," Quesada said.

I too was wondering why he put his trust in an ex-policeman who had forced him out of a hospital ward at gunpoint with no more explanation than that he needed to talk. The magistrate told me that he was being held prisoner by factions in the armed forces and the police who roamed freely through the streets of Buenos Aires but felt no loyalty towards what he termed "their natural commanders".

"Your audacity or your lack of awareness opened the cage door for me, Martelli. I'm no pet bird, and I don't like tiny, enclosed worlds."

The order to get rid of him, if possible without any show of violence, had come from on high. Believers know that beyond God there is nothing. Atheists are sure that beyond nothing there is still nothing, yet we Argentines will never know who exactly sits on top of the pile, even though the managers of the system boast of their omnipotence.

Quesada had been friendly with one of the magistrates who were quick to pass on the investigation into the explosion at the Rio Tercero military factory. There, one quiet and baking-hot summer morning in the province of Córdoba, an arms factory had gone up in flames. The results were nightmarish scenes that Hollywood special effects experts would have loved to use for their Rambo films. The debris bombarded the defenceless inhabitants of Rio Tercero like a biblical plague. The fact that it was a small city with wide streets and avenues was the only reason hundreds did not die, but such a shocking, brutal event left wounds that the apparent impunity of those responsible did nothing to heal.

The president of the day proclaimed to the four corners of the earth that the Rio Tercero incident had been an accident. As with Quesada's car losing a wheel, anything is possible. But suspicion and the endless investigations that followed, delayed at every stage by changes of jurisdiction and legal challenges as varied as the ammunition flying out of the arms factory that scorching November morning, eventually led to the exposure of a sordid deal. Argentina, a country, as one nineteenth-century hero once put it, "whose flag has never been draped on the triumphal chariot of any victor", was, in the dying days of the twentieth century, being used as an aircraft carrier to deliver supplies of arms to countries engaged in racial or fratricidal wars. This, despite the fact that all the world's bureaucracies had made solemn declarations supposedly banning them from purchasing such weapons.

Clink, into the till. Grab the money and run.

The rich world meanwhile applauded the economic and political miracle brought about by the most corrupt government on earth. It came to power promising to do the exact opposite of what it did, and was financed by drug traffickers – none of which was of the slightest concern to the world's policemen. In less than a decade, that model government transformed Argentina into a vast bargain basement, with people and goods sold on the cheap.

Quesada's friend had not lasted long in the investigation. A couple of telephone calls and an accident similar to the one Quesada escaped from were enough to quench his professional curiosity.

But a month ago, a visit to his personal doctor had rekindled the flame. He went with a pain in his chest, but came back with a heart attack, said Quesada. The cardiologist who looks after him works in the Santiago Cuneo hospital.

In addition to warning him not to smoke or overdo it in the bedroom, as he was writing out a prescription the doctor told him that the Santiago Cuneo, once a model teaching hospital where many eminent doctors had trained, had now been turned into an arms dump.

What the doctor told his patient corresponded exactly with what Don Quixote and Sancho Panza had discovered in their wanderings through a building that was no more than the shell of a hospital. While dozens of police were busy raiding the shanty towns that backed on to the hospital like parasite fish on a shark, enough weaponry was being stored in the newly built wards of the Santiago Cuneo for a second invasion of Afghanistan.

Unable to credit what his friend had told him, Quesada had decided to visit the hospital as just another patient. He took a number and then, like thousands of others who had been there since dawn, joined the jostling queues waiting to be seen by a doctor. Once hidden among this herd of people, it had been easy enough for him to slip away, supposedly in search of a toilet but in fact heading for the new buildings.

When he heard a command to halt, Quesada was reminded that to be an administrator of justice in Argentina is nothing more than a floral tribute. Every judicial ruling or verdict is a poem: sometimes it can be beautiful, at others nothing more than a string of clichés. But it is always something recited, and never carried out. The brute who blocked his path said his face looked familiar from T.V. He was searched for any hidden microphone or recorder, then told to go back the way he had come. "Go and get yourself seen to in a private clinic, only the poor come here," the guardian of the temple advised him.

Quesada had retraced his steps, but before the day was out he began a judicial investigation that had government officials awake well before dawn the following day.

The noise in the bar had become so deafening I had to cup my right ear towards Quesada's mouth to hear what he was saying. On that broiling afternoon of December 20, 2001, everyone wanted to be heard, but nobody wanted to listen.

"Many eminent politicians and businessmen are involved in this, Martelli. And military men too, of course, but they're the ones who have the most doubts."

"What do you mean by 'this'?"

"The president is resigning – he's on his way out out. He won't make it to the end of December, not even his wife listens to him any more. But these people fear that if the henhouse is opened and the cock has gone, then the steppenwolves will come down, eat the hens and steal all the eggs."

"But who are these wolves? Speak more clearly – and louder too, I can't hear you for all the row in this place."

"They have already deposited their money abroad and left more than half the people in poverty. Like the Santiago Cuneo, which looks like a hospital from the outside, Argentina looks like a country when in fact it's nothing more than a breaker's yard, Martelli."

"Yesterday people started raiding supermarkets," I said, struggling to make sense of all this. Quesada had the advantage of knowing the secrets of this huge labyrinth better than the minotaur.

"It didn't start yesterday, Martelli. The presidential palace, the parliament, and that decadent, empty palace over there," he swept round to indicate the Law Courts, "they're nothing but stage sets rigged with microphones."

"I understand," I said, lying. "The problem isn't the fact that this government will fall halfway through its term, it's who will take its place and announce for the *n*th time the arrival of a New Argentina."

"The steppenwolves," Quesada said again, his face as anguished as an addict with no fix. "They're already in the henhouse gobbling up the hens."

7

Just as there is no scent in dried flowers, just as butterflies no longer flutter when pinned in an album, there is no sadness in memories. Words sometimes capture facts or faces, the faint trace of a smile; they hold emotions we once thought of as everlasting as if in a bowl. But time ends up cracking the bowl, and in the absence of fresh words or faced with our inability to express them, all absolutes perish.

Your words, Mireya. Written on headed paper from a hotel in the south of Patagonia. "Don't let's ever leave," you wrote. You were afraid we had reached the end and that only the calm down there could save us. It was a perfect spot: a small lake, like a mirror flashing among the trees, a freezing windowpane from where we could spy on the harsh world outside.

Perhaps you already knew, and that is why you wrote those words. Bowls containing the poison that could put an end to despair, as we sat by the fire in the huge hearth of Los Machis Hotel. Words not to be repeated out loud, but dreamed of in a whisper. If we did not say them it would not happen.

But it did happen. And from that moment on we had no need of words to show our feelings. Words that spoke of a love that was, that should have been, our last.

*

Quesada asked me to make myself scarce.

"Crawl into your cave and don't come out, even to take your dog for a walk," he said. We were already on the pavement outside the bar, which like every other public space in Buenos Aires had become a meeting place for arguments between the deaf, for the most absurd assertions and political opinions that made biblical prophecies seem as uncomplicated as weather forecasts.

"You're more dangerous than the Unabomber," he said, clutching my shoulder. "If you were lured down to that place . . . what did you say it was called?"

"Mediomundo."

"It was to chop your head off."

"But Cárcano was my friend."

"There are no friends in this business, Martelli. Friends are pawns, to be sacrificed so that kings can grow stronger."

As I had already done inside the bar, I denied having anything to do with anyone involved in plots.

"You only look in your own mirror," Quesada said. "You don't see what others see. You were a policeman. And not just any policeman."

The hand on my shoulder gripped me like a claw. He held me back, but at the same time said, "No, don't stop, keep walking, make it look as though we're talking about football." There was a traffic jam in front of us, so we dodged round cars and buses to reach the opposite pavement.

"You said you knew nothing about me."

"What we don't know, Martelli, we find out. While you were handcuffed and dozing in my chambers, I went into the network."

Obviously he was not referring to the internet.

"It's all nonsense," I said. "A pack of lies written by bureaucrats trying to justify their fat salaries by cutting out little pictures and sticking them in files."

"I'm not accusing you of anything. The orange file exists, even if nobody talks about it."

I remembered he had mentioned the orange file when he had

borrowed the doctor's mobile in the hospital, so I asked what it was. Quesada kept on pushing me forwards, making me walk.

"It's a sort of bible for people who work in the law," he said. "And a safe conduct too. We judges are no fools, Martelli. The state has infiltrated the whole system. Not content with informers, it has installed its own judges in every court. They're the ones who worry about their ratings, the ones who put make-up on in the car when they see journalists with cameras. And they talk, talk, talk. They pull rabbits out of hats and fascinate the public the way dictators used to do in the days when there was no T.V."

The orange file had a restricted circulation among those magistrates who considered themselves honest, "career" jurists, the untouchables, the ones still resolutely faithful to the blindfolded lady with her balanced scales rather than to any clone the government might have produced to replace her.

Quesada's fine words, the arrogant way in which he spoke of himself and a chosen few others, did not entirely convince me. What was there in that orange file about me?

"What the intelligence services did not say. The true story."

Although he still had hold of my arm, I came to a halt there and then like a tree growing out of the pavement. I dug my heels in like a donkey or a stray dog refusing to be taken away to the pound and the gas chamber.

That afternoon, when the president resigned halfway through his term and abandoned the presidential palace in a helicopter, the same afternoon when his political opponents were celebrating the success of a civilian coup organised by mafia bosses and local gang leaders, financed by dirty money and with the acquiescence of the opposition and even some members of his own party, that December afternoon when the police fired on a crazed populace that swept through the streets like waves across the deck of a ship in a storm, that December 20, 2001, I discovered that my true story, the one I had never told anybody, the one I believed I had erased even from my own memory, was described from start to finish in the orange file.

8

In the early morning of December 21, 2001, lying back against the headboard of the bed it had made for itself, Argentina stared blindly into the darkness. It was taking a rest, stunned but satisfied by the great orgasm. It had rid itself of a worthless president, but had a dim suspicion that the vague, half-formed idea of replacing him with something different had already been tossed onto the scrapheap, and that other people were lining up, without even consulting it, to take part in the pagan rites of political speculation.

The front pages of all the newspapers were filled with the photograph of the helicopter taking off from the palace roof. Just like Isabel Perón in 1976, at the end of 2001 Fernando de la Rúa was escaping across the roofs of a city that had become too dangerous for him. Shortly before, while he was writing his own letter of resignation, the National Shame had shot at spontaneous demonstrators on the streets outside.

I put some fresh water and more of the balanced diet out for Félix Jesús, then locked my apartment and waited downstairs for the magistrate's car. It appeared before I had finished my first cigarette, approaching me slowly with Quesada himself at the wheel. He pulled up and got out.

"You drive," he said. "I'm worn out. I haven't slept for two nights."

"I haven't had much sleep either," I said. "But I can understand that you didn't want to bring a chauffeur."

"I've already lost one. He had a wife and two children. His name isn't going to be on anyone's list when they tot up how many people died in this madness."

As I slid behind the wheel, I myself felt like Quesada's chauffeur. I wondered if I should stop at a garage to at least get the tyres checked. I remembered how right Wolf had been when we came out of the National Library talking about Faulkner and made me sit on a park bench while Isabel's car went up in a ball of flames. But Quesada seemed different: in his world, if something got broken, it was replaced – even when it came to human lives.

Just as when I had received Edmundo's telephone call, I drove out of Buenos Aires in the dark, unsure of what I would find when I reached my destination. While Quesada lay sprawled over the back seat of this automatic Japanese limo, I thought about what I had learned from him.

"The orange file is like a database," the magistrate had explained. "It's not an intelligence network, and we don't have the latest generation computers. We are a club, a sect, a brotherhood of justice at bay. Magistrates also spend a lot of time in libraries, and in newspaper archives. Looking up matters of jurisprudence in a country that is constantly changing its laws so as not to have to abide by them is a job I wouldn't wish on my worst enemy. But it has to be done if we are to justify our verdicts and sleep with a clear conscience when we send criminals or murderers to jails they will come out of long before they even start to realise just what they are responsible for."

The name Pablo Martelli was among those chosen to go into the orange file as people who could be trusted. And alongside my name, the facts – not so different, according to what the magistrate told me, to the version the intelligence services had given. Whoever had supplied the information had not gone quite as far as Quesada wanted to believe, convinced as he was that he belonged to some post-modern Masonic brotherhood where the nation's 21st-century heroes were being groomed.

After its great orgasm, Buenos Aires was exhausted. On street corners we saw the remnants of park benches torn up in angry protest at police repression, tyres still giving off the acrid stink of burned rubber, shreds of posters demanding that the government resign, gas canisters, and smaller cartridges from hand guns: all the paraphernalia left over from an afternoon spent fighting one another, only to hand ourselves over the next day to the latest miracle worker, the messiah who first got his name onto the list. Someone who overnight had already been trying on all the attributes of power, pulling faces in front of the mirror, trying to decide on his less cretinous profile, rehearsing the next scene in our unending national farce.

I drove out towards the south-east again, and headed down the coastal highway. There was little traffic apart from a few lorries and buses. For long stretches there were no oncoming headlights. I had the feeling I was piloting some ship into the depths of an unexplored ocean. I searched for Lucila Davidson's voice on the radio, but all I could find were early morning charlatans, religious pastors who howled their psalms like ravenous wolves. At that time of the morning, the sheep were dreaming that they had broken into the pastures of power at last. Contented, their bodies light, they muttered and plotted as they slept, buoyed by a non-existent victory, by an uneasy dream that would rob them of their illusion soon enough.

I enjoyed driving out of Buenos Aires, putting my foot down on the highway while Quesada, another little sheep, dreamed he was a wolf. Before dawn we would be in Mediomundo, a quiet beach where the people who owned or rented the few chalets dotted among the sand dunes would by now be arriving for their summer holidays.

The judge said something in his sleep; probably even asleep he was studying cases and delivering verdicts. I wondered how he would react when we got there, when we opened the door we should not be going anywhere near, when we turned the handle and pushed the door open. What would happen when my upright believer in jurisprudence found what we were looking for.

9

The woman I loved the most only loved me a little. Nothing new there: we always love what does not love us, and are loved by those we do not love enough. Perhaps the woman who only loved me a little was right: what is the point of loving a policeman? People love winners, those who are lucky, poets, madmen even. But who loves a policeman?

I was nothing to the magistrate fast asleep behind me, although he expected me not to fall asleep at the wheel. I was less than the crooks, rapists and murderers he locked away, or more often allowed to go free for lack of proof, or anywhere to put them.

Yet I have never shot anyone in the back. I always kill face to face, staring into the eyes of the person who is going to die at my hands. I never give them any advantage, of course, or I would not be here.

The magistrate needed me, the woman I loved the most needed me, the murderer needed me. I was their shadow, the echo of their voices when they were alone and told the truth. If I did not exist, what justice would the magistrate dispense? What love would the woman who only loved me a little learn to forget, and who would put an end to the serial killer's compulsion?

I put my foot down. The speedometer whizzed round into the red. The slightest mistake, if I nodded off for a second or if a wheel touched the verge, and it would be no more magistrate, no more memories for the woman who does not remember me; goodbye, shadow; goodbye, echo; even when they are on their own they can lie. That is all death is: darkened rooms and blank sheets of paper that will never be written on, impunity for those who survive.

We were heading for Mediomundo. Quesada thought that if we searched my friend's chalet we might find something the forensic team had missed, for the simple reason that there had been no forensic team carrying out a search in the first place.

"It's a beautiful day," I heard from the cradle in the back of the car, where after four hours' deep sleep the magistrate had woken up as pink and rested as a baby.

"We'll be arriving in half an hour," I said, like a pilot telling his passengers to fasten their seat belts for landing.

The sun was just coming up over the horizon, spreading across fields full of crops and hundreds of cows, the fertile pampas, the untold wealth of our colonial country. Meat and soya, wheat and maize, sunflowers, pigs and sheep, horses that sniff the ominous odour of the slaughterhouse and gallop off until they are forced to stop by the barbed-wire fences. All of them Argentine, even if they are not human: compatriots watching life go by in a state of contained despair.

"Did you bring a gun?" I said.

"There'd be no point, I don't know how to use one."

I opened the glove compartment and passed him Isabel's .38.

"You'd better learn – we're going to need it."

At first he looked at the gun with horror, but then began to examine it.

"If you're not shooting, make sure the barrel is pointing upwards. That lever you're about to press is the safety catch. As soon as we get there, I'll teach you how to load it."

"What about you?"

I showed him the other gun in the glove compartment, an old .45 that was National Shame issue when I was thrown out.

"It's old, but effective. It belongs to Félix Jesús," I said, not bothering to explain who he was.

To enter Mediomundo, you have to turn off the highway down a dirt road that is scarcely more than a track, although it is gravelled. Lining it are plumed palm trees that look like the Swiss Guards at the Vatican.

"We should have stopped for breakfast," the magistrate mused.

The track wound past a vineyard, then climbed a sandy hill from which you could see the sea. There was a line of gentle waves rolling in, the sky was an intense blue, and the sun was rising like shares on the New York stock exchange when the Republicans win.

"It's a beautiful spot," Quesada said cheerfully.

The track broadened, and we drove into the village. No more than two houses to each block, everywhere well looked after, young pine trees planted to fix the sand dunes. Although that day was the start of the summer holidays, there were only a few cars parked outside the houses: the Argentines were resting from their labours. The day before, they – and not the armed forces – had ousted a president. Nobody knew what was going to happen now: in fact, nobody ever has. Especially not the people who get rid of their presidents. A beautiful day, a beautiful spot.

Edmundo's house was small: my friend was never ostentatious. It was a simple chalet, like the ones that Italian immigrants have built all along this coast, facing out to sea, towards Italy. The grounds, though, were spacious, and it looked as if a gardener had been to cut the grass only the day before.

I still had the key Lorena had entrusted me with the night we left. Quesada gave me permission to use it. He was being serious: "Of course, I should have spoken to the magistrate in charge of the case," he said. "But I'll take responsibility."

Inside the chalet there was a strong smell of damp, as though it had been shut up for far longer than my last visit. There was still a blood stain in the middle of the floor; nobody had bothered to clean it up. "It's evidence," said Quesada. "It's my friend's blood," I corrected him.

"Did he have a safe?"

"I don't know the house. I didn't even manage to spend a night here," I said.

He did have a safe. It was in the wall behind a painting. Of course.

Edmundo cannot have had much to hide if it was that easy to find. And to open: it was empty.

"I think we're wasting our time here," I said gloomily.

"Look under the furniture, in the kitchen, in the bathroom."

I started with the bathroom. Traditional fittings, old-fashioned taps, a bath bought from some house clearance. If Edmundo really did have funds in Switzerland, he should have come to me to refurbish the room.

We were both so occupied – the magistrate in the kitchen and me looking for heaven-knows-what in the bathroom – that we did not hear the front door opening. Whenever somebody enters a house without knocking, they are not doing it to pass the time of day with the people who happen to be there at that moment.

*

There are ways of being violent without being rude. What is the difference between a louse who kills for a few pesos and a licensed killer? Their way of going about it.

"Welcome to Mediomundo," said one of the two gentlemen who appeared behind us, brandishing automatic rifles.

"Today's the first day of summer, although high season only starts after the 31st," said the other.

"If you're looking to rent the place for January or February, the owner is away at the moment. He left a few days ago, and we don't think he'll be coming back."

"He was murdered," I said, staring at the bloodstain on the floor. Every time I say something stupid, I promise myself I will never do it again, but you cannot change bad habits from one day to the next. "I bet he didn't even get a chance to defend himself."

When one of the gentlemen hit me I crashed through a rattan table and ended up on the floor. The magistrate took a couple of steps back, worried he would be next, but our friends knew who he was and respected his office.

"We hit him because he's used to it," one of them said. "He's one of us."

"You've taken it out on prisoners in your time, haven't you, Martelli?" said the other, kicking me in the kidneys with the toe of his boot.

"The police are like fairies: they wave a wand and the innocent become guilty," they went on explaining to Quesada.

"Get up, you son of a bitch," they said, talking to me this time. "We don't want you to die lying down."

"Remember, whenever you take a statement, nothing is what it seems, and everybody is a liar," they advised the magistrate. Then one of them knocked me to the floor again with his rifle butt.

The first thing you should always do when you are beating someone up is to take their gun. Our two visitors were so concerned with being polite they had forgotten to do so. Face down on the floor, gasping for breath, I clutched on to my .45 like an asthmatic reaching for his inhaler.

*

The magistrate stood there as cold and transparent as a stalagmite. He could not believe his eyes: the shots, the violent jerking of our visitors' bodies, their eyes rolling up as blood spurted from the neck of one and the middle of the forehead of the other, then the two collapsing together in one heap.

"It was luck, not my good aim," I said with false modesty, trying to see if I could breathe in again.

The magistrate knelt down and put his head between his knees.

"I feel sick," he said.

He was right, we should have had breakfast before we got to Mediomundo, but the cafés along the way were shut.

At first I thought he was going to pass out, but he recovered, took a deep breath, and went onto the attack.

"There was no need to . . ."

"If I shoot from such close range, I shoot to kill. Besides, I only did what they were going to do to us."

Quesada did not say it, but he obviously thought they were going to spare him.

"Who are they?"

"Hounds of the Baskervilles. Dogs with badges, the guardians of the temple. Where's the .38 I gave you?"

"I left it in the car."

"It's not a torch, Quesada. We're past the point of no return. We have to cover each other's backs. These people don't faint at the sight of blood."

"But who are they?" he insisted. "What's behind all this?"

"You should know. Look at your infallible orange file. I'm a complete nobody, so if even I am in there, you must have at least some idea of who we're looking for."

Quesada could not get over it. He was still more affected by my marksmanship than he was by the mess he had got himself into by coming here.

"Lock the door and we'll carry on looking," he said eventually.

All of a sudden he seemed to have forgotten the two fresh corpses on the floor. A strange force was driving him on: he was sure that there must be papers. Magistrates are lawyers, and lawyers are attracted to papers like moths to a flame.

We had talked about it before we left Buenos Aires. A plot had been hatched to depose the president. At the same time, though, there had been another plot, and this one won. A power vacuum is essentially a vacuum, and if one lot do not fill it, another group will.

So who were the ones who had got in first? Those who any newspaper reader already knew about. Nothing new there. People on the streets of Buenos Aires were shouting "Kick them all out!", but none of them would do it. The protesters would go home or back to work, and when they were asked to, they would vote again for the same people. Anyone who got in first had won the game.

"Who are 'they'?"

They are no better than the others, Quesada had told me the previous evening. The Trotskyite left; Peronists who felt betrayed by their own party; military officers cashiered for taking part in previous coup attempts; other officers still on active service, who boosted their wages with a little arms dealing; the police mafia; port bosses who dealt in drugs; shipping companies supplying chemical happiness by air, sea, and land; managers in crisis like Edmundo.

"Why don't they join parties or form new ones? Why not do things democratically?"

"Because they don't."

I had spent more than twenty years selling bathroom appliances, but I still had better reflexes for shooting two men with a gun I had never fired before than I did for selling a bathroom suite. We never change, we cannot expect anything new from what seems new, we are suspicious of promises because we have made them before. We know perfectly well we always let down anyone who believes us.

"Here it is!" Quesada shouted from the kitchen.

I ran to see what he had found. He was standing in a small pile of rubble. He had spotted a tile projecting slightly from the wall, had pulled at it, and half the tiles in the kitchen had come down around him.

"Congratulations, you found the treasure!"

"Thanks. But it isn't going to make us rich."

10

On the road again. This time Quesada was driving. About a hundred kilometres from Mediomundo we stopped at the service station where I had filled up on the way down. This time the cafeteria was open. The magistrate looked at me intently as we ate our sandwiches. I asked him if I had food on my chin, and he said no.

"So what is it?"

He hesitated. He had seen me in action and was probably having some difficulty trying to overcome his fear and repugnance. He could not bring himself to ask how I could be eating when I had killed two people barely an hour earlier.

"It's been a long time since I killed anyone," I said out of the blue. He choked on his ham, cheese and tomato special. "You don't get to do that sort of thing when you sell bathroom appliances. That's why I changed my job."

He insisted that perhaps they had only been trying to frighten us.

"Were they only trying to frighten Edmundo?"

"Your friend was one of them."

"Well, if that's how they treat their own people, what can the rest of us expect?"

"I don't think your friend called you at midnight and asked you to drive four hundred kilometres just to kill you."

"If you have a gun barrel pressed to your head, you're apt to betray even the noblest feelings, including friendship. You're right about one thing, though: I don't think he was luring me into a trap. He needed me. But I got there too late."

"Do you want revenge?"

I swallowed the last bit of my sandwich.

"Not at all. He did what he did. But he never intended to hurt the people he cared for. Now look: his daughter has been kidnapped, his former wife is too scared to go out, and here I am dodging bullets."

"The people he worked for are not going to get away with it that easily," the magistrate said.

In addition to dyeing what little hair he had left, Quesada was having trouble chewing his sandwich. His false teeth wobbled when he spoke, and he must have been taking bucketfuls of pills for rheumatism and impotence. Yet he still thought he was the masked avenger of Gotham City. I could just see the board of C.P.F. in London quaking in their boots at the thought of Patricio Quesada launching his crusade against them.

"Let's go," he said forcefully.

"Show time," I said.

*

We did not know if the two corpses in Mediomundo had been alone, if they had seen us arrive, or if an obliging neighbour had sent word. There might be others following us, I warned Quesada. "Make sure you pay as much attention to your rear-view mirror as to the road ahead. It's another two hundred kilometres until our next stop," I told him. "I'm going to try to get some sleep."

The magistrate woke me in Tres Arroyos. The journey had been quick and peaceful, the road empty, with nobody behind or in front of us. Argentina was like some huge, sleeping beast, a mythical elephant like those the ancients believed held up the world. It had just shaken off a president and all his ministers. It got rid of them because they did not know how to steer it, could only torment it with their absurd decisions on a journey to nowhere. Today the beast was resting, digesting, occasionally regurgitating its favourite, its only nourishment: madness.

Quesada parked in the main square and began to study the papers he had found, his treasure trove. An inventory, a complete list of names, the organisational structure, confidential reports and even proclamations written by a famous T.V. journalist. It was a shame to throw all that effort and talent down the drain.

"They'll deny everything," I said. "Nothing is signed. Anyone can write what they like and then attribute it to anybody else. It's one person's word against another's, and there are too many of them for my liking."

Quesada admitted it would be ridiculous to accuse them of trying to overthrow the constitution. People would laugh in his face. We were in the third millennium now, there were no more military coups in Argentina. But he said they could be tried for their everyday activities: trafficking, bribery, buying favours from the state so that they could profit time and again, always at the cost of the people.

"Oh, sure," I said.

"Will you help me?"

"I suppose I've got nothing better to do, have I? Let's go."

This time I took the wheel and drove slowly out in the direction of the farmhouse where they had shot the dog. It had been a long detour, I told myself, I should never have left that night. But I was on my own then: not that I was exactly coming with competent reinforcements this time.

I could scarcely recognise the route in daylight, but fortunately among Quesada's papers there was a map showing the way. Everything was in the documents, although there were only pseudonyms, *noms de guerre*. The journalist who had written the group's unused communiqués was probably at that very minute presenting his radio show, editorialising, pontificating, counting the dead, sowing the greatest doubt possible among an audience spellbound by the tricks played to avoid the endlessly slow, complicated processes of democracy. I tuned in to his station, and yes, there he was, criticising both the government and those who had risen against it, quoting Greek philosophers, unfavourably comparing Argentina to the civilised nations of the earth. He condemned the irresponsibility of those who stoked the fires of easy solutions, but also inveighed against a government that cheated ordinary citizens of their hopes, behaving with impunity and arrogance in its bubble far from life as lived on the street. When we reached the first gate, I switched off the radio.

"What are you looking for?" I said, and since the magistrate did not seem to understand, I repeated: "What is it you're looking for?"

"If only I knew."

"If you tell people what we find here – if we do find something and you live to tell the tale – nobody is going to believe you."

"You're good at boosting morale, aren't you, Martelli? You should have been a soldier."

"I'm a policeman, not the Pied Piper. There's the farmhouse."

A low building with a wind-pump next to it. Nothing like the luxurious main building of a rich *estancia*. There were no vehicles in sight, nor any living dogs. Nor were there any trees, still less a hillock to hide the car behind, so I drove on slowly and parked in front of the veranda as calmly as if I were a stranger stopping to ask for directions.

The first bullet smashed the windscreen. Quesada and I had got off to a bad start. Both of us were already bleeding.

I threw the car into reverse and roared back, away from the hail of bullets. All of a sudden the only word I could utter was "Bastards". I tried to steer backwards up the track, but too late saw a tractor pulling out of its hiding place, blocking our escape. I had no time to brake, and the impact jerked the two of us like dummies in a simulated accident. I cannot tell you what happened next, because I was unconscious.

*

I came to in a room lit only by a bedside lamp that stood on the floor. I was also on the floor, although someone had been kind enough to throw a blanket over me. My whole body ached, but the pain was so diffuse it felt almost pleasurable. I guessed I had been drugged, and immediately wondered why I had been kept alive.

I sat up and checked my body. I was not seriously wounded, it was mostly cuts from the shattered windscreen. My clothes were stuck to me with blood, so gingerly I pulled them away from my skin.

The lamp and I were all alone. The room was empty and cold, hence the blanket. After trying to kill me, it seems they did not want me to catch a chill. When I looked up at the roof, I saw that there wasn't one, only stars.

It was like the old neighbourhood cinemas I went to as a kid. They had sliding roofs, so that on summer nights we watched Westerns beneath real stars. Sometimes, if we had just fallen in love with the blonde girl down the road, we forgot all about the shoot-outs between Palefaces and Indians, and plunged contentedly into distant galaxies, certain we could reach the far ends of the universe. Isn't that what childhood is: throwing yourself into an exploration of the impossible with complete disregard for all distance?

The door opened and someone looked in at me from a dark corridor. I recognised the voice of the man who had shot the dog.

"He's awake," he said to someone beside him.

A shadow whose outlines I could dimly make out – thanks to the starlight – came into the room. Soft outlines, curves which anticipated a woman's voice.

"Leave me alone with him."

"He's dangerous," the man warned her.

"We've given him a horse tranquilliser. I'll be alright on my own."

The door closed behind her, and as she stepped into the pool of light I realised who she was.

I don't believe it, I admitted to myself, for once being honest. Who would have thought it?

PART FOUR

Hired Brains, Unpunished Hearts

1

"Mireya."

"Shhh . . . Not Mireya. Not even Debora. Here I'm known as La Negra."

She pressed her finger to my lips to silence me. Her finger was all I managed to kiss before she pushed me away with the flat of her hand.

I made an effort to sit up, but she used the same hand to signal I should stay where I was.

"What are *you* doing here? What *is* this?"

Her only reply was a smile.

Her flowing hair covered her otherwise bare shoulders and cascaded down the front of the short, flimsy dress she was wearing. The outline of her breasts was like an abyss. When she leaned over me I felt them calling out from the depths. She saw the glint in my eye.

"None of that," she said. "There's a man out in the corridor who gets nervous if he hears noises."

"I called you. Christ, I called you so many times."

"But you never said a word, Gotán. You never spoke, even when you should have. I had to find out from others."

"I'm not Gotán any more, I'm Martelli."

"You're a bastard, that's what you are."

There was no furniture in the room, and no roof. She strolled up and down, circling me like a tiger that has already caught its prey.

"I didn't expect to find you here."

"But I expected you."

"This was the last place on earth I thought I'd see you, even though I've no idea what all this is about."

"Yes, you do. That's why you came. That's why I was expecting you."

I could not help but feel pleased. It always gives one's self-esteem a boost to be expected, even if it is only to be killed. Eventually she came to a halt and sat cross-legged in front of me. Her scent enveloped me like a huge, beautiful spider's web. I would not have minded dying then and there.

"We're going to seize power anyway," she said, before I had asked her a thing. She really thought I knew more than I did.

"'We're going to . . .'? I thought you weren't interested in politics any more."

"Not politics as politicians practise it. You know how much I despise that clique."

"They are our representatives."

"Yours, you mean."

Talking about politics aroused her. Her nipples hardened, her lips came to life. To her, hatred was like passion.

"Where's Isabel Cárcano? What have you done with her?" I asked her point-blank. The surprise in her eyes seemed genuine. She seemed to have no idea who I was talking about, she must have thought I was trying to trick her. "She's the reason I'm here, not to try to wake you from some kind of revolutionary nightmare."

"Nobody here knows our comrades' real names," she said reluctantly.

"From the way she was 'recruited', I don't think Isabel was exactly a comrade."

With the same calm authority as a surgeon calling for a scalpel, she opened the door and asked the man on guard outside for a chair. She sat astride it in a masculine pose which did not fit my memories of her, but it excited me nonetheless.

"I can see it," she said, amused.

"My fear?"

"No, your erection."

"Can only be the side effects of your 'horse pill.'"

"That's your most potent weapon, Gotán, your incredible instinct for self-preservation. You just go for it, no matter who you leave in your wake."

"Why am I here, Mireya?"

"You should know."

"And if I don't?"

"Why else would a horse gallop happily to the slaughterhouse?"

"I'm such an old, weary horse. I confuse alfalfa with straw, love with desire."

"But you always leave chaos in your wake. You shoot first. You wouldn't have killed our comrades in Mediomundo if all you wanted to do was sell toilets."

"News flies, I see. But is it so wrong to put a couple of trained criminals out of action, Mireya?"

"La Negra, Gotán, La Negra."

I could not help smiling: my old need to distance myself whenever I felt threatened by something, even if that something was happiness. I scarcely believed any longer in what was happening to me, still less in what people told me was happening.

"If I'd known I would find you here, I wouldn't have come."

"You knew, Gotán, you knew. The cry of the wolf has been haunting you since that other night. That's why you came back."

"Was that you?"

"There you were, scuttling along like a cockroach in the dark. Stumbling along as ever, spying on love, scuttling away."

"Who were you . . . ?"

"Fucking? I don't even remember. There was no light, a poor dog had been killed, and a blind man was shuffling around with his eternal white stick. Why didn't you kill us then? I don't think you would have flinched, unless you really have grown old."

Again, I tried to get up, but Isabel's .38 appeared like magic in her hand.

"Stay still. Let's talk: we need to."

Sitting on the floor, I picked up the blanket and wrapped it around me. A drop of blood trickled from my left eyebrow to the corner of my mouth. I licked it.

"I'm cold and I'm wounded," I said.

"You could be dead, Gotán. Thank La Negra you're not. And start talking."

"What do you want me to tell you?"

"The truth."

2

But which truth? The one I had been constructing as a sparrow builds its nest, twig by twig? A short-term truth, simply to shield me from the storm, the most convenient truth, composed of small, everyday details, a superficial, promiscuous kind of truth?

No, it was the other truth you wanted, Debora, Mireya, or La Negra.

That was why there was so much tango, so many promises of eternal love, so much rowing upstream to discover the sources. You knew all this. Once I had thought you were on the journey with me, but you were here expecting me all the time.

"The good thing about being part of a plot in Argentina is that you have access to all the archives," you said, playing with the revolver once owned by Isabel, whom you said you had never met. Every so often, the barrel of the gun was pointed directly between my eyes, but it was only for a moment, there was nothing premeditated about it. It would have been pure coincidence if the gun had gone off.

"You're right, Mireya. Some of the bigwigs found out too late that you gain power from the inside, not from the other side of the street. By the time they decided to do a deal with the dictatorship they had already lost. A couple of bastards succeeded in making the deal, then vanished with all the loot, stepping on a stageful of corpses on the way."

"What's all this historical revisionism for, Gotán? Who cares?"

"I do. I was a policeman in those days. And yet, when the shooting started, I was on the other side of the street."

"As now."

"Now I'm not even part of the picture."

"You wouldn't be here if you weren't."

You found it hard to understand that the pawns could be taking other pawns who were on their own side, or that bishops betray, or that the king is a cuckold, or that the queen sleeps with the opposing knight.

"I'm here because I'm an idiot. I'm here because I answer the phone after midnight, because I believe in nostalgia, because I wanted to help the widow of a friend who was killed like that poor dog here the other night."

"You're good at it, aren't you, Gotán? I'm in tears."

You stood up and went to the door a second time. This time it was documents you were after. The person outside must have been very close, because it was only seconds before you were back, holding a thick, orange-coloured file.

"Do you know what this is?"

"Only from hearsay. Gaddafi's Green Book, Chairman Mao's Red Book, President Chávez of Venezuela's colourless Constitution, and now the Orange File. I never read bestsellers."

It is strange to find yourself written about by others. Even if the stories are dreamed up by the intelligence services, it is still odd. You resent the intrusion. They are full of old photographs, apocryphal facsimiles that look like authenticated documents, handwritten documents someone else has scribbled on our behalf. But Mireya was right: there were also some real letters, sheets of paper left lying around at the end of a marvellous night.

In this case, there were only three sheets of paper. There was not that much to tell. Almost nothing, if the facts written on three yellowing sheets of thin airmail paper were all there was.

"You told me you left the force because being a policeman disgusted you."

"I was never disgusted by being a policeman," I corrected you.

"But that's what you told me."

"Only because you fooled me. You made me believe you hated the police in general, and I didn't want you to hate me."

Furious, you got to your feet again. The barrel of the gun was like a black well, or the dark window of the world before my eyes.

"And it was true," you said, too close for me not to think once more that this was all unreal, that you were somewhere else and that we would never meet again. "Can you deny what it says here?"

You tore the three sheets out of the orange file and waved them in my face.

"Deny everything and I'll believe you again. We women in love are stupid. I'll believe you, Gotán. Tell me it's not true, that it wasn't you who wrote this."

But it was me, and would always be me, as long as the .38 in the hands of the woman who called herself La Negra did not blow my head off. And the information about me handed to you on a plate by the orange file, the information Quesada took into account when he took me along with him, made you angrier still.

"What did you do with the magistrate?"

"That's nothing to do with me. Other people take care of the logistics of our prisoners. I don't know who comes and goes. For reasons you'll understand, it's your case I'm dealing with."

"I don't understand, but I'm grateful anyway."

You took my hand and I felt like a king on the topsy-turvy chessboard. The cuckolded king, of course, one aware that in his own bedroom the queen was fornicating with her lovers, one who wrote all their names in the equivalent of an orange file so they could all be executed the moment the queen announced she no longer loved him, had never loved him, that power is a labyrinth of whispers in corridors, a constant exchange of picture cards, a game of poker in which honour and life are the beans you use to tot up the scores. Who cares anyway, when there will always be another round?

"Come and let me introduce you," you said, still holding my hand, allowing me to follow you wrapped in my blanket. "You couldn't get far anyway, barefoot and with no clothes."

You know me, you know I hate inspiring pity, that I never appeal to anyone's better nature because I don't believe in it. Conquer or die – that was a good slogan, a shame nobody uses it today, or even knows what it referred to.

We left the roofless room where I had come round. I walked along groggily because of the horse pill, while the guard stared at me with suspicion, as if killing me there and then would have been a weight off his shoulders. Mireya, though, seemed to be some kind of leader, an overseer in the madness she was enveloped in, as I was in my blanket.

"This is Rata," she said. "He prefers shooting to talking. He doesn't know the meaning of a question mark; he never asks himself a question before killing."

"We're colleagues, then," I said to him, but I did not hold out my free hand or bother to look at him.

We went into another room. This one was big and well lit, and it had a roof. It was the one I had been in several nights before, examining the maps by torchlight. In it were two men who smiled but seemed tense. They were paunchy, broad-shouldered, and wore smart uniforms. They had taken off their balaclavas out of politeness, and because it was too hot to wear them anyway. The uniforms were new, obviously bought in an army supply store.

"Cain and Abel," Mireya introduced them. She let go of my hand and put hers on my shoulder: "Gentlemen, this is Gotán!"

"*Chan chan,*" Abel said dismissively.

Cain took a couple of steps back and stood surveying me, like someone buying a slave. He was evidently disappointed.

"So you're the fancy dancer?"

"And you're the one in the bible who ends up killing his brother," I said.

"Kill him, Negra," said Cain.

Abel lifted his right arm in what looked like a cross between a papal blessing and a Nazi salute.

"Who is behind you?" he said.

I whirled round to look. Not to poke fun at him, but out of pure instinct. I took his question literally: for the past twenty-five years, I had never imagined I was working for someone else.

"Finish him off, Negra," Cain insisted. "There's nothing we can do with him."

I recognised his voice.

"You killed that farm dog, you bastard."

Cain threw himself onto me. He tore the blanket off so that I was left naked, staggering and dizzy. He pushed me hard so I would fall. I heard them laughing, making fun of my tiny prick. La Negra started to defend my manhood, which only gave rise to more jokes.

"Who sent you, Tanguito? You didn't come here on your own account, so who's behind you? I'll count to three: one, two, three."

"Barboza!" I said, like someone shouting "royal flush!"

I heard a whistle of admiration, a throaty cough. Mireya said nothing to contradict me. She was as surprised as the other two.

"That castrated pig, I should have known!" said Abel.

Nemesio Barboza was a caudillo in the south of greater Buenos Aires. He was a leader of the most repugnant kind of Peronism, someone who had handed over worker militants, the friend and accomplice of military goons and prominent businessmen, a drugs trafficker in the '90s. With his Alzheimer's kept under strict medical control, he was still the boss in many of the crowded shanty towns that sprawled around the capital.

"And they call me Gotán, not Tanguito."

But this clarification, or anything else I might have to say from then on, was apparently of no importance. Abel took Cain by the arm and led him off to another room. They had decisions to take which were none of my concern. It seemed as though my invented revelation had caused such an impact that my execution had been postponed.

The woman who called herself La Negra congratulated me.

"You always have an ace up your sleeve, even when you're stark naked."

She picked up the blanket, put it round my shoulders, and we set off back to the room without a roof.

"If you're one of Barboza's men, I'm surprised you came on your own."

"I came with a magistrate, for Chrissake! What's happened to him?"

"Don't worry," said Mireya, alias La Negra, who had once been Debora. "The most important thing now is to get you out of here unharmed."

"I'm not leaving without my dead friend's daughter, or Quesada. Did you kill them? Does everyone who ruffles your feathers finish up like that dog?"

I began to feel very cold. I started to tremble and must have turned blue, because all of a sudden Mireya put down her gun and hugged me tight.

After a moment's surprise, desire flared up in me like a cigarette butt dropped carelessly in a field of scrub when it has not rained for months.

Mireya's dress was little more than a napkin tied around her neck. There was nothing to undo or tear. It slipped over her head in one swift movement, then up over her long, raised arms. Her breasts flopped against my chest. I cupped them in my hands, warming them and bringing them to life with a tongue I quickly lost control of. My body declared its joyful independence from all the political plotting, all the threats, the pressure and even its own imminent demise. It had been caged for far too long, a prisoner of memories no-one shared, of an image as false as that of me belonging to Nemesio Barboza's hordes, or the story written on the three sheets of paper in the orange file. My body was like the effigies we used to burn on the feast of St Peter and St Paul when I was a child: made for this, for this night, this woman.

You did not say "I love you"; that was never something you said. At most you agreed to dance the tango with Gotán in some out-of-the way dive in Boedo: "Women in love are stupid" you had said earlier in that same room.

"So it was true, then," you whispered in my ear while your tongue licked my wound, the lobe of my left ear and then probed deep inside. Your head rolled downwards, rolling almost forever, crushing my throat, my chest, stopping only to lap at the prenatal dreams curled in my umbilical, then on, down again, sated, warm, down, down, down. "Everything the file said was true, everything people say to each other and you never said to me, yet there I was with you, they wouldn't laugh at your prick if they saw it now," you said, clinging to my buttocks like a lifebuoy, what if women were not so stupid after all, what if when it came to sacrifices they were the high priestesses and not the offerings? Your head resurfaced, and you were wet, Mireya who wanted to be called La Negra and who was once Debora, you slipped through my hands so I could not catch you, you slid off as easily as your dress. My hands could not really strip you bare, uncover you, catch you and hold you.

"Tell me it isn't true," you said as I penetrated you almost without meaning to, just because we were so close, because of the imminence of what we already knew, the collision of one world into another, the fusion of matter, atmosphere and suffocation.

"Tell me you didn't shoot him in the back. Tell me you at least gave him the chance to defend himself, that you risked something that day."

"The eyes of an unrepentant murderer are unbearable, Mireya. How can you know that is what he really is, or that, despite all appearances, he didn't kill anyone? Why talk about that now: are you recording this, is there a hidden camera in your clitoris, Mireya? After twenty-five years, who cares what happened? It was not professional, it was revenge."

"Do you love me?"

Your question did not surprise me, and nor did the cynicism I glimpsed behind it. I needed to believe that at last you wanted to know what had really happened.

"I do, but you . . ."

"The last love, Gotán."

Then the cold once again, a sharp, definitive chill as the stiletto pierced my heart.

3

You do come back.

They are lying, the ones who say there is no return and those who talk about dark tunnels with a light at the end of them.

You do not come back because of any faith in God or Stephen Hawking. You do not come back because of all the virtues or vices you have accumulated: there are no rewards or punishments. You do not come back because there is something called reincarnation.

It is not exactly death you come back from. You come back from a dark place full of sounds and sensations which, given the circumstances, are impossible to make sense of. When you lose as much blood as I did, part of you has been emptied, like a wineskin poured onto a table which nobody is sitting at any longer because the banquet is over.

In the hours between when I was murdered late at night and the early morning when I was rescued, I had more than enough time to die properly and put a stop to all the mess I was making in this world. The advantage of being unconscious is that you do not feel the weight of any remorse or regret: with a litre or two less of blood and memories, your body feels light. It floats off aimlessly, until the moment when other arms enfold it, and someone else's blood brings a different kind of emptiness.

"You had a lucky escape, Martelli."

Inspector Ayala did not sound convinced. The sight of a corpse coming back to life can unsettle even the most cynical policeman.

"Your heart is over to the right."

This time it was not Ayala speaking: what did he know about hearts? It was Burgos, floating like a fluffy cloud in my hazy vision.

"Ang gow goo u kno?"

With all the tubes supplying me with air and liquids, this was the nearest I could get to a proper question.

"Because I cut you open with a hunting knife I use for wild boar. I thought you were dead, and I was curious to see what the guts of someone from the National Shame looked like."

Ayala burst out laughing. I was in no state to tell whether this was at the doctor's scatological sense of humour or because it was really true. It was in this hospital bed at Tres Arroyos that I discovered the inspector had a metal tooth.

I felt no urge to speak. I could not have said anything intelligible anyway. My throat hurt, and just breathing made me choke. I would quite happily have slipped back into death again, but for the urgent need I had to know. Burgos and Ayala took it in turns to fill me in.

Nobody had been arrested because nothing had been reported, either to the authorities or to the press. Parrondo had got in touch with Mónica from his Uruguayan retreat. He told her that "sources within the G.R.O." had informed him that Isabel had been abducted because they thought she had information about documents Edmundo Cárcano had deposited in Geneva, together with the money he had siphoned off to enable him to enjoy his twilight honeymoon.

"Gwat er fug zzz er gro?"

"Don't try to talk. You could perforate one of the tubes, and if oxygen got into the saline solution there would be such a build-up of gases you'd burst like an airship," said Burgos.

"G.R.O. are a sect financed by a group of big businessmen who want it all ways," Ayala explained. "They support democracy as long as it lasts, but they don't rule out alternatives. It was all in a bunch of papers we found in that roofless ranch we fetched you from – or rather, what was left of you."

There were no names amongst the documents, apart from mine on the three sheets of paper in the orange file that Quesada had been clinging to. When I heard his name, I almost tore out the tubes to ask what had happened to him, but my rescuers did not give me time to do so.

"He is in the mortuary of this very establishment," Burgos said, apparently under the influence of the rhetoric within the files they had discovered.

"He was not as lucky as you," Ayala said.

Burgos promised there would be a proper autopsy, although it hardly seemed to matter if he had died when they first started shooting at us, or later, perhaps under torture. The poor magistrate: in the end, he knew no more about what was going on than any low-grade stool pigeon at work in the corridors of the Law Courts.

I closed my eyes while Burgos and Ayala went on explaining. I wanted to believe it was all a stupid nightmare, that in this first dawn of the twenty-first century it could not be true that the Argentines were at it again, searching for or offering themselves as cheap messiahs. Still thinking they were unique, better than all the rest of humanity, kicking over the table like provincial hoodlums, like small-town schemers who ruined their neighbours' reputations with the same pleasure as they stuck toothpicks into bits of cheese and salami while drinking themselves silly in the only bar on some ghastly main street.

In Buenos Aires they had already brought on a substitute president who, after receiving a standing ovation from Congress for declaring a moratorium on the country's debts to the pack of foreign hounds baying for blood, was to be kicked out through the back door only a week later. In the midst of this farce, political parties and popular organisations were boasting how they had got rid of a constitutional president as if he had been the very worst banana republic dictator.

I closed my eyes and disguised myself as a corpse again, but I could not avoid hearing the details of how Burgos and Ayala had made their way to the roofless ranch.

When they had reached Bahía Blanca, they found the real serial killer, the family man, waiting for them at the police station. He signed his confession and asked to be left alone in his cell until the trial had been prepared. He said he was tired of arguing with his wife all the time. He decided in the end to make her his final victim, although he claimed in his defence that this murder had been a *crime passionnel*: fights between husband and wife start easily enough, but you never know how they are going to end.

When the serial killer turned himself in, Inspector Ayala saw his last chance of promotion before retirement vanishing out of the window. So as not to get too depressed about it, he suggested to the doctor they try to find Isabel's kidnappers. The closest place for them to start looking was the ranch I had been to, although they had to get the estate agent to show them the way. After they pitched up there, they not only had to give me mouth-to-mouth resuscitation to make sure I made it to hospital, but they also had to revive the poor estate agent, who almost had a heart attack when he saw what had been going on in a property he had been trying to sell as unoccupied.

*

In the end, nobody even knew there had been a plot. The businessmen who had included the G.R.O. as part of their portfolios dismissed the idea the same night the president was taking his last trip with official bodyguards. The arms stored in the Santiago Cuneo model hospital would be duly shipped out to an unknown destination on a caravan of trucks that did not even attract the notice of the staff working there, used as they were to daily shoot-outs in the neighbouring shanty towns, the constant toing and froing of the police, and to seeing notorious gang leaders swaggering along the corridors with the assurance of top surgeons.

One day Argentina should seriously consider exporting the sophisticated know-how behind the way it strips governments of power without waiting for them to complete their constitutional terms. Throughout the twentieth century it has had more practice at this kind of thing than any but a few countries in Africa. We are world leaders at it.

My saviours had little more to tell. Ayala seemed glad to have discovered I did not leave the National Shame out of a fit of the vapours: "That's for pregnant women, not police officers," he said. Burgos was more aseptic and sceptical. He said he was reserving his opinion until I either recovered or died, which would be obvious soon enough. I am not sure whether he was trying to encourage me or finish me off.

After announcing that Argentina was going hell for leather for disaster yet again and that there was nothing I could do about it, they said they would leave me to rest or breathe my last. They would be back the next day to say goodbye, whether I was still in my bed or by then being fitted for a wooden overcoat. The tubes supplying me with air and sustenance prevented me from cursing them roundly for all they had done for me.

I closed my eyes, and in the middle of the night dreamed that someone came and took all the tubes out of me and bundled me away into the boot of a car. From there they took me heaven knows where, and two "male figures" unloaded me while a "female figure" issued instructions and talked on a mobile to a fourth person whose sex I could not determine.

I woke up in even more pain and feeling weaker than on the previous day, only to find that certain dreams are the confused prologues to even worse nightmares.

*

There are two ways of immersing yourself in violence: either of your own accord, or by letting yourself be swept along by it, like somebody falling into a raging torrent. I would have preferred the former, but found myself in the latter.

When I woke up, I was in a different bed. I had no tubes stuck into me any more, which chiefly goes to show that all this costly medical apparatus is often unnecessary, and only adds to the health service's bills.

I did not try to move, but I was not tied down either. I was in such poor physical shape that my captors must have decided I was in too much pain to attempt an escape. Flat on my back in the hospital bed, I consoled myself with the fact that at least the room had a roof. This gave me a surge of optimism: if I had been abducted from Tres Arroyos hospital and taken in a car boot to another one, that must mean someone was interested not only in keeping me alive, but also in staying in contact with me.

It was not you, Mireya. That was my first disappointment when I came back to life, thanks to having my heart in the wrong place. Who was it then? Who had taken the risk of secretly abducting me and transferring me to another hospital?

The door to my room opened. Finally I got the answers.

4

At the end of June 1978, while the Argentine football team was winning the World Cup, to the euphoria of the populace and the satisfaction of the military dictatorship, one of the top police chiefs, Anibal "Toto" Lecuona died in an ambush in the Tigre Delta outside Buenos Aires. The commander of the First Army Corps gave immediate instructions to the owners of the national newspapers and news agencies that nothing about his death should emerge. That night crowds poured onto the streets to celebrate winning a manipulated tournament lavishly promoted to show the world an Argentina that had returned to peace, had an economy that was growing as fast as savage capitalism allowed, and was exporting middle-class tourists flush with money from all the exchange-rate and other fiscal juggling going on.

The murdered police chief was far from having been the dictatorship's blue-eyed boy, but to order his death in the midst of all the patriotic rejoicing must have seemed like a dangerously dissident initiative to the monolithic armed forces. The man had in fact been a fifth columnist for the Peronist *guerrilleros*, but he enjoyed the protection of a big cereal wheeler-dealer who, like the good progressive bourgeois he was, made sure he was affiliated to the Communist Party. He donated as much money to their campaigns as he did to the Rotary Club, of which he was also a member, just in case. The Argentine Communist Party had swapped its copies of *What Is to Be Done* by Lenin for colour pamphlets of the Kremlin, whose gerontocracy were delighted with our dictatorship because it had disobeyed the underhand boycott imposed by the Carter regime in Washington, and sold them wheat on better terms than it had to the European Community.

Only a loose cannon, or a fundamentalist in the murderous crusade known as the Process of National Reorganisation, could have thought it would be a good idea to shoot the police chief on the same night as the football triumph was being celebrated, and anyone who did not dance was a Dutchman.

Whoever drew up the orange file was generous with the space devoted to that hidden episode, giving it the equivalent of a centre spread in a newspaper. My name and even my nickname Gotán figured prominently in this well-thumbed document originally intended for a restricted circulation, which Burgos and Ayala had prised from Patricio Quesada's dead hands. But why, almost a quarter of a century later, was anyone still interested in an episode that in no way altered anything written about the last Argentine military dictatorship? Did some eager, democratically minded researcher into those atrocities want to shed more light on the shadowy goings-on of that period, to expose me to public condemnation, and send my weary bones to jail?

My involvement in the affair made it less of a surprise that Toto Lecuona was still alive than it was to see him coming through the door, healthy and smiling, with the apparent intention of embracing me.

"None of your bones are broken, and the blood you lost was partly replaced in Tres Arroyos hospital. They finished pumping up those flabby muscles of yours in here," he said by way of a greeting, even though we had not seen one another for almost a quarter of a century. He came over and hugged me. "You old crock . . . I had to get you out of that provincial hospital – they were planning to kill you."

"What, again?"

He guffawed and sat beside me on the bed. He was right, I was well enough to sit up with his help and lean back against the headboard, even though a sharp pain in my chest reminded me of Mireya's reappearance in my life.

"You're an inconvenient witness, the missing link in a chain rusted by time, Gotán. If you are killed now, there is no-one who can contradict what it says in that orange file."

"I've no intention of contradicting it. I was happy selling toilets."

"But you put on the masked avenger's cape and flew off to bring justice to Gotham City."

"Don't talk to me about justice. Tell me instead why you came back?"

"I have my pride, even if I've retired to the Canary Islands with my adolescent girlfriend."

"All my friends seem to be doing the same. Why can't they settle for the truth, that they're nothing more than living mummies?"

"Look who's talking, the tango dancer."

"Mireya is thirty-nine, almost an old woman."

"And it's because of her that you're here instead of enjoying a happy retirement."

"Where is she?"

"Disappeared without trace. Everyone in the G.R.O. has vanished, and left me in the lurch."

Since this time I had no tubes, I asked once again what on earth G.R.O. stood for.

"'Group of Revolutionary Officers' . . . Until a few hours ago, they hoped to seize power. Now they're the initials on a rubber stamp."

"The military again?"

"But these are youngsters, Gotán. They're the internet and mobile phone generation. They admire Chávez in Venezuela, and they support Evo Morales in Bolivia."

"Bingo!" I said triumphantly. "But what brings you here?"

He stood up and paced round the room. He lit a cigarette, filled the air with smoke, and then asked if I minded him smoking.

"What I mind is dying without finding out why nobody will let me go back to my peaceful job, why they keep bringing up the past, why they want to make me guilty, why they make up a story I can no longer be bothered to deny. And I'd also like to know who Mireya – or La Negra, as she calls herself with these people – really is, where Edmundo's daughter is, and more than anything, why Edmundo was murdered. He was a good guy, he also put his money on a less crappy world once upon a time."

"That's quite a list of questions," Toto said.

I refused the cigarette he offered me. "I'm choking already," I said, and smiled. As hare-brained as ever, Toto Lecuona: someone who could be boasting about his latest conquest as the bullets were whistling around him.

"The G.R.O. recruited Edmundo. He liked the idea of shaking up our subservient democracy."

"Off his head again. I honestly thought he was becoming more mature, and only wanted to be happy. Instead, they made mincemeat out of him."

"Don't talk about your best friend that way, Gotán. Don't pretend to be cynical. Dreams don't grow old; revolution is eternally a fifteen-year-old who is worth risking everything for."

"Go fuck yourself, Toto. Tell me everything, and let history judge me, as Fidel and Admiral Massera both said in their time."

Toto stopped pacing and stared at me, taking a few moments to decide whether to go on talking to me at all, or to abandon me to my executioners. The fact that he spoke meant he had given me another chance.

"Edmundo called you that night from his beach house. He was happy there with the girl . . ."

"Lorena, another *nom de guerre*."

"That's right: Lorena, I'd forgotten her name, poor thing. Edmundo was willing to risk everything, and wanted to bring you in too. 'He's a good friend, and an even better killer,' he said. 'I can vouch for that,' I said at the meeting we held just before Edmundo called you, 'and a good conjurer too.' I told them about the trick you played that night back in 1978 when all those cretins were celebrating a football championship played on the graves of all our comrades."

"Nobody questioned your death, Toto. That Communist Party Rotarian who protected you was dispatched the very next day. They shot his daughter first, in front of him, after two marines had raped her: the same two that I saw being feted recently as heroes of the Malvinas campaign."

Toto Lecuona took a deep breath of the air he himself had poisoned, as if he were about to dive into an oceanic trench and needed reserves of carbon dioxide. He knew that to submerge oneself in memory is to mutate, to change not your skin so much as your species.

"La Negra, or Mireya as you call her, is a big shot in the organisation. She was the one who rang me in the Canaries and convinced me that this time it was for real, that we could seize power by taking advantage of the weaknesses and contradictions among the squabbling morons in government. We were going to announce the start of a new stage in Perón's unfinished revolution, blah, blah, blah . . . The young military men are angry because they are never taken into account and told to wait before they are brought any new toys to play with. They're sent to let off fireworks in Central America and before that in former Yugoslavia. Just put yourself in their shoes: they had nothing to do with the dictatorship."

"You put yourself in them, Toto. Of course, nobody in Argentina had anything to do with anything. I can't believe what you're telling me: what did you think you were going to do – bring socialism to Argentina?"

Toto Lecuona stared hard at me, as lost as ever.

*

It was just like the night when I engineered the farce of his murder by a police squad I was in command of.

We came to his house, a small prefabricated place in a working-class part of San Fernando where he lived on his own. We smashed in the door without any difficulty and found Toto stark naked with a girl. He started shouting nervously, "You bastards, who sent you?" while we kicked the girl out like a dog caught sleeping on a bed. I made the three numbskulls with me leave too. "I'll handle this on my own," I said, "we've got old scores to settle." They were pleased: it meant less work for them, fixing the body so it looked as if he had resisted arrest, writing up reports, all the paperwork.

When we were alone, I told him what was happening. In two or three days' time he was going to be quietly arrested, then slowly tortured in the Olimpo or the Escuela secret prisons. After that, an injection and then he would be food for bottom feeders in the widest river in the world. He could not believe they knew everything. "It was you who told them," he accused me, beside himself with fury, impervious to fear because he was so sure of his own invulnerability. I had a hard time convincing him they had let him grow like a tropical plant in the Antarctic base of Marambio. "If you only knew how far you've been infiltrated," I told him that night as I helped him gather up two pairs of trousers, a sweater and a jacket and put them in a bag. I gave him the money I had collected: enough for him to get by for a couple of days, to reach a frontier or find a hiding place. "Better to leave the country though, because if they find you alive, I've had it," I said. He vanished cursing everyone and everything.

*

As soon as he left that night, I set fire to the bed and the cheap wooden furniture in the house, emptied my revolver at the smoke while the flames leaped up, then walked out calmly. Before I climbed into the patrol car I lit a cigarette, "Let's go," I told the others, as if I had just been to take a pee in the undergrowth. "That's another one who won't cause any more trouble."

*

"Who gives a fuck about socialism these days?" Toto said at last. "Russia is governed by mafias; China by gangsters desperate to make fortunes at the cost of millions of Chinese begging in the streets; North Korea, a medieval country with nuclear warheads; Cuba, a Sweden without a penny, even taking in a crazy guy like Maradona. No, Gotán, to talk of socialism now is like wanting to get to the moon in a hot-air balloon. Jules Verne wouldn't consider it for a novel."

Beyond this, even he grew confused trying to explain the complicated alchemy the G.R.O. theorists were trying to work. "They were all highly educated," he said, "with Masters degrees from First-World universities. Brains, Gotán, brains, what we never had. That's why we ended up in the National Shame."

"So they had lots of good ideas," I said, "but they used them in the service of criminals. Why did they kill Edmundo, Lorena, and someone called Cordero? Why try to finish me off? And why try to bring a poor serial killer into it, a family man, a loving husband who could not bear to see her love him so much, and decided at the last moment to include her on his list. He's in a cell at Bahía Blanca, as depressed as hell."

"Mireya was the one who personally planned all that. It's something you'll have to ask her, if you ever see her again."

It was my turn for a hollow laugh, but the sudden pain in my chest reminded me once again that unrequited love leaves its mark.

"My Mireya isn't someone you'd call a stable personality, Toto. She's not what she was yesterday. And she can be the opposite of what she seems today."

"For now, you're among friends. The pair who rescued you from the ranch are outside, watching over you like guardian angels. I don't know where you find your friends, Gotán."

"Or my loves."

At that point, Inspector Ayala and the doctor made their theatrical entrance. With Rodríguez still absent – they thought he must still be wrapped in the embrace of the police museum attendant – Burgos and Ayala seemed to complement each other admirably. No sooner had they come in than they apologised for not having warned me about my traumatic transfer from Tres Arroyos hospital.

"We didn't want to wait for your executioners to find out they had come up against a rare specimen with a heart over to the right," Burgos told me.

"Where am I now?"

"In the Santiago Cuneo."

"But don't worry," Ayala said, afraid I might react badly to the news. "All the weapons have gone; there's not so much as a penknife left. They took everything."

"Where to?"

"Paraguay, probably," Toto said. "They're big arms buyers, and they pay with top-quality drugs. The G.R.O. never really owned those weapons, they were only leasing them. If we had seized power, there would have been no problem paying for them."

"While they're busy plotting, Argentines are expert administrators. Their problems start when they get their hands on the state budget."

"The people at the ranch fled south," Burgos said.

"How do you know?"

"Just a hunch, Martelli," Ayala said. "Nobody ever knows anything for sure. Not even the Pope – I bet when he looks out of the window at the Vatican and sees the crowds in St Peter's square, he must be shit-scared and wonder: 'Shall I tell them or not God doesn't exist?'"

We all laughed at that. I laughed as gently as possible, because I was still meant to be seriously ill, but very early the next morning, before the duty doctor made his round, we left the Santiago Cuneo model hospital and warehouse for weapons in transit. Shortly before we left, a nurse who was quite happy to co-operate – thanks to the generous tip Toto gave her in euros – supplied me with another horse pill, this time for the pain in my chest, although even that was not as bad as it had been the day before.

Although we left at 5.00 in the morning, the corridors on the ground floor of the hospital were already teeming with people hoping to become patients. They were queueing to get a number at 8.00 which would enable the chosen few among them to be seen by late that afternoon, the next day, a week later, or in a month's time. Those who were late would be lucky to get an appointment after their death.

I only learned all this from my friends' comments as I lay in the back of a Japanese 4×4, rented and driven by Toto. He had decided to join the hunting party for the G.R.O. because, after the failure of their coup, they had neglected to pay him.

"One of those at the ranch was the G.R.O. treasurer. And La Negra's lover, in fact," Ayala said, oblivious to any damage he might do to my chances of recovery. "That's why they chose what they thought was a safe spot. Who would have thought that the brains behind an armed revolutionary organisation would hole up in a tumbledown ranch in the middle of nowhere."

"I did," I said from my uncomfortable position on the floor of the 4×4. "Though I thought they were common criminals, not social redeemers."

Loud snores from the doctor. Apparently he intended to sleep all the way.

"He was snoring like that when we drove from Bahía Blanca to

Buenos Aires," Ayala said. "The problem was that he was driving. 'It's my angina from smoking,' he told me when I shook him to make sure we didn't crash into a farm truck waltzing all over the road as it came towards us."

*

As we left Buenos Aires and headed south again on Route 3, Toto switched on the car radio. The provisional president was declaring an end to all historic injustices, the arrival of a new era, a veritable cornucopia of jobs and riches for everyone. The eternal hope that dawned with this "new era" was to last four or five days; the new president managed only a week.

*

We headed south. I knew I would find you.

Once upon a time, the south was inhabited by dignified, tough, religious men and women. Afterwards, others arrived, with more religions and symbols: first the cross, then, in its wake, capitalist accumulation. And the fate of what these others called Patagonia was sealed.

I did not get far in my crazy drive to nowhere with Lorena, and yet, without realising it, I had been close to the place we were on our way to now.

Piedranegra is a ghost town, a one-horse place once swarming with adventurers and seasonal workers who stopped off there on the way to the apple harvest in Rio Negro, to try their luck for a few weeks as gold prospectors.

Somebody had discovered a secret, or invented a legend – it is all the same today: buried beneath the barren land was gold. Just by dipping a pan into the waters of a tributary of the Rio Colorado you could find precious golden flakes. Back in Liverpool, an English company had loaded a boat with all the machinery needed to open a mine. The miners travelled on another huge cargo boat with an indistinct flag: two hundred blond bears with watery eyes who only spoke their own dialect, humanoid beasts who could drill stone with their fingernails, or if need be smash it with their fists.

There was no time to lose. As in the Malvinas in 1982, when the British arrived the party would be over. But the party never even started. It simply faded away when the would-be prospectors left the area, covered in nothing but mud. The British boat never arrived, and in less than a year the deserted town had all but dissolved back into the harsh Patagonian uplands.

We reached what was left of Piedranegra at nightfall. It was nothing more than a street two hundred metres long, lined by at most a dozen derelict wooden buildings. The wind whipped up a dust storm.

Toto Lecuona stopped the 4×4 before we got to the street that gave shape to this mirage that would otherwise go unnoticed a good many kilometres off Route 3. When he switched off the engine, the wind ran the whole gamut of howls and groans.

I sat up in the back seat and looked around. We were here because Piedranegra had appeared on one of the sheets of paper Ayala and Burgos had found in the roofless ranch near Tres Arroyos. Although isolated, that place was far more exposed than this ghost town. We were soon to discover though that until only a few hours before its ramshackle walls had harboured all the life and ambitions normally found in trade union headquarters, political activists' offices, or barracks where conspirators encourage one another to take to the field in that other Argentine national sport: the search for absolute power.

Toto and Ayala got out, opened the boot, and came back with two rifles each.

"They're Yugoslav," Toto said.

"But be careful, they might be Argentine," Ayala warned. "During their war we sold the Croats shiploads of old scrap with their serial numbers changed. If they *are* Argentine, they could easily backfire on you."

Burgos had never been interested in any weapon other than the scalpel, and he only dared to use that on the dead. Still, he took his rifle and examined it with great curiosity. Ayala tried to make sure he was not pointing it anywhere inside the vehicle, then showed him how to slip off the safety catch. Burgos followed his instructions like a diligent pupil.

"What are we facing? Death. But who? How many of them? Why here?"

"If they have hostages, they must be here," Toto said. "I didn't ask for money up front because I was a supporter of the cause. But they cheated me."

Once they had seized power, the plan had been for them to keep their V.I.P. prisoners in Piedranegra. Not the president: "We knew we could leave him free, because he doesn't have the slightest idea where he is anyway," Toto had explained during the journey. "The party bosses, the heads of the intelligence services, gang leaders from around Buenos Aires who, because of the control they have over the masses of unemployed, are as powerful as generals in the regular army."

But now their only captive, if she was still alive, was Isabel.

"Why did they take Isabel?"

"They thought they could put pressure on Edmundo's wife, or Isabel herself if she knew, to tell them where Edmundo had hidden the money. Money that belonged to the organisation."

"As far as I know, nobody has asked Mónica for anything. All they asked her to do when they called was to warn me not to stick my nose in their affairs. They couldn't pin Lorena's death on me, and they failed to blow me up in Isabel's car. But what has C.P.F. got to do with all this?"

"For fuck's sake, this is no time for an interview, Martelli," Ayala said.

"The C.P.F. supplied the finances," Toto said anyway. (He had never liked the Bahía Blanca inspector: he could not stand provincial cops:

"They're even more stupid and bloodthirsty than the National Shame," he had said more than once.) "C.P.F. gives food to the poor, pays for literacy campaigns, helps overthrow weak presidents. Big oil companies are even more efficient than the F.A.R.C. in Colombia, plus they're welcome on stock exchanges round the world."

"Of course they are, they extract our oil for next to nothing, then sell it in the First World at O.P.E.C. prices."

"The struggle for power is an expensive business, Gotán. When we were young, we thought all we needed were a couple of kidnappings and a bank robbery. Look where that got us."

"If Mónica said nothing, why did they put a quarter of a million dollars into a Spanish account for her?"

"Ask the G.R.O. treasurer. He's one of the guys hiding out in Piedranegra. I just want my money."

During the twelve-hour journey down an interminable, dead-straight road through the pampas and then the Patagonian desert, none of us had said much. Toto did not like to talk when he was driving; Ayala wanted nothing to do with the National Shame; Burgos was snoring; and I was floating in the sargassos of all the drugs I had been given. But now, as we stood outside a ghost town peopled by phantoms, we realised we could not just wade in shooting. We needed to make some kind of reconnaissance.

When I volunteered, the others laughed behind their hands.

"Forty-eight hours ago you were skewered like a piece of meat, and now you want to play the hero," Toto said dismissively.

"Somebody can come with me then," I suggested. "I'm not waiting here. You lot are capable of killing La Negra before I even get the chance to talk to her."

"The only one we should spare is the treasurer, at least until he signs my cheque," Toto said.

Burgos was still gazing at his rifle as if it were the newborn child of a pregnant corpse. He seemed more inclined to slit it open than to pat it on the backside to help it breathe. Ayala seemed equally reluctant to share with me the privilege of being the first to die. There was nothing to discuss. Toto and I would cut the ribbon for the official inauguration of the battle, or whatever came next.

My excuse was wanting to find Isabel. My wager in the void, my suicidal dream, was to be alone with you again.

5

The town, or what was left of it, was in a dip, a crater hidden in the desert wastes as if a meteorite had fallen to earth there, the fragment of a comet which as it smashed into pieces left these wooden houses as a memento. Among them was what once must have been a chapel, with a sloping roof and a iron cross at the top. It was still erect because the Holy Spirit was holding it up by a thread from the sky. But it swayed alarmingly from side to side, threatening to fall across the entrance and throwing a shadow that from the fear it cast must have been the fear of God.

There had been, or was, a bar, a chemist's – with its own kind of cross outside – and the remains of several houses. Probably they had no roofs either: it seemed as though the members of the G.R.O. liked to choose hiding places in which they were still in touch with the universe.

Toto and I each took one side of the street – he was on the left, I was on the right. At the first shot we could unite our forces, if we had any left. We also had a walkie-talkie (part of the equipment meant to have been used to overthrow the president) that we could use to alert our companions if we needed reinforcement.

The wind roared down the street, driving us back. The first block we came to had two houses on my side, and only one on the other. Typical, whenever there's work to be done, I get double. The houses were not as delapidated as they appeared from a distance, although some of the rooms were missing roofs, and elsewhere there were no walls, only doors. Like an idiot, I opened one or two of them, going from emptiness to emptiness.

When I saw Toto still standing on his street corner I cursed him under my breath, then out loud. The wind whirled my words away. Toto could read my lips though: he gave me the finger with his right hand and waved his rifle in the air, looking for all the world like Gregory Peck in *Only The Valiant* (Cinema Eden, Villa Urquiza, 1957, the last film in the matinee) where a U.S. army colonel surrounded by hundreds of Apaches shoots them one by one until he has nobody left to talk to.

We crossed the side road that was no more than a patch of sandy earth, and reached the second block.

This time there were three buildings on the left and four on the right, although Toto had to deal with a two-storey construction, of which only one and a half were still standing. It looked like a Wild West saloon, with swing doors that strangely enough still banged together, and a wooden sign which read B R G LD N CH M R, as if someone had stolen all the vowels. The bar had two large windows with their panes smashed, either due to the ravages of time or because the last rowdy drunks of Piedranegra had been thrown through them.

Toto appeared and disappeared in the swirling sand, but I could tell he was signalling for backup. I pointed to the radio he had stuffed into his belt. Why were those other two still in the 4×4 if we needed them here? Perhaps we did not have time to wait for them to arrive. Toto must have seen something to arouse his suspicions, because he went on gesturing at me like an excitable monkey.

I jumped down into the street, but the wind immediately knocked me off my feet. I rolled in the dust still clinging to my rifle. In an instant, twenty-five years' experience of selling toilets vanished, and I could feel the controlled adrenalin of a professional killer taking over. Rifle in front of me, I crawled towards the far side of the street, feeling the ground tremble as the bullets slammed all round me. They came closer and closer, and would eventually have hit me had I not managed to reach a small, life-saving cement wall. It was only about half a metre high, but I could take cover and return fire.

From my vantage point I could see what had happened. Toto had been caught by surprise. Several guns were trained on him from inside the bar, and while one was aimed straight at his head, others were firing heavy-calibre stuff at me through the broken window. I could hear voices, probably telling me to throw down my weapon and surrender, but the howling wind was too strong for me to make out the words. I saw Toto throw down his rifle and raise his arms, signalling to me to do the same. I pressed the radio button to tell Ayala and Burgos we needed them (if they too had not been captured). A well-aimed shot blew it out of my hands and smashed it.

It was logical they would be good shots: after all, they were the leaders of a coup that never happened. It was equally logical that they would not ask for or give any mercy, as Mireya's loving embrace had eloquently shown.

I flattened myself behind the wall. I could have been shot in the legs, but there are two situations in which I need to feel comfortable: when I am making love, and when I am killing. I took careful aim, squeezed the trigger, and behind Toto there was a cry of pain. He flung himself to the ground and started turning somersaults into the middle of the street. But he was not as young as he would have claimed, and the bullets from the bar with no vowels put a stop to his gymnastics.

I should have killed him that night back in 1978, when I had stepped in to save him before his planned abduction. I would have cut short a life that ended with one final pirouette, while he was still stubbornly dreaming of some kind of revolution, only to be defeated without glory, cut down by a bunch of clowns who – to add insult to injury – had promised him money he would never receive.

I stood up and fired again, offering such an easy target to Toto's killer he must have been licking his lips in anticipation. When I saw him stand up too behind the window, I gave him no time to aim, but sprayed the bar with bullets. I was shooting from a long way off, but I heard his body crash to the floor, passing from life to death. I ran towards the bar and crashed through the swing doors. If there had been any more armed men inside, that would have been the moment to shoot me.

But there was nobody in the bar still breathing. I was pleased to think that one of the two I had shot must have been the dog killer from Tres Arroyos.

My instinct for self-preservation is strong and persistent. The bureaucrat's voice inside me was telling me to get out of there, out of that sinister building, that imitation Wild West saloon, before death stripped me naked again and tempted me with a well-rehearsed fellatio.

Of course, I had not come this far, half-dead already and with the stabbing pain in my chest, merely to finish off the jackals who had killed an old colleague and a defenceless, loyal farm dog. Nor had I come to put an end to a bunch of revolutionaries recycled like organic waste, people who refused to see that, however much it cost to admit it, in Argentina we were living in a democracy ruled by crappy governments elected by the people.

I had lost my radio. Toto's was beneath his body sprawled out in the street. There were no signs of life from Burgos and Ayala: they must have set off in the 4×4 in the opposite direction, and would by now be racing back up the highway to Bahía Blanca, which they should never have left in the first place. I was all on my own, and yet again I was treading on dead bodies.

But I was sure there was someone still alive, on the " PST RS" floor of the wrecked bar with no vowels.

It was time for me to end that life as well.

6

Stairs so rotten they crumbled underfoot, and the inevitable creaking that competed with the gale of sand beating against the banging shutters.

You were expecting me. You could have come out as soon as I burst into the ground floor and shot me from up here. I was so busy trying to rid myself of our attackers, and so furious I had not been able to save Toto Lecuona from death a second time, that I would not have had to time to react.

Inexplicably, I no longer felt rage. I would have been disappointed not to find you, although that feeling soon changed.

The upper floor was little more than an attic. I had to bend my 1.90 frame to walk along the corridor. This part of the building was better preserved. I could tell from the little details that a woman must have lived here: flower pots with the dusty remains of once pretty, exotic plants, woodcuts and a pair of watercolours of lovers who invited the spectator to join in their game. Decay had left some lines untouched. Beauty resisted defeat.

I checked out two small, empty rooms without doors. I wasted no time on the locked door of the third. I fired at the lock and kicked it open. As it bounced back towards me, I prevented it from closing with my foot. A shot from inside the room skimmed my head.

I could scarcely make you out, but I knew you had missed on purpose. I would not have had time to take aim if you had fired again, at me this time, but you lowered your rifle and I stepped inside the room.

"This time you did know I would come."

"I did the last time, too. I know you, Gotán. As I once told you, you pursue your prey like a man possessed. You're a killing machine."

"Look who's talking."

"We have a cause. Everybody kills for a reason. For ideals, money, passion."

"I'm the exception to the rule. I did not come here for you."

You turned your back on me and stared out of the window at the deserted street invisible in the storm of sand and dust. I wondered if I could wound you with words, if they were your weak point, if a word could be the *coup de grâce* I would never dare give you.

"Isabel is alive," you said, still looking away from me. "We were going to let her go. She can't harm us any more."

"How could she have harmed you?"

At this you turned to face me, weary of the game, knowing how absurd it all was.

"She knows the security code to Edmundo's account in Europe. He had money from the C.P.F. that never reached the N.G.O. it was destined for, which meant we didn't get it either."

"I didn't know. She didn't tell me."

"I'm not surprised, and neither should you be. What girl could trust someone with your record?"

"Isabel doesn't know anything about it. My past is my own, I don't advertise it."

"You advertise bathroom appliances. But her mother did not know the code either. That's why she made that deposit in Spain: she must have been afraid of what might happen and that $250,000 was all she had time to transfer."

"Not a bad haul."

"Both of them are rich. You could marry whichever of them you managed to seduce."

"Where is she?"

"I'm not going to tell you. You find her, if that's what you really came for."

"Who put Lorena's body in my room? And who shipped around that transvestite Cordero?"

"The G.R.O. has its intelligence unit, Gotán. The dirty war in the '70s left a lot of highly trained personnel who found it impossible to live on unemployment benefit. But they weren't the ones who disposed of Cordero. That was a group of disillusioned Muslims who passed the death sentence on him from Paraguay. The difference between ordinary crime and political murders is that the latter make it to the front pages. The serial killer on the coast acted as a shield. In the end, Edmundo Cárcano and his young lover, who was so devoted to Edmundo she betrayed Cordero and our organisation along with him, chose to be common crooks rather than revolutionaries. They must have known nobody can double-cross an organisation like ours."

"So it was you who made love to Lorena?"

Your face lit up joyfully. You laughed silently, staring at me, waiting for me to laugh as well or ask you for details. We men are aroused by lovemaking between women, and you were expecting me to ask why and how you seduced her, how you lured her to your secret corner, the same one perhaps as the one I had stumbled into . . . but before I could ask, you told me anyway.

"We made love in your room at the Imperio Hotel in Bahía Blanca. The night porter gave us the key."

"Mónica was told Lorena came in with a man. Was the porter one of you as well?"

"We don't recruit service personnel, but in hotels they get paid like immigrant workers, so they try to make money on the side by allowing prostitutes in. When I gave him the equivalent of his Christmas bonus, the porter was happy to let us do whatever we liked. The Bahía Blanca police were ordered to keep you away that night you went and got drunk in the local dive. They did their work well, because you didn't turn up until the next day."

"I was back before dawn, in fact," I said, as if it mattered.

Ayala and Rodríguez. So they had picked me up outside the bar on orders. Cervantes would never have written *Don Quixote* with those two as his main characters.

"Who gave the order?"

"A top mafia man in Puerto Belgrano. He controls all the white-slave traffic in the region. He makes his contacts internationally each year when he sails with the navy's training ship. They say the whores in Jordan are especially hot."

You laughed openly, defying me, then like someone raising their champagne glass, you raised the rifle level with my face.

"Are you going to kill me?"

"There would be no point, Gotán. I am death."

"You tried it once before."

"Do you think I would have failed if that's what I had wanted?"

"The doctors told me it was because my heart is over to the right."

"You should never believe what doctors say."

*

And then, as I had guessed and feared it would, it all started to happen again. Mireya bent her knees slightly, and let the rifle drop gently on the floor, pushing it to one side with her foot.

I did the same. I did not trust her, but thought I had no right to be more mistrustful than she was. That was the strange path we took, and although nothing was said or promised, it was written that nothing between us would come to an end if one of us was still alive.

The two rifle butts bumped into each other, spinning round and then coming to a halt, each one pointing straight back at its owner.

She straightened like a flower bathed in sunlight and early morning dew, and began to take her clothes off. I waited until she was naked to do the same. I had none of her arrogance, though: I felt like a befuddled old man, or humiliated like a prisoner forced to strip off in jail. Perhaps that really was my situation, and for the first time I felt afraid.

"Did you take all your clothes off with her too?"

She nodded.

"And with you as well, the last time," she said defiantly.

The pain in my chest surged again, forcing me to hunch up.

"Why did you leave me?"

"Pain makes you look pathetic, Gotán. I left you because I have no idea who you are. A good tango dancer, a toilet salesman . . ."

"Bathroom furniture in general: bidets, washbasins, fittings. But I'm not on a sales trip to Patagonia, I didn't bring my leaflets or price list. Do *you* know who *you* are, which bosses *you're* serving, Mireya?"

The pain in my chest turned into a burning fire. Mireya standing there naked telling me not to call her Mireya, me saying I was not just a salesman, that I risked my life when necessary, that they could have put me through the meatgrinder while I was making my clandestine attempt to save colleagues like Toto Lecuona.

"Just so your school chums could gun him down. That treasurer of yours you screwed while I was sniffing round the roofless ranch like a timid mouse. If I had known it was you I would have peppered you both with bullets in bed – then we wouldn't have been here like this today, and poor Toto would still be alive, instead of lying out there in the street with sand and brushwood blowing over him."

"That's his fault, Gotán. He had instructions to finish you off, but instead he wanted to help you, to pay you back for the favour you did him that night in '78. Like you, none of your friends have any ideology, only nostalgia."

She moved around the room on tiptoe, as though she were wearing high heels. Each step made her breasts quiver, and as she turned away I saw her firm, wonderful backside. She shook her head as she turned towards me again, her hair alternately covering and revealing her features, while her breasts seemed to grow firmer at the touch of her long tresses, as her pupils grew in the semi-darkness. It was only when she whispered to me to come closer that I realised the wind had dropped. Closer, she begged me. Closer.

I tried to concentrate on her hands. I was never very good at spotting conjurors' sleight of hand: anything can grow from a closed fist, from the passing of the palm of a hand. Any trick of the light can lead to a string of handkerchiefs, a rabbit, a dove, a stiletto. She insisted she could have killed me if she had wanted to, that she told her "comrades" I was dead. That was why when they saw me arrive in the ghost town they stopped trusting her, and locked her up in this room on the top floor of the bar with no vowels.

"Aren't you going to come here?"

She held out her arms. I took hold of her hands, feeling every pore, trying to discover betrayal in every cell of her skin. I asked her again why she had reacted the way she did when she found out I was a policeman. "What did you expect to find apart from ugliness?" I pleaded that night, my real face is not beautiful, running after her until she dived into a taxi. This ugly mess is my true face, the same as that of all the living dead who thought we were fighting for something, but we were merely scratching the surface, digging our own graves.

"Don't think," you said. "Put your arms round me."

I relaxed my grip and slid my hands slowly and gently along your arms, still wary but already yielding to the pressure of desire I could feel in my body. "Only your stomach is flabby," you said, your own hand seeking out my sex. Your fingers closed around its taut urgency. In the end Eros and Thanatos search each other out like neighbourhood gangsters on every corner of the human condition. There is nothing we can do to separate them, to prevent the inevitable clash, the blind duel that is no more than a pretence, the fake death of the Messiah who, while everyone is crying over him, comes back to life without a word and like you tiptoes out of the back door or climbs out through the skylight and makes a beeline for heaven, from where he can look down on us.

Anybody would be happy to die if they could guarantee an outcome like that.

"And yet you're scared," you said, as if you could read my mind, that other ruined bar with no vowels or chimeras where a couple of ideas scratched themselves for fleas, as bored as the whores in this same room when the prospectors for easy gold realised their mistake and left them without customers. "Don't think. If you feed your fear, it will only grow. Come closer, Gotán. Everything in your life is bringing you to me. You and I were born for this. I never stopped loving you."

My hands reached your shoulders. Your hand on my prick would bring it to its natural berth. You are that berth, but I know there is no solid ground, no shoreline, that it was just a word spoken far too long ago for me to believe you now, a word tossed into the void, with no possible echoes or resonance.

Then there was the pain.

I took hold of your hands, as if by wrapping mine round them you could not hurt me, as if by halting the magician there would be no more tricks, no more doves or knotted strings of coloured handkerchiefs. But the pain was unbearable: my heart was not over to the right as the roly-poly doctor had said, it was where it should have been, but there was a stiletto shard still in it, that same stiletto you had used on Lorena and Cordero. That was why you had put your weapon down, calling for an armistice that ended in this other pretence.

"The doctor at Tres Arroyos did a good job," you whispered in my ear. "He was one of us too. But don't think, Gotán. Just fuck me, that's what you and I were born for."

Terrified, I suspected my stiff prick was simply an anticipation of the rigor mortis of my whole body. You removed a hand and grasped me behind my back to pull me towards you, as if you wanted to penetrate me again, but this time with your entire body, to devour me so that our insides would merge and become one, howling their dismay in a single, androgynous being. I would have played along, Mireya, but for the tearing pain in my chest: nothing I had left to lose could be more important than you. This time, I hesitated. I could kill in cold blood, but looking in the mirror at my own death was suicidal, impossible. My rifle, though, was too far away, and seemed to be locked together with yours as desperately as the two of us were, steel and gunpowder strained to the limit.

The only way out was an explosion. Almost unconscious, I slipped inside you. It was you in all your fury and ragged despair who opened yourself to me, tearing yourself to pieces. The groans when I reached orgasm were the groans of death. I ejaculated a trickle of blood which fell from my mouth onto your face.

After that there was a long silence, as if my tomb had just been sealed. I did not have the strength to open my eyes, and was too frightened to confront my horror. Then I felt something moving, and it was not my body but yours freeing itself from me like someone throwing off a blanket because they are too hot.

I can reconstruct what happened next because it is not hard to imagine.

You got up, still full, in a vampire-like trance that must be a genetic trait in women like you, Mireya. A no less authentic or treacherous reply than any other to the painful questions of love.

You picked up the Kalashnikov the G.R.O. had given you to help force your way into trade union headquarters or government offices if your coup had succeeded. You aimed at my head, still undecided whether finally to put an end to my agony. Farewells are impossible, Mireya. We do not want to admit that whatever we do we will end up as we began. Alone.

"Ciao, Gotán."

Paralysed by the pain in my chest, I closed my eyes. My voice, faint but steady in the rubble of my collapse, failed me. I wanted to thank you.

7

Later there were other voices happy to supply the details of what occurred between my brief absence and my stubborn return to those who think they are alive.

"When we heard the shooting, I tried to convince Burgos it was time for us to join the assault on the Winter Palace," Ayala said. He had read the history of the Russian Revolution in a weekly serial.

But Burgos had still not worked out how to get the safety catch off his Czech rifle, "reconditioned" – that is to say disguised – in the military factory at Azul, in Buenos Aires province, before being shipped abroad again. He had cheerily lifted the rifle to his shoulder, though, and closed one eye to take aim. He must have chosen some target in his subconscious, because the bullet ignored the jammed safety catch and perforated the roof of the 4×4 in which he and Ayala were bringing up our rear.

"You missed my head by *that much*," Ayala said, holding up his thumb and forefinger as he stretched out his other hand and clipped the doctor round the ear.

"We decided to make a detour round the town, to at least confuse them if they were lying in wait for us with heavy artillery," Burgos said. He had got behind the wheel and hurtled off into the countryside, the 4×4 ploughing through the swirling sand like a ship through fog.

"We couldn't see a thing, so when we came across a gunman armed to the teeth I thought it was one of those apparitions you sometimes get in the countryside, especially after you've eaten meat slaughtered by rustlers."

Robocop turned out to be Rodríguez, our Sancho Panza presumed lost in the arms of the police museum spider.

"Love is luggage in transit," Sancho said with a hint of melancholy. His only similarities to Schwarzenegger were his lantern jaw and an unshakeable fascism that left him invulnerable even to a tragic love affair. "As soon as I split up with her, I called Inspector Ayala: 'I'm once again at your command,' I told him. She used the idea of me joining the federal police as bait to seduce me, but I can't get on with Buenos Aires women, even if they're the same rank as me. 'You smell like a farm labourer,' she told me the first time we fucked. When she compared me to an inspector from the capital who wore Paco Rabanne perfume, I realised that even if I did join the National Shame I would always be a bumpkin, the sort of lumpen from the provinces they send in to shoot other lumpen in the shanty towns, not to fight crime, but to try to get us to wipe each other out."

"I ordered Rodríguez to follow us," Ayala said. "I didn't really trust your friend Lecuona. Nor you either, mind. But I had to get to the bottom of all these crimes, and when the serial killer handed himself in I was at a loss."

Ayala had managed to steal to steal Burgos' car keys, so Rodríguez was able to follow us from Buenos Aires to Piedranegra in the V.W. When the doctor saw Rodríguez standing there like a centaur in the middle of the desert next to his beloved vehicle, he thought the time had come for him to give up not only drink but his post as forensic expert too, although everything seemed far too real to be simply a case of delirium tremens.

The bond forged between them from having served together in the police priesthood and sharing so much shit in their provincial town meant they wasted no time debating what to do. Instead, the three of them advanced on the ghost town like a troop of cavalry, entering the other end of the street from Toto and me. Burgos demonstrated that he would have made an expert tank driver, while Ayala and Rodríguez fired out of the back of the 4×4 at anything that moved – "Which wasn't a lot," Rodríguez admitted. "We shot more at tumbleweed and birds stunned by the wind than we did at the enemy."

The defence of Piedranegra could not compare to the siege of Stalingrad or Madrid. Not even to that of the Malvinas, where starving young conscripts with medieval weapons faced a N.A.T.O. country's army. Half a dozen gunmen posted on the town roofs quickly decided discretion was the better part of valour, and sped off in a half-track they had inherited from the Argentine military.

It was enough thereafter for the three musketeers to reach the bar with no vowels, even if they had to pass the disagreeable spectacle of Toto face down in the dust, the involuntary donor of his old, weary blood to an earth than can never get enough.

"By the time we arrived, the mysterious lady with the dagger had disappeared," Burgos took up the narrative. He had stayed in their vehicle while Ayala and Rodríguez shot their way into the bar. "As seems to have become a habit, they found you half-dead and carried you out to the car."

At this point I instinctively felt my body for signs of bullet wounds. It gave me a tender jolt to realise that Mireya had left without shooting me. Perhaps she had the wild idea we could do it all again.

"On the outskirts of Piedranegra there are some old mineworks," Rodríguez said. "I discovered them because I came cross-country to get here. That V.W. of yours is a tank, Doctor."

Burgos closed his eyes and gritted his teeth as if he could hear the creaks and groans from his beloved car's long-suffering shock absorbers, but he did not interrupt Rodríguez's tale.

"I told Inspector Ayala what I had found. We headed straight there, reckoning that the best place in the world to hide one or more prisoners would be an abandoned mine."

"And what happened?" I asked with the faintest of voices, still struggling with the incessant pain in my chest.

Ayala and Rodríguez exchanged glances like experienced hustlers. Burgos, who had been driving the 4×4 at walking pace along a dry river bottom, drove it up an incline and came to a halt. Fifty metres away, I could see the entrance to the mine.

"Nothing happened," Ayala said.

"But it's going to," Rodríguez said. He was used to closing sentences and doors for his superior.

8

The only living thing we are likely to meet if we enter the mouth and penetrate the innards of a fetid body are worms.

"I want to go in alone," I said.

Toto was dead, and I was about to follow him, so it made no sense for the other three to risk their lives.

*

In the event, the other three accepted my suggestion without demur – which did not exactly please me either. They were to wait half an hour, and if I did not reappear, they would set off in search of reinforcements, although by this stage it would probably be impossible to get anyone to stir themselves for something that was swiftly vanishing into thin air like another conjuring trick.

"Do your best not to die," was Ayala's laconic advice.

Weak from loss of blood and in so much pain I could hardly breathe, the Kalashnikov weighed like an artillery shell in my arms. For a moment, and perhaps due to the sense of distance which those about to pass on are said to experience, I saw myself advancing through the desert like an explorer contracted by the Discovery Channel to find evidence of a lost civilisation.

I stopped seeing myself this way, and in fact as soon as I entered the tunnel, I stopped seeing at all.

The first conclusion I came to when I found myself in complete darkness was that this had never been a mine. That was why the British boat never arrived, and why the prospectors had left empty-handed.

Thirsty for mirages, human culture accepts any story that goes a little further than "once upon a time". The predators who arrived in Peru from Spain, centuries ago, tore apart the stones and heart of Potosí. The bleeding remains of a millenary culture were left drying in the sun. There was once a continent that was even shaped like a cornucopia. Its inhabitants thought the looters and executioners were gods. They realised too late that all the psalms, revelations and holy tablets were a farce.

More recently, the lure of gold brought a swarm of men to this area. They built what was now a ghost town, Piedranegra. These useless mineworks were the vestigial reminder of that fever. But the town continued to grow for a while, even after the hope of finding gold had been extinguished. What were they looking for then, if not an acceptance of defeat, of growing old?

I stroked the walls of the cave as if it was the skin of a woman's body. It was smooth, even warm in places. I was moved rather than afraid: if I was finally going to confront death, this seemed as good a place as any.

For several minutes, I completely forgot I was looking for someone I was hoping to find alive. That no longer mattered. Something was affecting my limited perception of the world around me. Like Jonah, but without a God who had sent me, I wandered through the darkest shadows.

My only guiding light was pain. Touching the cave walls had given me some relief, but as soon as I groped for my rifle on the ground, I could feel a searing pain in my heart once more. I dropped the Kalashnikov, which would not have been much use in the darkness anyway, and put my hands back on the wall. The pain eased again.

Without intending to, I was touching and caressing the insides of a living being, a geological female who had absorbed my pain and was leading me to her centre. Lost to myself, I stumbled along thanks to a life that was not mine.

A faint groan stopped me in my tracks.

It could not have come from far away, although the darkness was so complete I could not fathom from where.

The ebb and flow of my pain was my guide. I moved forward when it lessened, stopped whenever it reappeared, as solid, as merciless as ever. With each tiny but firm step I regained control over my body, and the pain withdrew.

All of a sudden, the groaning seemed to come towards me from a tiny glow, a capsule of light at the far end of the gallery. By now the pain had completely gone, and I ran towards the light. I could breathe as easily as if I were in the open air, although the walls of the gallery narrowed sharply, so that for the last few metres I had to stoop down.

"Isabel!" I said.

*

She was lying at your feet like a slave or a penitent who had reached this furthest corner of the earth, lost in the wilds, a hole punched in the desert by scrabbling hands desperate to reach the veins of riches that only existed in the greed and delirium of extravagant adventurers, irredeemable loners condemned to a journey that ended only in death.

"Isabel," I said again. But there was only an intense silence, until finally I heard a muffled groan.

I stretched out my arms and brushed her freezing, wet face with my fingertips. I collapsed on top of her, enfolding her in my embrace. I smothered her moans until they went out like a fire, then tore off her gag with trembling hands.

"Oh, my God," she said, and her feeble cries rose like a tattered flag in the darkness.

We recognised each other through the touch of our hands. We needed to confirm what we were seeing, to prove this was not simply another trick.

As my fingers ran over Isabel's face, as they had done along the walls of the mineshaft, it was your face I was searching for. I could not accept that it was you lying there, at the end of the gallery, face up on a stone altar, your eyes open, staring into who knew what abyss. A light still gleamed in your eyes, like a guttering candle in an airless room. It was the fullness of life being snuffed out, the stubborn reflection of your need to fight against yourself, to conquer yourself. If, as you boasted, you were death, then perhaps in this defeat you had reached some kind of immortality.

I do not know if you succeeded, Mireya, but this was the end of the game.

You hid Edmundo's daughter in here like a spider dragging its prey to the corner of its web. Then, without a word, you drove the stiletto into your own heart.

Isabel thought you were going to kill her, and that was no doubt your intention: to pile up one more dead body in order to postpone your own death. This time though, something went wrong. Staring down at your lifeless, ice-cold body, the open mouth and eyes that only a short while earlier had been peering down a gunsight, searching for my misplaced heart to shatter it, I accepted your decision to quit and, since my instinct for self-preservation is even stronger than my desire, I celebrated it.

*

Although more than half an hour had gone by, the three musketeers were still waiting for me outside the mine. Shielding themselves behind the 4×4, their recycled guns trained on the mouth of the tunnel, they said they were disappointed when they saw us come out alive.

"We were hoping for a good shoot-out," Ayala confessed. "A serial killer who hands himself in, a lady with a dagger who spares your life when she has the chance to finish you off, and now you two – strolling out of there arm in arm. It's not fair."

"We need action," Rodríguez said in support. "We kill people. We draw up our report, the doctor here writes his, then the three of us head off to Pro Nobis for a few drinks."

Despite his profession, Burgos behaved like the most human of the three. He came over, took off his jacket, and draped it round Isabel's shoulders. Still trembling from fear and cold, she found it impossible to speak.

"How do I explain all this, Martelli?" Ayala said, taking me to one side. "What can I tell my bosses when they ask me why we were away from our posts? How will I justify the expenses?"

"Argentina has imploded again," I said, trying to calm him. "A government has resigned. Everyone has been buying dollars to hide under their mattresses. The people who toppled the president have taken over without the slightest notion of the consequences . . . And you're worried about how to justify two days' absence and expenses that would not cover the bill for a lunch any of those politicians might have had in a swanky Buenos Aires restaurant. Give me a break, Ayala."

To boost his morale, I went on to suggest that we call a press conference in which he could be the star. He would be the brains behind an operation that had foiled a plot against the constitutional order, and succeeded at the same time in putting a stop to the activities of a serial killer who had turned out to be two different people.

"Who would believe us, Martelli? The serial killer handed himself in, as meek as a lamb, and at this very moment is probably reading the

Bible in his cell. That impostor friend of yours did herself in, and the plotters failed – not because democracy triumphed, but because others beat them to it. Fuck your constitutional order."

Inspector Ayala was right. He was a practical sort, a man who hunted down poor wretches. A policeman.

We buried Toto Lecuona at the entrance to Piedranegra. Protesting all the while, Rodríguez dug the grave with a spade Burgos always carried in the boot of his car.

"For a doctor of the dead, the scalpel and spade are as essential as a stethoscope for a doctor of the living. You don't always have a refrigerated room to put a corpse in, and they can't be left out in the open. Buzzards would pick at the evidence," he said.

"With this simple act, the burial of this unexpected and unsuccessful defender of justice, I declare the cemetery of Piedranegra open," Ayala said solemnly in his capacity as the most senior officer present. I threw the traditional first handful of earth onto Toto's face, where surprise still perched like a crepuscular crow.

We drove away in silence. Burgos took Don Quixote and Sancho Panza in his V.W., while Isabel and I left in the 4×4 Toto had rented. Still shivering with fear and cold, she gave me her version of the whole sad story on the way back to Buenos Aires.

9

"Daddy told me who you are, Gotán, but I couldn't speak openly with you without betraying him. 'Men don't help each other just so they can boast about it afterwards, or expect to be repaid,' he told me. When he realised he was up to his neck in trouble with C.P.F. and was certain that he was finished whatever he did, he came to see me one night when Mummy was at a mass in her church, the one where they provide you with the papers to pass from one world to the next without having to go through customs.

"'Your mother is half-crazy,' he told me. 'Look after her, but make sure you don't catch it. Here, take this, in case you should need it.'

"He gave me the security code of his account, which was why they kidnapped me. He also deposited a quarter of a million dollars in a Spanish bank for my mother."

"She thought they were trying to buy her off," I said.

"She wasn't wrong. It was too late, but Daddy was in love with her again when he died. But obviously, after all he had made her suffer, he couldn't tell her."

"What about Lorena?"

"A fleeting passion, 'fresh meat', as you would say."

"Who do you mean by 'you'?"

"Dirty old men. Stupid '70s idealists who grow old thinking that 21st-century revolutions can be brought about by fooling around with girls the age of their daughters or granddaughters. Paedophiles."

"'To each according to his need.' We're still loyal to Lenin."

"You're old cretins who can't stand retirement and crawl back for whatever crumbs you can get. But I'm not one to judge."

"Thank God for that. How did Edmundo get involved with the G.R.O. in the first place?"

"Initials," Isabel said. "In Argentina four people get together, think up some initials that sound good for the group, and believe they've started a new political movement. For C.P.F., the G.R.O. was no more important than any other N.G.O. they support financially. Capitalists are big gamblers. They take over the tables and couldn't care less what the croupier calls. They always win – they're the bank. Daddy was playing a double game: he took on the New Man Foundation to siphon off C.P.F. funds, but at the same time they were using the money for arms trafficking. But while he was playing his game, others were playing him."

"Like the Relusol cat," I said. I explained what I meant: in an ancient advertisement for scouring powder, there was a picture of a cat staring at itself in a gleaming frying pan, with the reflection of an infinite number of cats also staring at themselves in an infinite row of frying pans.

"I wasn't born when that ad appeared," said Isabel.

"Nor was Félix Jesús, but I stuck a copy I rescued from *El Hogar* above his litter tray, and he seems to like it."

In the game of mirrors that C.P.F. and state officials play, the cats are being watched when they think they are staring at themselves as they plot mischief or crimes against humanity.

"What did that stupid '70s idealist tell you about me?"

For a moment, Isabel held her breath, then exhaled deeply. That was how she prepared to tell someone something they did not want to hear, a way of relaxing while she considered whether it was worth saying or not, if the other person would listen without flying off the handle.

But in this case that person was happy to listen. He could have told Isabel everything she found out from her father, but for the moment preferred to hear somebody else describe what he did all those years ago.

"You've always had a weakness for shooting people at close range, haven't you?" Isabel said, quite bravely: it is no easy matter to call someone who has just saved your life a murderer.

"I had not used a weapon since I was thrown out of the National Shame."

"Then nostalgia got the better of you."

"I was tempted by the .38 I found in your glove compartment."

By now, Isabel was driving. The pain in my chest had returned as soon as we left the mine works, though less intense than before. Burgos said I needed to be opened up to find the piece of stiletto still in there. I hoped he would not be the one to do it.

"When you were sacked you left a lot of bodies behind."

"Killing is part of the job; that wasn't why they sacked me."

"No, they were suspicious because you never caught any *guerrilleros*."

"True – somehow they all managed to escape. That was my job, too: to cover the backs of idealists like your old man, people who still believed it was Silvio Rodríguez and Pablo Milanes who made the Cuban Revolution. Why did you have a .38 in your glove box? For self-defence?"

"It was Daddy's. He gave it to me with the account number, when he realised he was trapped. Lecuona had suggested you join the G.R.O., and Daddy liked the idea. It meant you could be together again in something that was worth the effort, like thirty years ago. But the G.R.O. high command, and La Negra in particular, had other ideas."

"Debora is her name. It's about time we stopped all this *noms de guerre* nonsense. We're nothing more than killers."

The speedometer climbed to 150 kilometres per hour. In a few seconds, Burgos' V.W. was a distant blue speck in the rear-view mirror. I asked Isabel to take her foot off the accelerator.

"Listen to me, then. If I can't talk, I accelerate. I'm fed up with silence, Gotán. I grew up with it."

There was not much more for me to listen to, but I did not like what I heard. Isabel Cárcano, a magnificent 23-year-old, told me all you had kept quiet about, Mireya.

She told me you recruited Toto Lecuona. You sold him the lie that it could all begin again. He left his Canary Island paradise hoping to construct another in his home country. Before that you sold the same lie to Edmundo, who was as dazzled by the idea of returning to his revolutionary youth as he was by Lorena the blonde.

"It's true that I loved Debora too. But I have no idea who she really is."

"Who she *was*," Isabel said.

"She appeared in my life one night, at one of those sordid tango dance halls I used to go to when loneliness became too much for me. I never told her I had been a policeman."

"So you really thought she fell in love at first sight with a toilet salesman?"

Isabel laughed out loud and slowed down until Burgos caught us up. She flicked the indicator in response to his flashing headlights. I did not reply, but sat staring out at the empty countryside, the vast, sandy plain. We were still travelling at 120, but it felt as though we were stationary.

I lit a cigarette. Isabel took another that I passed to her, "Even though I've given up smoking," she said. I told her the doctor's theory: that two or three a day help prevent cancer. She agreed, we can't give everything up. The world's gone crazy, nowadays nobody smokes, nobody eats fat, people care more about whales and penguins than they do about street kids, homeless and dying of cold. They want to ban the bomb, but they dream of somebody wiping out the entire Arab world.

"Debora left me when she found out I had been in the National Shame during the dictatorship."

"That wasn't why she left you. You'd already been hoodwinked."

"You call falling in love being hoodwinked?"

"While I was her prisoner, she told me one of your exploits had been to shoot an army officer, a brigade commander."

"That's true, although there's no report about it, so I don't know how Debora could have known. After the '76 coup the guy organised death squads in Morón, just outside Buenos Aires. They hunted people down, looted their homes – nothing remarkable in those days. The *guerrilleros* in the area began to drop one by one. I didn't ask anybody's permission. I knew him, and I knew where he lived, so one day I went to his place. He showed me in: "What a surprise, Martelli," the bastard greeted me. "We haven't seen each other since Caracas." We had been together at a congress for the military and police in Venezuela, organised by the Yankee intelligence services. We came back with diplomas and everything, wc looked like university professors. I still have the pictures in a trunk somewhere."

"I heard he was pleased to see you. You shot him in the back of the head while he was pouring you coffee."

"What was I supposed to do, read him his rights? Who told you all this anyway? He lived alone, he died alone."

"No, he didn't live or die alone. He was separated from his wife and had a young daughter. Over time she grew up and learned to dance the tango."

10

Burgos flashed his lights and signalled for us to stop at a service-station café.

"I'm asleep at the wheel," he said, staring into his mug of black coffee. "I can tell because what I'm dreaming about has nothing to do with the road in front. All of a sudden I find myself on a Caribbean island, stretched out on the beach, surrounded by dead bodies. I don't have to do the autopsies because in a couple of hours the sun splits them open like the sharpest scalpel. That's the life!"

Ayala and Rodríguez were fast asleep in the back of the V.W. Isabel told Burgos that perhaps he should have a rest too.

"No, I prefer to nod off on the straights," the doctor replied. "You stay close behind me, and sound your horn if I start doing zigzags."

*

So we set off again. It was still three hundred kilometres to Bahía Blanca, and night was falling. We did not try to stop the doctor driving. We trusted to fate. "Nothing will happen that is not already written," Isabel said, although she confessed she was worried, not about Burgos and his companions, but about me.

"I thought I knew you, Gotán. Daddy had such a romantic view of you."

"He kept the truth from you. Nobody is proud of having a policeman for a friend. We're the hidden face, the Mr Hydes for all those Dr Jekylls with secretaries and the latest mobiles. And worse still, even if the revolution we were fighting for had triumphed, we would have gone on being policemen. At least capitalism gave me the opportunity to sell toilets."

*

Isabel had learned all she knew from the person the G.R.O. called La Negra, when she was still convinced she would be killed. La Negra had been made responsible for her; she had to decide what to do with Cárcano's daughter if she did not reveal the number of the account where the New Man Foundation money was deposited.

"I don't think any of the top people wanted to get their hands dirty by killing me. If there was blood to be spilled, they preferred to have someone else do it."

"That's why they are leaders."

"Your tango-dancing friend had been with them right from the start, when they first began to plot against the recycled pseudo-left they thought were behind the people who won the 1999 elections. They were children of military fathers, like the one you did away with while he was serving you coffee. Nostalgic for the past. A small organisation, but well financed. They soon realised that harking back to dictatorships was not going to win anybody over, because today even the most Neanderthal fascists claim to be democratic. So they changed their tune to try to recruit people from the other side who were similarly nostalgic."

"The 'national revolution'," I said. "Empty slogans like that sent a whole generation to the slaughterhouse."

"Daddy believed in something like that."

"So did Toto Lecuona – and so did I, if it comes to that. Socialism, but with limits, capitalism, but kept under control. We were told there were officers who refused to serve the oligarchy and wanted to place the armed forces at the service of the people. We were shot in the back."

"Why did you join them, Gotán? To make a better world, to get shot in the back?"

"Religion. I always had metaphysical doubts. I wanted to believe, although it's obvious I failed. I am a policeman, Isabel. Ever since I was a kid I liked the idea of arresting someone who steals an old lady's purse. I was always a policeman when we played at cops and robbers; I never hesitated to thrash cheats, or to kill birds with my catapult. I come from a proud working-class family: my father never stole from anyone. He was a railway worker who got sacked under Perón. For going on strike – one hell of a supporter of popular movements Perón was. That was why I could never believe in those mutants either. Evita the saint who became a devil after Perón was toppled and we were forbidden to even mention their names. My father never recovered: in those days, to be a railway worker was to be part of a privileged caste, like being a military man. When he was kicked out it was like losing his stripes. The day after I graduated from police academy, he used my service revolver to kill himself. 'A policeman for a son, that's all I need,' he said – and shot himself. If you wanted me to sing you a tango, I have a good one. But I don't want to talk about the past any more."

"What have you just been doing, then?"

"Talking about love, Isabel. Don't be surprised, even the most ruthless executioners fall in love. Who can escape it?"

*

When we reached the turn-off to Bahía Blanca, I said goodbye to Don Quixote, Sancho Panza and the doctor. We swore to meet again one day. Democracy owed us, but since she was never likely to pay up, we said we would meet at least to celebrate the fact that we were still alive.

"Take care eating that rustled meat," I said to Burgos.

"And you, Don Gotán, stop hunting for girlfriends in your box of memorabilia."

"Carry on selling toilets," Ayala recommended.

"Now I understand why you didn't make a career of it in the National Shame," Rodríguez said. "You're a great guy, when you're not killing people."

"And you two, make sure you stick together," I said. "You still have a great future as a comic double act."

*

There was a sort of shuffle, a warmth soon stifled by embarrassment, arms half-raised for an embrace, mouths twisted in our lined faces, weary from our absurd odyssey. In the end we said and did nothing more, but turned on our heels and refused to look back as the sky-blue V.W. and the 4×4 rented by an already-dead companion set off in opposite directions.

11

So your childhood dream had always been one of vengeance. While other girls were playing with dolls, you were playing with my dead body.

After that you grew up, fell in love, thought you had forgotten.

The night we met was a card played by the great cardsharp in the sky, the one who never shows his hand, the one who comes back to life just when everyone thinks he is dead. Your disgust when you discovered I was a policeman, your horror when you found out what kind of a policeman: it was all there in the cards, so how could we not go on playing?

You see, lady-who-danced-the-tango, nobody knows exactly what they are up against. The people who compiled the orange file did not find out half the details of my unofficial biography. Patricio Quesada would not have been butchered like the cattle Burgos enjoyed eating so much if, before he set off for Mediomundo, he had been aware of just who he was allying himself with. But free will is a farce: the only freedom we have is to choose our enemies.

*

From the time we said goodbye to the three musketeers until we reached the outskirts of Buenos Aires, Isabel and I hardly spoke.

Strikers had cut off access to the capital. Tyres were burning in the streets, there were men with sticks and placards, some with their faces hidden under balaclavas like decaffeinated Chiapas *guerrilleros*, others with their faces bare, unkempt-looking women, kids who had gone straight from their mothers' milk to cartons of cheap wine. They all seemed to be beating drums or dustbin lids and handing out leaflets – even the dogs were handing out leaflets. They were celebrating the great victory of overthrowing a constitutional government which they claimed not to have elected. There are no heroes in Argentina, because nobody ever admits to having chosen to play on the losing side.

A tall man, unsteady on his feet and with a face that would have terrified the serial killer kicking his heels in Bahía Blanca jail, called for a round of applause for the supermarket looters. He told all the cornershop Koreans to go back home and eat dogs. He laughed at the candidates queuing up outside the presidential palace, and prophesied a short stay for whoever was ultimately chosen. Applause, shouts, *chamamés* from northern Argentina, red flags, black flags, Argentine flags, huge banners and small posters, "United we will win!", "Las Golondrinas", "Popular justice!", "Kick them all out!" Just when it seemed we were doomed to listen to a wearisome stream of speeches and a whole C.D.'s worth of *chamamés*, the barricades were suddenly lifted and we could proceed into the capital.

The people up in arms in the centre were the middle classes. Wearing balaclavas was definitely not the done thing for these hoarders of dollars and fixed-term deposit rebels, all ready to lay down their lives for the right to carry on flying to Miami. Well dressed and with fashionable footwear, they refused to accept the government's excuses as to why they could not have access to their money in the banks. They knew they would never get their hands on it, but in defeat found a dignity they had never shown when they thought they were different and better than all the dark-skinned inhabitants of Latin America.

On the other hand, there were no upper-class protesters on the streets of Buenos Aires. The arse-lickers of power had fortified their positions and dug their trenches in the Cayman Islands, Switzerland or Panama. In the streets of the so-called elegant neighbourhoods it was the smallest petits bourgeois who were walking along like zombies expelled from Port-au-Prince, or vampires thrown out in the midday sun from a certain infamous boarding house in Transylvania.

*

"Why didn't you give them that damn code?" I said when Isabel pulled up a block away from the house of Mónica's friend, where she was going to meet her mother. "They could have killed you: is it worth dying for money?"

"Your tango-dancer friend was not going to kill me," Isabel replied. "Nor you either."

*

Shortly after Edmundo's call in the early hours of December 15, 2001, his killers left the chalet in Mediomundo.

With the old, old excuse of going to the toilet, Lorena had managed to escape. She ran through the deserted streets of the resort until she found a public telephone that did not swallow all her coins. She told the police not only what she feared was going to happen in the chalet, but also about the G.R.O. plot to overthrow democracy. The officer at the other end told her to calm down and go back home: "We cannot guarantee the safety of a woman on her own in such a desolate place," the voice said. The same concerned voice immediately got through to my reception committee and convinced them they had best make themselves scarce before I arrived.

Lorena fled Mediomundo, but came back the following night in the hope of finding some trace of the money that Edmundo had set aside for them to enjoy. When she stumbled on me, she decided to use me as a chauffeur to take her to Piedranegra. She thought the G.R.O. high command assembled there putting the finishing touches to their plan would protect her from the jackals who had eliminated Edmundo. She thought the internal war going on was between pawns for the loose change. She may have been right, but she did not get the chance to prove it.

"Poor Lorena," I said.

Another useless *nom de guerre*, Catalina Eloísa Bañados, seduced by a '70s revolutionary who, unable to accept the passage of time, had tried to double-cross a gang of ideological murderers so he could buy his fountain of youth.

With Edmundo dead, the tango dancer received orders to take care of his lover and Cordero, the other corner of the triangle Lorena had formed to make sure she would not be left without savings in her old age. Edmundo knew nothing about Cordero: he, too, was a believer in love at first sight.

"If only you could see yourselves in the mirror," Isabel said. I discovered, six hundred kilometres too late, that she still had Burgos' jacket wrapped round her shoulders. She took it off and asked me to make sure I gave it back if and when the famous reunion of the four musketeers ever took place.

"If Debora killed Lorena and Cordero, and if she drove that stiletto into me without bothering with an anaesthetic, and would have killed me too if my heart had not been over to the right – why do you say she wasn't going to kill us? I'm disgusted at the thought of her making love to Lorena before she sacrificed her, and the games she and the others played with Cordero's corpse."

"You're disgusted because she was unfaithful to you. You were happy enough to make love to her again yourself, though, even if you knew it might cost you your life. Your heart isn't over to the right, Gotán. She could have pierced it without you even knowing, and had her revenge."

"So why didn't she? Why didn't she finish us all off?"

Finally she looked at me. Her eyes were like yours, staring at nothing, or at a God in the wrong place too, a God whose son has died but is alive, in a heaven as dark as those mine works, where no-one has ever found what they were looking for.

"She was expecting you. When you arrived at last, something went click. She realised something that shook her to the core."

"She realised her father shot people in the back as well, Isabel."

"She isn't, or wasn't, any different from you, Gotán. Twin souls existed long before cloning came into fashion. She left you to avoid having to fulfil her promise to avenge her father's death. She left hoping you would never come looking for her. But you went on calling: how could you accept such an insult to your macho vanity?"

When the G.R.O. retreated to Piedranegra after their defeat, Isabel thought her time had come.

"But the tango dancer saved my life. After all the shooting, instead of finishing me off she dragged me to the far end of the mine works. She no longer trusted anyone, but she knew you would come looking for her."

"Get out of here when everyone outside has finished killing each other," she told me when we reached the place where you found me. "There's only this one shaft. It's three hundred metres to the tunnel mouth, and Piedranegra is less than twenty kilometres from the highway proper. When you see him, tell him the truth. I'm sure he will survive. Even if I had pushed the blade right in, he would survive with a severed heart."

She tied me up so that I would not stop her doing what she had decided to do. She gagged me so I would not cry out in horror, then leaped like a panther up onto a rock that one of the miners had carved out there, the one that in the dark looks like an altar. Then silently, without a word, she plunged the stiletto into her heart."

"But why, Isabel? Why didn't she finish me off instead, if that had been her reason for living?"

"Remember, she could dance as well as you. It wasn't out of respect for another person's life that she didn't kill you. Think about that when you get out of the car. I've nothing more to tell you, and please, don't contact me. I need to have a rest from you for a while. In fact, I would probably prefer never to see you again."

When a beautiful woman tells me I am *persona non grata* I accept the verdict. I got out, and only turned round to remind her that the car wasn't hers.

"The person who rented it was called Aníbal Lecuona. We used to call him Toto, but I expect they won't be too concerned about that at the car hire place."

Isabel switched on the engine, and I set off towards the avenue. I stopped when she caught up with me and wound down her window to thank me for saving her. I could not help imposing on her politeness one more time by asking the stupidest of questions:

"Did she tell you she loved me?"

She gripped the wheel and stared straight ahead, as though she were on a Grand Prix grid.

"No-one loves a policeman," she said, hurtling away in reverse.

I walked on. I would have liked to be able to take giant strides to get as far away as possible. I walked steadily, furious, my heart in the right place aching more than ever.

Some day someone will pass through Piedranegra. Thinking they have found a short cut, they will stumble upon the scene of yet another tiny hell. I should have buried you there, alongside Toto Lecuona. After all, it had been your idea to go and find him, to persuade him that social justice could once more be the banner leading to victory. But I decided to leave you where you had chosen to die, on your improvised altar, like the unprincipled, unscrupulous high priestess you were.

Someone will pass through and sound the alarm. The press will fall on the dry bones strewn round the ghost town, and the stories of your comrades or accomplices will be mingled with those of the miners who in reality had been hired hands on their way to the apple harvest in Rio Negro.

But they would not find your body.

I should have buried you, even if poor Toto would have cursed me for having to spend his eternity next to you. If I had, I would not have arrived home and seen, correctly parked and polished as though for sale, my car that had been stolen along with Lorena in the far south.

I resisted the temptation to go upstairs and get the spare key. Nobody who wants to grow old should accept gifts from the mafia, even if it is only something they are returning.

I called the police and the bomb-disposal squad from a public telephone. The police do not like anonymous tip-offs, so I hung up before they could ask for too many details.

I was not sure they would come, but they did. They could hardly ignore the report of a booby-trap in a car parked in the heart of the city. The political situation was tense. Nobody knew who was pulling the strings of all those scrambling for power. They had to cover their backs.

They arrived in two trucks and three patrol cars. They closed the road to traffic, mobile T.V. units appeared out of nowhere, the police started shouting, nervously giving orders. Curious neighbours gathered to see what was going on. I joined them. We watched as the bomb-disposal experts set to work, the watch-repairers of terror.

When they had cleared the area and prepared everything, bang! Up went my car. I was not too happy thinking the police might identify the owner, and was hoping that the fierceness of the blaze that engulfed the car would help me avoid having to make a statement, tell stories nobody would believe, run the risk that my insurance company would find an excuse not to pay me.

There was a second, smaller explosion. The boot flew open. A know-all in the crowd pronounced that cars running on gas were dangerous even when they did not have a bomb in them. When I went closer I saw that it was not gas cylinders. It was a woman's body.

A policeman stopped me going any nearer. I was on the point of telling him that it was my car, and nobody had asked my permission to put that woman there, but the flames had reached her too, a blue flame enveloping her left arm as it fell out, pointing downwards.

EPILOGUE

We open our eyes thinking we are waking up, hoping that when we rouse ourselves and get out of bed everything will make sense again. That everyday reality will gently put things back in their proper place, and the dead crawl back into their graves.

Zulema, my cleaning lady, left a note warning me that Félix Jesús had come back that morning the worse for wear.

But I find him sleeping quietly in the laundry room. When he notices my presence, he yawns and stretches. He comes to me, tail erect, and rubs himself against my leg. Then he jumps up on top of the tallest piece of furniture in the kitchen, where he sleeps during the day.

I should say that Zulema is a good, discreet cleaner: but she sees visions. She does not distinguish between night and day, and her dreams get mixed together. She can be crossing the road to the bus stop while at the same time (in her mind's eye) she is calmly watching a lion with a camel's hump devour a blond boy on the pavement opposite.

I have no doubt that if Zulema saw it, Félix Jesús was hurt. From his day-time perch on the blue cushion, he stares down at me, though his slant eyes are not fixed on mine. He seems to be staring at something at my chest level that has caught his attention. He yawns again, then curls up to go back to sleep.

I follow his lead. I turn on the T.V. with the sound off and switch the fan on. I doze off listening to its hum, while on the screen they drape the presidential sash across the chest of Argentina's fourth president in a week.

The ring of the telephone wakes me. I do not need to look at my watch to know it is past midnight.

Let it ring, let them keep on calling until it goes dead.

FINIS